More Than
I Asked For

Book One in the More Than DC series

By: T.J. Tims

Copyright: 2014 by T.J.Tims
First Edition: May 2014
Printed in the United States of America
ISBN: 978-0-9903625-1-7
Cover design by: T.J. Tims
Formatting by: T.J. Tims
Editing by: Jacquelyn Ayres

Dedicated to my husband and son. Without you, this would not have been possible. xo

Table of Contents

Chapter One

You are strong. You are fierce. The world is "your cup of tea." *No, that's not right.* The world is your oyster, Genevieve Westley, time to open your eyes and take a closer look at life.

"Ma'am, your cup of tea."

Startled, I smile at the waitress, "Oh, thank you!" I say.

Great, now the waitress is giving me peculiar looks. I glance at my watch. *Twenty minutes late.* What's new? At least I have my tea. Tea always has a way of calming my nerves. The hostess walks into the dining area; thankfully, escorting Brad to the table. I watch his approach, noting various women around the room stopping mid-sentence to stare.

Of course, at six feet one inch, the blond, athletically-built god, dressed in a perfectly tailored power suit would draw attention from practically every female in the room. As Brad reaches the table, I stand to greet him. With flair he leans in and kisses both of my cheeks in greeting. It always annoys me whenever he does that. I want to scream that he's not European and in fact, has never even been to Europe, but of course, I don't. I have an even bigger issue I'd like to discuss.

"Sorry I'm late, a meeting with a client went on longer than expected," he says, taking his seat.

Brad is always late being that he is a lawyer working towards becoming partner at DiNardo & Rossi, a prominent law firm in the city. He works longer and harder than most; always making sure he is ahead of the race, putting his job above all else. The waitress brings my usual glass of water to the table. I'm not much of a drinker. She also brings Brad's scotch on the rocks. After coming here at least twice a month for eight straight months, I'm not surprised that the waitress anticipated our drink order. Brad begins to drone on about his day, his clients, and his fellow associates. All the while, gesturing with his perfectly manicured hands, around his perfectly moisturized face, and his perfectly styled hair.

It's just too much.

"Are you gay?" I blurt out somewhat forcefully.

Shock registers on his face for a moment, but only for a fleeting moment. I'm sure I have my answer.

I press on. "We've been dating for eight and a half months. We've never progressed passed holding hands and goodnight kisses. That's not normal! I know how important it is to you to make partner. I am aware that image is a big part on your way up the ladder, but I need to know—are you using me as a cover? If so, you need to tell me."

Brad stares at me with what I call his *lawyer face.* Impenetrable. Direct. It makes you shift nervously in your seat and want to break eye contact.

"Well this is not how I planned to, eventually, have this conversation. I was hoping for a more private setting," he sighs, looking around the restaurant. Clearing his throat, he leans closer to me from across the table. "Gen, I need you to know I never meant to hurt you, and I fully intended on disclosing the nature of our relationship when the time was right."

Anger flashes through me. He never meant to hurt me? For a smart man, he's really stupid. I bet he never gave me much thought at all when he made his decision.

"When would have been the right time, Brad? After you made partner? After you wasted one, two, or maybe even three years of my life? That certainly wouldn't have been the right time for me! Thanks, but I'll pass. You are a selfish asshole! And just so you know, you are not European!" I stand up, take a sip of my water before slamming it back down, and stride out of the restaurant.

Why? Because I'm strong, I'm fierce, and I've been living in my own little world for too long. It's about time I start seeing what this oyster business is about.

I make it back to "The Brownstone", as my roommates and I call our little home. Well, not really little; it's a large brownstone located in the Georgetown section of D.C. I kick off my boots in the foyer, toss my jacket in the coat closet, and head towards the kitchen, swinging my bag full of goodies the whole way.

Standing around the island in the kitchen are my roommates, though that title doesn't give justice to our relationship. I've known these girls since kindergarten. They've known each other their whole lives, considering they are cousins and come from a very tight knit family. Hailey and Tara Trenton, though related, looked nothing alike and have opposite temperaments.

Barely grazing the five foot mark, Hailey is tiny with delicate features. She has waist length, blonde hair and crystal blue eyes. Hail is the writer in the family and prefers the quiet lifestyle that her career provides. Her personality is as sweet as her looks, but she has a backbone made of steel when it needs to make an appearance.

Firecracker is the best word I can use to describe Tara. She doesn't take crap from anyone and speaks her mind, often before stopping to think. She's five foot five inches with rich chestnut hair, cut into a pixie style and emerald green eyes that openly flash with defiance. As a photographer, she's a complete adrenaline junky. The more difficult the locale to shoot, the more she enjoys jetting off to those exotic lands.

"Well how'd it go? Does good old Brad have a sweet tooth for the man candy?" Leave it to Tara to launch right into it.

"Shush, Tar, let her finish walking into the room before you jump all over her." Hailey is always the reasonable one.

"Well he does indeed have a sweet tooth and thought he'd use me for his diet plan while still sneaking some goodies. Oh, but the upside is that it was only supposed to be until he made partner." I smile when Tara snorts and continue to walk into the room with my bag full of Ben and Jerry's.

My goal is to finish the whole bag or develop diabetes trying; whichever comes first.

"Oh, Gen, I'm so sorry," Hailey says sympathetically.

"It's okay, I'm not. I'm just really glad I have you two. Otherwise I would have continued in my own little world, not noticing that something was off. Really, though—I'm okay. I have a date with a few cartons of my two favorite guys and I'm going to enjoy them fully. Although, I may be persuaded to share, if you're lucky." I wave the bag to tempt them.

"I knew this wouldn't get you down! Now don't get into a huff, but I planned for this eventuality." Tara beams

Hailey and I exchange "the look" and groan. This is nothing new. Tara always has some plan to shake things up. Some turn out really great, others we try to forget. The first plan is what set us on the road to life-long friendship in kindergarten.

Throughout the first three months of kindergarten at the exclusive private school we all attended, I kept to myself, but noticed so much. My Grand-pop always said I was a born looker. I took this literally and made sure to always watch everything.

One day during recess, I noticed a little girl with pretty, long brown hair. I recognized her from being in my class. I observed her sneaking up behind a second-grader. I continued to watch, curious to see what she was up to. It didn't take long before she pulled his pants down and pushed him into the mud puddle that he and his friends were throwing sticks, rocks, and bugs into. When the boy stood back up, the little girl was nowhere in sight.

I'm not sure why, but when I saw pretty brown hair disappear around the side of the building, I decided to follow. After I rounded the building I found her with another little girl who was also in my class. They were whispering to each other. The other little girl was what Mother would call "dainty". I know this because I am the opposite of dainty. Mother was always sighing about that when we went shopping for new clothes. When they noticed me standing there, the dainty one looked worried while the brown haired girl frowned at me.

"What do you want?" Brown haired girl said in a snarly voice. I don't think she's happy that I found them.

Not sure why I did it, but I said, "I watch lots of police shows when I visit my grandparents. You're going to need an alibi."

Dainty spoke up. "What's an alibi?"

"Well, I think it's when you lie and say you were doing something okay when you were actually doing something naughty, and if you have a good enough alibi, you don't get in trouble."

That's the best I could explain it from the shows I'd seen. I hoped I was right or the brown haired girl was going to get into a lot of trouble.

"My name is Genevieve. We're in the same class. I saw what you did." Before I could say any more, Ms. Locke, our teacher, rounded the corner.

"Tara, I was just informed that someone saw you push another student into a mud puddle. I am going to have to call your parents to the school, and have you explain to us why you would do such a thing."

Before she could drag the little girl away, unsure of where all of the courage came from, I spoke up.

"But, Ms. Locke, it couldn't have been Tara!"

"Why is that, Genevieve?" She looked at me questioningly.

"Well, she's been here with us this whole time, telling me about her trip to England this summer to visit family and how they spoke different, and used words like arse!" I rushed to say this so fast that by the time I was done, I was out of breath.

It was a good thing I happened to overhear a conversation Tara, had a few weeks before with Dainty girl.

Ms. Locke looked confused for a moment, but let go of Tara's hand. "Well, it looks like I have to apologize and go find the real culprit; however, we do not use words like arse. They are inappropriate and proper young ladies should never say them."

After watching our teacher walk away, I turned back to the other girls.

Tara extended her hand towards me. "Thanks, slick. That was a close call. I'm Tara Elaine Trenton, and this is my cousin, Hailey Rose Trenton. We're of the D.C. Trenton's." We shook hands like adults. "Tell me more about this alibi stuff. I have a feeling I'm going to need to know what that is. Mama says trouble always has a way of finding me."

I found out that the second-grader, whose name was Micah, bumped into dainty Hailey without the gentlemanly "excuse me". From that day forward, he became enemy number one. I also finally had friends who included me in all of their plans, for better or worse.

Two hours after coming home, I'm seriously wishing I was eating my Ben and Jerry's. Tara has crammed me into this gorgeous bronze dress that barely covers the essentials. We're built differently, so her dress is leaving me feeling exposed, especially in the topside region. Let's not mention the fact that I am four inches taller than Tara, so much of my legs are also on display this evening. I do have to admit that the color of this dress makes my light brown eyes stand out, appearing more gold-toned. And my black curls, swept into an up-do, add a nice contrast.

"Well look at you! I'll never be able to wear that dress again after seeing how you put me to shame in it!" Tara is always dramatic. "You look like walking sex! You'll inspire many wet dreams tonight!"

I don't need to look in the mirror to feel the flush crawling up my neck.

"You know, if you put as much passion into finding a man as you do your paintings, you'd be leaving broken hearts all over town," Tara says, giving me a thoughtful look.

I roll my eyes.

"I definitely have to agree with her about that, Gen. I'm in the same boat. I get lost in worlds of my own making. You throw everything into all of your paintings." Hailey slips into the room wearing a white dress that floats around her with her long blonde locks swaying at her waist. "I think going out tonight will be good for all of us. I know I need to try and shake things up a bit."

For about a month now, Hailey has been slumped at her desk with a major case of writer's block. Maybe going out is just the thing we all need. They're completely right of course. I spend so much time in my studio painting, and when I am around other people, besides Hailey and Tara, I'm wishing I were in my studio painting. Going out to this club will give me an opportunity to scope out potential oysters.

If I had paid closer attention, I probably wouldn't have wasted so much time on Brad. I definitely should have realized what was going on when his "old college buddy" kept giving me dirty looks at a party we attended for the law firm.

The town car we called pulls up and we pile in, which is an apt description considering the heels we are all wearing. I'm not sure how women get into the back seat of a car gracefully, but that does not seem to be something any of us have mastered, though Hailey's entrance is the most graceful of the three of us.

"Where are we going again?" I ask Tara

"Well I met this girl while getting a pedicure. She's a bartender at this really posh club named *Eloá*. Her boyfriend is the bouncer at the door. I explained to her our potential situation. When she told me she'd add us to her VIP list just in case and could hook us up all night, I said *hell yeah*. Oh, and don't even think about giving each other that *look*! We're going to have a great time!" Tara bops in her seat with giddy energy.

As soon as we arrive at the club, Tara walks right up to the door. We flash our identification, and after a quick look at the list, we're in the door and heading straight for the bar. The bartender, Heather, who actually turns out to be really nice, starts us off with our cocktails of choice and a shot on her, to get us going.

After spending an hour dancing, I quickly realize that oysters aren't my thing. They're slimy and gross, and the men here tonight all seems to have a close resemblance to that description. I'm still having a good time, though. The three of us aren't able to do this too often. It's nice to let loose a little and enjoy being with my girls.

Standing at the bar, we get ready to do our fourth shot with our fifth drink in hand. I feel, only what I can describe as, a heated look scouring my body. My gaze goes to the VIP booth, and is drawn and held by the most gorgeous man I've ever seen. It has nothing to do with artistic appreciation, he's raw masculine beauty. Definitely walking sex, as Tara would say. When I realize he's grinning at me, probably due to my open stare, I toss my shot back and let the burn of vodka snap me back to my friends. Hailey and Tara are both staring at me. They observed my moment.

"Wow, I got wet just witnessing that!" Tara doesn't fail to comment, of course.

"I need a pen and paper." Hailey puts her shot in my hand and turns to push through the crowd.

Looks like she found her muse again. The uncomfortable thought is that I may be the reason for that.

"Toss that shot back, and let's get back on the dance floor to give that wickedly, good looking man a show." Tara yells over the music.

My gaze drifts back to the VIP booth where the gorgeous man is with his group of friends. He's still staring at me and does not seem to be interested at all in the conversation that is going on around him.

Tossing the shot back, I make my way with Tara towards that side of the dance floor. I am ready to see what the rest of tonight brings us.

Chapter Two

Goodness…when did my head decide that sunlight was enemy number one? Why was I ever a fan of sheer curtains? What possessed me to drink like a sailor on leave last night? Despite my raging hangover, I am happy to say I'm not nauseous while lying here, and I am really comfortable. What is that incredible smell that is making me want to burrow into my bed, indefinitely, just to enjoy it?

I crack my eye open, carefully, due to my current enemy: sunlight. I push my hair out of my face, glance around, and look down. *Holy crap on a cracker!* I'm wearing a man's shirt. A really large man's shirt! Screw the hangover! I sit up with both eyes wide open and swing my head around the room, looking for the man that owns the shirt!

My heart beat begins to slow down—just a little— once I realize my room is empty. Next to my bed, my cellphone's message light is flashing at me. I pick it up and read it. It's from an unfamiliar number.

Unknown: *Sorry I had to run before you woke up. I had an early flight this morning. I can't wait to see you in two days. Have a great day, Beautiful. L.*

Oh my. I'm not sure if I want to smile or frown. I guess I really want to smile because this text message is totally cute and frown because I don't know who L is!

After a quick inspection, I see that my underwear is still in place under the shirt. I don't feel different in any suspect areas. At least I can feel relieved about that. I put on sweat pants and one of my old t-shirts before I stumble my way to the kitchen.

Gratefully, Hailey is already there, not looking much better than I feel. And—thank all that is holy—there is a cup of coffee waiting for me. Groaning, I throw myself at the mug and suck down its liquid goodness.

"Tell me *everything* I did last night," I command, unable to make eye contact just yet.

"I left early, after I went searching for a pen and paper. I had things I needed to write. When I found you after I came out of the office, you and Tara were in the VIP section with some guys. You told me to go ahead and that you'd catch a cab home, so I left." She murmurs.

When I finally look up Hailey is blushing into her own coffee mug. Hail isn't much of a drinker, so the few she had accounts for her state. However, that certainly does not tell me why she's blushing.

"Where's Tara?" I question.

When she doesn't answer me after a few moments I wave my hand in front of her face.

"Huh?" She finally looks at me.

"Tara?" I ask again.

"Oh, she ran out. She said she'd be back in time for our girls' night. She'll be bringing the Chinese," Hailey says yet she doesn't seem to be focusing on our conversation.

I'm used to Hailey being distracted, but this seems to be different. I wonder if I should question her about it now or let her tell me in her own time.

I go to brush my teeth before I head to the studio to try and get some work done today. Before I can reach the bathroom, the doorbell rings.

"Hailey, are you going to get that?" I yell out.

She must have slipped into her office already, which means she won't reappear for hours. I trod to the door, holding my breath. I don't want whoever is on the other side to run away from my morning breath.

I swing the door open. I definitely wasn't expecting to see a massive bouquet of sunflowers. Behind the bouquet is a little Asian delivery man who looks like he's about to fall over from the weight. This might be because he is precariously leaning to the right to try and see around the large, beautiful blooms. I couldn't hear the man from behind the flowers, but signed for the delivery anyway. I walk back into the kitchen and set them on the island. I hop on a stool and sit back to admire for a moment.

When we get flower deliveries it's usually because one of Hailey's books did really well and her agent is sending a congratulations, or Tara left another broken heart in her wake.

Fetching the card from among the blooms, I'm more than a little surprised when I realize it has my name on it.

I heard it is going to be overcast this afternoon and wanted you to have sunshine all day. L.

Stunned. I met a guy I don't remember and so far he's made me smile and feel special *twice*, within the space of an hour, too. I think maybe it's time I text him back. I snap a picture of the bouquet and send it to the new number in my phone.

Me: *Absolutely amazing.*

Not even a minute passes.

L.: *Me or the flowers??*

Ha, there's another smile. He's on a roll.

Me: *Maybe both?*

L.: *I feel that I should be allotted extra points for not buying cheesy roses.*

Me: *Well in that case, you are definitely more amazing. How's your trip so far?*

Maybe I can find out some more about my mystery man from last night through these text messages.

L.: *New York is a little dreary today. I should have stayed to say good morning, but I promised to have breakfast with my mother and sister.*

Ah, a family man. That's a plus. This whole situation is incredibly confusing. I'm actually contemplating going on the date I made while drunk with someone I don't remember meeting. I need more information before I go through with meeting this guy. I will also talk to Tara when she gets back tonight.

Me: *I completely understand.*

What can I add to that to not make me seem completely boring? I should pay more attention to how Tara holds a man's attention.

Me: *Besides, eating in New York is much more exciting, and possibly safer for your health, than eating anything I may have cooked for breakfast. :)*

Ten minutes pass with no reply. I knew I'd sound like a complete dork. I go into the master bath suite connected to my bedroom and get ready for my work day.

Is it weird that I'm feeling incredibly disappointed?

I walk through the kitchen on my way to my studio and take my flowers.

Despite my disappointment, I want to keep these flowers to myself a little longer and in a place where I can view them all day long. My phone pings from my work bench. I rush over, nearly tripping over an easel.

L.: *That's a risk I'd be willing to take.*

Wow. He just made me sigh. I put my phone down. I need to get to work before my heart flutters right out of my chest.

Going through my routine of setting up my canvas, brushes, and paints, is very comforting. It relaxes me like nothing else does; not even a cup of tea.

Before I discovered the perfect release painting provides me, I was socially awkward; much to my mother's disgust. That may sound a little harsh, but that was my mother. She was elegantly beautiful; tall and willowy with classical features, along with the ever popular, blonde hair and blue eyes.

Me? I favor the Westley side of my father's family. That even left me at odds with my father, in terms of coloring, since he took after my Gram's family with their blonde hair and clear green eyes.

I certainly wasn't the child they expected to have. One: I was female. After a sonogram, they eagerly awaited the arrival of their son. I arrived instead. This was their first issue. They were completely unprepared. Luckily, my Gram stepped in and gave me a name. Otherwise, I'm not sure if I would have been named before leaving the hospital. After seeing me, I'm sure they questioned if a switch was made in the nursery. I didn't quite live up to their expectations of having a fair-haired child. So that was two strikes against me, from the very beginning.

I completely lacked social grace, as well. I, either was not able to speak at all, or once I gathered the courage, spoke too much with zero filter; even for a child. I was a total disappointment to my mother, and even more so when she had multiple miscarriages and was unable to provide my father with the golden son they both desired.

My father was better than my mother. He had genuine affection for me. When he was home, he'd read to me and tell me stories about the countries he'd visited on his business trips. I hated when he went away because it would mean spending multiple days alone with my mother's constant critiquing, ranting, and moods.

Father never called when he was away. I think he did this to avoid having to speak to my mother. Their relationship was very strained during my childhood. By the time I reached my early teens, they barely spoke when in the same room.

I remember the last time I saw them; vividly as if it happened hours ago. Mother and I were in the dining room, eating in silence, as usual. I was hoping the courses would go by quickly, so that I could escape to my room. I wanted to call Hailey and Tara on three-way, so that we could discuss our math homework. Well, Hailey and I would discuss math and Tara would tell us about the latest boys vying for her attention.

Before dessert could be served, Father strode into the dining room, looking purposeful yet agitated. When he reached my mother's side, he dropped to one knee, taking her hand into his.

"Let's go for a drive. Let's just walk out of that door like we used to, leave all of this between us behind for a few hours, and simply be together." My father visibly relaxed when my mother smiled.

She glowed, looking young, and eager for their adventure. After they both kissed me goodnight for the first time in my entire life, I watched them walk out to my father's car, hand in hand. I sat and daydreamed a little about us finally being a happy family when they got back.

That dream came crashing down just four hours later when the police officers arrived on our doorstep. My parents had been in a car accident. When I reached the police station to wait for my grandparents to arrive, I overheard some officers discussing the crash.

My parent's vehicle was riding the center line and accidentally crossed over; striking a tractor trailer that was heading in the opposite direction.

My father's side took the brunt of the accident. He didn't survive the impact.

Witnesses said that my mother was stumbling away from the vehicle when she realized my father was not behind her and went back for him. She crawled back into the car and was holding him when the car exploded, due to gas leaking from the tank. When I heard the final moments of the accident, it eased the loss for me.

That may seem weird, but it really did help. After years of not being able to grasp happiness together, they finally had each other and their love. That was enough to comfort and help me through the following days.

After my grandparents picked me up, everything seemed to whirl together. After the funeral, my parents' will was read. My father's parents were named my legal guardians.

Gram and Pop became my anchors. My grandfather and his accountant handled the estate, but kept me informed of their actions. They paid off my parents' debts and saved a few properties they felt would be worth keeping. The Brownstone in Georgetown was among them. They sold everything else and placed it in an account for me.

I knew my grandparents were concerned for me. Weeks after the funeral, I still seemed to drift through their house, clearly in shock. I hadn't even come out of it when Hailey and Tara visited.

My grandparents had the back parlor of their house converted into a paint studio. My grandfather liked to "tinker with paints" as he'd say. I'm not sure what made me pick up a paintbrush one afternoon, but before I knew it, I had spent hours in front of the canvas putting every emotion churning through me into paint strokes of moody colors.

I finally came up for air when the natural lighting in the room faded to darkness. After I set the brushes down, the lights came on in the room.

I turned around to see my grandparents there with tears in their eyes. However, their focus was beyond me, at what I had put to canvas. I'm not sure how long they had been standing there for, but they had seen what I had done. My grandfather stepped up behind me, putting his hands on my shoulders.

"You have a raw talent, Genni-V. I think you may have found a way to finally find yourself," Grand-pop whispered over my head.

Gram grasped my hand and I finally looked at the whole of what I painted. For the first time since my parents' sudden deaths, I cried.

I turned into my grandparents embrace and let out weeks, maybe even years, of pain that I had not realized I held so deep inside of myself.

"Genevieve Viola, you need to sign your work. Every great artist does and this is a masterpiece that deserves to have your signature," Gram said encouragingly.

In the bottom corner with stark white paint, I boldly scrawled *Genni-V.*

It became my signature from that day forward, in thanks to my grandmother for naming me, to my grandfather who fondly gave me the nickname, and to both of them for providing me a loving home. Without them helping me, I don't know if I ever would have found my outlet— *or myself.*

Chapter Three

"Gen! Girls' night! Chinese! Let's go!" Tara's bellowing startles me out of my trance.

When I step back from my canvas, to see what I've done, I'm not shocked to find sunflowers arranged throughout my work. All day I've been sneaking glimpses at the flowers and smiling to myself.

True to the note that came with them, when noon arrived, the skies became overcast and the wind howled outside. This was nothing unusual for a D.C. winter, but inside my studio I had a bit of sunshine.

L. and I continued to exchange the occasional text discussing likes and dislikes. I'm still calling him L. since I'm too scared to ask his real name. It is a little more than embarrassing to admit that I was so drunk last night, I can't remember our encounter.

So far, everything is good. He has a sense of humor similar to my own and doesn't seem to mind my, more often than not, unsophisticated replies. At least, judging by the LOLs and smiley faces I've received. I sigh to myself.

I need to go get cleaned up before Tara comes in here and drags me out by my hair.

After a quick shower and change into the usual girls' night attire of yoga pants and a tank top, I wear sleeveless shirts every chance I get so that I can flash the guns I earned from hauling heavy canvases around. I start walking towards the den while trying to pull my hair back into a pony tail.

"*Gen!*" Hailey and Tara both roar.

Okay, I'm a little late for girls' night, but not enough to have Hailey yelling at me, too. I pick up the pace, and by the time I reach the den, I'm practically running.

When I skid to a halt inside of the room, both girls are standing in front of the couch. Chinese food is spread out on the coffee table. The T.V. has on one of our favorite girls' night shows and it's paused. Thank goodness for DVR because I hate missing out on the latest celebrity gossip.

Hailey and Tara both look worried.

"What's going on? I know I'm a little late, but thanks for pausing." I glance back and forth between the two of them.

"Okay, don't freak." Tara saying that guarantees that I will freak out.

"Maybe you should sit down for a minute," Hailey whispers.

Okay, so now I'm really worried. I have no idea what's happening, but it can't be good. Someone died or is dying. I take a deep, calming breath and sit down on the couch. They each take a seat beside me. Tara picks up the remote and takes a deep breath before pressing play.

Holy crap on a cracker! That's me and the guy that was staring at me from across the bar!

I'm on the celebrity gossip show. The screen is showing a picture of me wearing the shirt I woke up in. Add to that the fact that I'm practically wrapped around the most gorgeous man I've ever seen.

Judging by the picture, he's easily six foot three with a pretty spectacular athletic build. His tattoo covered arm is around my shoulder and he's grinning down at me like he's completely focused on what I'm saying.

I look breathless in the photo, but considering I'm practically breathless just seeing his picture, I'm sure last night I was hyperventilating and that's the cause of his grin.

The host of the show is asking one question right after another. *Who's the mystery girl with Lucas Alexander? Is Lucas Alexander, rock star turned music mogul, cheating on his on again off again girlfriend, pop singer, Lissandria?*

A picture of Lucas and Lissandria flashes onto the screen briefly before flashing back to us. The picture of them together is striking. They make a beautiful couple; her stunning warm blonde beauty opposed to his cool, dark, good looks.

The show goes on to give a little more background info about where we were and speculate about what we did.

The club we were at last night is apparently owned by Lucas's brother, Micah Alexander.

That's interesting. The girls and I went to school with Micah Alexander.

I can't believe *my* L. is actually Lucas Alexander. This is way out of my league. *He* is so out of my league.

I don't know when, but at some point, I laid my head in my hands and started whispering "Oh em gee" over and over.

"I knew he looked familiar last night! Girl, you spent the night with Lucas Alexander! Damn, I'm jealous," Tara says, grinning. She's attempting to coax a smile out of me, I'm sure.

I think I may be a little lightheaded at this revelation.

"I can't do it," I say absently. "I'm supposed to see him in a few days, and I can't do it."

"What do you mean you can't do it? Of course you can do it. Last night you had a great time with him. You two sat in the corner of the V.I.P booth away from everyone else and chatted with each other like you were the only two people in the entire club!" Tara throws her hands out in emphasis. "Hailey, talk some sense into her."

"I'm going to have to agree with her. I wasn't there for long, but from what I saw, you looked very cozy with Lucas. Plus, if you think about it, he's just a man like any other. Last night, you invited him home with you, which is not something you would ever do with just anybody, despite the alcohol." Hailey has always been my soft-spoken, voice of reason.

"I don't know. I don't even remember meeting him! Why did I have to drink so much? Maybe if I remembered something, I'd feel differently, but I don't!" Rubbing my hands over my face, I jump up and start pacing. "He's way out of my league. I'm a twenty-four-year-old virgin and the closest I've ever come to a man's anatomy is handling my paint brushes and he's—" I break off, sighing. "He's international, stud muffin, Lucas Alexander."

Tara snorts. "If you handle him as lovingly and as often as you handle those paint brushes, he'll be a very euphoric man."

Thankfully, I'm not as pale as Hailey or I'd be as beet red as she is right now. She can write erotica, but can't handle Tara's comments. *Such a contradiction.*

I pick up my phone and start texting before I can think twice about it.

Me: *I just saw the picture of us on TV. I can't do this. I'm so sorry.*

I hit send and set my phone back down on to the coffee table.

"I need to paint. Don't let me ruin tonight for you two." I excuse myself and walk out of the room, leaving Tara looking annoyed and Hailey looking sad.

That's fine. At this moment, I'm feeling rather sad for myself. I have no confidence—I know this. Maybe I knew all along Brad was gay and that's why I was so comfortable with him. I stop in the kitchen to grab a bottle of water and then head back to my studio, so I can get on with my pity party.

I don't know how long it took me to put my emotions to the canvas this time, but the finished result is very bleak, except for the stupid sunflower. I can't seem to stop myself from painting it.

Just like in my life, the sunflower is depicted distantly; within view, but unattainable.

The front door opening and closing pulls my attention from the canvas.

I glance at my watch. That can't be right, it's one a.m.? Who would be leaving at this time?

I thought someone left until I hear Tara whisper outside my studio door for someone to wait a minute.

After knocking on the door, Tara pokes her head in. "Can I come in a minute?"

"Sure." I look at her questioningly.

She steps in and closes the door behind her.

"You know I love you as much as a sister. Maybe more than a sister since I got to choose you and you can't choose sisters. That just goes to show how special you are to me and how much I love you," she rambles.

A rambling Tara is never a good thing, so just hearing her going on and on is making me a little anxious.

"Okay, I get it and I love you, too. Please tell me what you did." I can't help but smile.

I really do know that she loves me as much as I love her. She makes sure that life never becomes completely boring.

"Well after you walked out of the den earlier, your phone rang. I know I shouldn't have answered. And I know that I poked my nose into something that wasn't my business, but you looked so happy last night. So I did—I answered. With that said, I am completely willing to take all of the blame." She gives me a quick hug and kiss then walks to the door. "Someone is here to see you."

She opens the door to reveal Lucas standing on the other side.

He is looking mind numbingly gorgeous wearing a tuxedo. Being sober and in the same room as him is really bad for my respiration.

I turn around to find my stool, so that I can sit down before I pass out from oxygen deprivation. I don't want to make myself look like a complete idiot.

Giving me a hesitant smile, Tara slips out of the room at the last second, shooting me a thumbs up from behind Lucas's back.

"Hello, Genevieve," he says, looking intently at me.

"Hey," my voice barely whispers back.

Breaking eye contact, I stare down at my hands, clenched in my lap.

I hear Lucas cross the room to me. Still unable to look up, his feet come into view. I jump a little when he reaches out and grabs my hands from my lap.

Startled, I gaze up at him.

"I thought you were in New York?" my voice squeaks.

"I was." He grins down at me. "I know this is going to sound crazy, but when I got your text, I decided I needed to come back to see you. I know last night was a little intense, but it felt so right being with you. I don't want the press to scare you away. This can't end before we give it a real chance." His hands warm my cold fingers and his husky voice warms everything else.

What should I do? Should I tell him I don't remember last night and send him on his way? Should I play along because I kind of really want to get to know him?

When he doesn't say anything else, I take a moment to confront the devil and angel on my shoulders.

Unsurprisingly, they look like Tara and Hailey. My little devil is telling me not to let this man go so easily, that it's time to grab life by the balls. *My inner voice really needs to quit with these inspirational quotes since they're what got me into this mess in the first place.* My angel is currently agreeing with the devil. Darn.

I find the courage to do something I would normally never do—not in a million years.

I don't grab life, or Lucas, by the balls (thank goodness for that restraint). I *do* grab Lucas's face between my hands and lay a kiss on him. I know I'm never going to forget this moment.

It doesn't take long for Lucas's shock to wear off from my initial lip assault.

Boy, when he starts responding, he turns me into gelatin. I am quivering all over.

I never knew kissing someone could be so passion-filled. I may be a virgin, but I've had my fair share of kisses. Okay fair share may be an over exaggeration.

I've casually dated four guys. Kissing was never an issue. They were pleasant. Things just never got heavier than that.

I pull back, taking deep breaths to regain my composure.

"Why did you come back?" Crap, I still sound out of breath. It was a doozy of a kiss.

Lucas runs his fingers through his hair. I'm now craving to do the same.

"Last night was so different for me. I finally met a woman I could talk to. You have no idea how rare that is when you become famous. Girls flock to me," he says without modesty. "Not that I should complain about that, but they're there to be seen with me. They want what I can do for them."

He takes another step away from me and rubs his hands over his face. "Hell, honestly most of them are there to be fucked so they can say they fucked Lucas Alexander. I have always had it easy with women because of my last name. Once I became known for being the lead singer of Scarlet Anarchy, shit got crazy. After a while it left me with this numb feeling."

He whirls back around and grasps my shoulders. "Meeting you last night filled a void inside of me that I didn't realize existed. Shit, will you please stop me now? Before I sound even more like a whiny pussy." Spilling his guts to a girl must be a new experience for him. He looks a little ill at ease doing it.

I can't help it. I start laughing. Before long, he joins me. The tension in the room abates.

He pulls me up and leans his forehead against mine. "Give this a shot. That's all I'm asking. We'll do our best to avoid the media. Please don't throw the towel in that easily."

What woman in her right mind would turn down a man begging to give being with him a shot? Especially, when that man can melt the panties off of every woman in a thirty mile radius with just one look. Add his voice to that and increase the mileage by more than triple.

"Okay. I'll try," I promise.

"Great!" He looks relieved. I didn't realize he was so tense and worried I'd say no.

Grabbing my hand, he drags me off of my stool and towards the door.

"So, I'm starving. I left the party before anything but those little cocktail weenies were served. Tara already told me that you didn't eat anything tonight and I know this great little place that's open late." He pushes me towards the stairs. "Go change. Dress casual. I'm going to run out to my car and grab my change of clothes."

"Change of clothes?" I question

He grins at me. "I had my hopes you'd be merciful. Besides, I'm a little over dressed in this monkey suit. Don't you agree?" Chuckling, he steps out, closing the front door behind him.

After that kiss, a panty change is definitely in order. I think if he keeps coming around, I'll be doing that often.

Half way up the stairs I notice Hailey and Tara leaning over the banister, grinning down at me.

"Genevieve and Lucas sitting in a tree," Tara croons.

I shoot her the finger and skip the rest of the way up the stairs.

"We're going to grab some food, so don't wait up for me." I continue as I pass them.

Hailey throws her hand over Tara's mouth, "Have fun tonight." She gives me her support "Ouch!" she screeches as Tara bites her hand.

"Don't forget to blow him…I mean blow the socks off of him!" Tara's laughter echoes down the hall behind me.

Shaking my head, I hurry to get ready. What would I do without those girls?

Chapter Four

We turn on H St. and park outside of a restaurant called Big Wang's Bar & Grill. I had to stop myself from giggling out loud like a little girl. After Tara's parting comment and the name of this place, my mind is firmly in the gutter, which was also happily assisted there by the kiss we shared in my studio.

Apparently this is a hot after-hours spot around three in the morning when all of the other bars and clubs close down.

After opening the car door for me, Lucas drags me into the virtually empty bar towards a booth in the back. This is the second time he's dragged me behind him tonight. I'm going to have to discuss this tendency with him. I might not though since it does give me an unrestricted view of his grade A behind. He wears those jeans so well. I've known him a little over twenty four hours and I'm already turning into a complete pervert.

"What do you want to drink? The appetizers are awesome here." He glances up briefly from his menu and then looks down again. "Please tell me you are not a grass eater," he says offhandedly, and completely misses my look of confusion.

"Um, grass eater?"

He looks up to explain. "You order a salad and maybe eat a piece or two the whole time we're here. Then you just push it around your plate the rest of the time because you don't want me to think you eat or have a normal appetite for some odd reason."

I throw my head back and laugh. Loud.

People are starting to stare at us.

"Have you looked at me at all? These curves are NOT maintained by a few pieces of grass and air."

He's staring at me. It makes me blush. I can see the amusement in his eyes. "You are incredibly beautiful when you laugh like that, and yes."

I blink. "Yes what?"

He shifts in his seat and clears his throat. "Yes, I have looked at you and your curves. They're just as mesmerizing as you."

He turns his attention to the waitress that is waiting on our selections. We order our beers and he orders a lot of appetizers. I may eat real food, but I don't know how he expects us to eat all of that. Is he expecting company?

After our beer arrives, I take a sip. "So why were you in New York again?"

"Well it was a two purpose trip for me. My baby sister started her freshman year of college there, so my mother decided to visit her for the day. Since I was going there for business anyway, Mom dragged me by my ear out with them for the morning and afternoon." He plays with the label on the beer bottle. I have noticed he likes to keep his hands busy. "The evening was supposed to be spent at a social gathering. Kind of a mix and mingle, be and be seen type of thing."

I'm getting the vibe that those are not his favorite events to attend.

"Now that I'm in the business end of music, I do a lot of those between New York and LA." Our appetizers arrive and we both dig in. He was right, this place is great for their apps. I'm in love with their pizza egg rolls, which are filled with oozy mozzarella cheese and yummy pepperoni.

"I'm sorry I messed up your plans tonight." I do really feel sorry. I try to avoid looking at him, but our gazes lock anyway. His eyes are like magnets for mine.

"I'm not. So don't you be. I'm sitting here with a beautiful woman that makes me laugh while enjoying delicious fried foods and beer." He holds my hand, lacing our fingers together.

"There, I would have been served champagne and hor d'oeuvres so small I would have needed to order room service as soon as I got back to my suite. As far as I'm concerned, this has been a win-win for me." His smile is spectacular. I'm smiling back at him like a complete goof ball.

"So tell me about your family. You mentioned a mom and sister." I change the subject so I can stop smiling goofily at him.

"Well as you know, my whole family is from around here. There are five of us. Four boys and one girl. I have an older brother, Kaine. Well technically a twin brother. He's a dick for beating me out of the womb by ten minutes. He never lets me forget it either. Then there's my brother, Aryan. He's two months younger than Kai and I." My disbelief must have shown because he elaborates for me.

"Technically he's a cousin, but his parents passed away on a mission trip to Africa when he was three. Where they went wasn't as civil as they were led to believe. So my parent's adopted him and he became an official Alexander. We were raised as brothers, never anything less. After having three rambunctious boys, I'm not shocked there is a four year difference between us and our youngest brother,

Micah. They needed a gap." His voice has a soft edge when he speaks about his family. The fondness is apparent.

"Then after eight years, our family was surprised with little Lilah. She's the baby in the family but never lets us do anything for her. She has a back bone of steel, a lot like our mother's."

A girl with four brothers would have to. Goodness gracious!

"Mom still lives in our childhood home. She makes sure we are all in line and know who's in charge of our family. No matter how big our egos get."

As he talks, something occurs to me. Holy moly there are two of these walking panty droppers around?

He's done talking and is waiting for me to say something.

Focus, Gen, focus!

"Wow. That sounds so amazing growing up with that many siblings. I am an only child." I clear my throat and glance away. I don't want to talk about my family. I redirect the conversation. "You didn't tell me about your Dad?"

I watch as he reaches up and rubs his hand across the back of his neck. "I don't really talk about him."

"Oh, sorry," I mumble.

One of these days I really need to learn how to not take my foot and insert it into my mouth.

Lucas gazes down at his beer, almost like he's deep in thought, maybe reliving a memory. Whatever it is, I don't think it's a very pleasant memory. Two little lines are between his eyes brows.

"My dad and I didn't really get along," he starts, still not looking up.

"You don't have to tell me." I try to stop him. I feel guilty now, he's willing to share about his dad and I'm not ready to speak about my family.

"No, it's fine. I feel more comfortable talking to you about it than I have before with anyone else, including my family." I can tell he's anxious about the story he's about to tell me because he's rapidly drumming his fingers on the table in a rapid tempo.

Sipping his beer, he continues, "So my brother, Kai, and I were groomed practically from birth to take over the family hotel chain. Kai fell into line with this. I was much more rebellious. I lived and breathed music. From as far back as I can remember I loved it. My mother told me that even as an infant, when she would turn music on I'd start squirming like I was dancing." We both laugh a little at that.

"When I was fourteen I picked up my first guitar at a friend's house and taught myself how to play. I knew my father wouldn't pay for the lessons for my 'ridiculous obsession'. Especially when he felt my time was better spent learning things necessary to running a hotel empire." His expression is scornful at the thought of that.

"Don't get me wrong, the old man was a great father when I was a kid. The Alexander Hotels have been in our family for three generations. He lived for those hotels. He invested so much of himself into modernizing and making them an international empire. He took it to a whole new level when my grandfather handed the reins over to him. My brother, Kaine, lives for those hotels as well. He is happy to follow in the family footsteps. I never was."

His voice is pained saying that. There's more to this story to put that emotion in his voice.

"I wanted to play and I did every chance I got. I went behind his back and I joined a band. At first I just played guitar. We played local gigs in some dives. I knew my father would never think to look for me in those areas. No Alexander heir would be caught, let alone perform, in a rundown bar that barely had a roof and never bothered with legalities enough to check our identification." His eyes twinkle when he speaks of his act of defiance.

"One night our lead singer got sick and couldn't perform. I stepped up to take his place for the show. We had already been paid and the bar owner had a reputation of not taking kindly to acts cancelling. That night changed everything." He turns my hand palm up and traces the lines on my hand with his fingertip.

"There was an agent in the audience scouting the headlining band. He heard us before, but with me at the mic he loved the new sound. After the set I didn't think he was going to let us go home he was so amped up while going on and on about discovering us. His label reached out and signed us the very next day." He laces our fingers together again.

I can see why the agent would sign them. His voice is hypnotic. With his looks and talent, he is the full package.

"I was eighteen and a week out of high school. All of the things I only fantasized about were placed on a silver platter ready for me to feast on. I made the decision, I was flying across the country and recording a record and then going on tour. I walked around for weeks knowing I was leaving, but it didn't become real until the night before and I had to tell my parents. When I told my father, he lost it. We had our share of arguments in the past. This time he went completely ballistic. Mom cried the entire time. She tried calming us down, but it wasn't happening. I grabbed my clothes and slammed my way out of the house." I rub my hand over his to comfort him. He's gone into a sort of trance while retelling the story.

"I was so damn determined to prove him wrong. I told myself that I would make sure I was amounting to something. I wasn't throwing my life away. I was just making my own life, you know?" I nod to reassure him of my agreement.

"So when we reached Cali, we began writing and recording. I signed up for online college courses to get my business degree. I even kept up with them while on tour, too. The band stayed on tour non-stop for a few years. When we played in D.C., I'd stop in to see my family, but my father and I never really got passed that night. I worked my ass off on my music. We had a constant flow of new tracks and we kept winning awards. It took some time, but I eventually got my MBA. I wanted to shove that in his face so badly, but I took pleasure in silently knowing I proved him wrong." He finishes his beer and signals for another one.

"If things were going so great, why did you stop singing?" I ask him, genuinely curious.

His eyes become shadowed at my question. "I lost my music. We were in the middle of recording our next big album when we all noticed my vocal recordings were off and getting worse. I went to see a specialist and found out I had vocal fold scarring. My voice will never be the same, not even with therapy. My condition became a good excuse to cover the other reasons the band broke up. I was just the tip of the iceberg, the part everyone was allowed to see. There was a lot going on with a couple of the other members. An alcohol problem joined with drug addictions. Another member contracted HIV. He continued to shoot up and hook up while on the road with groupies and fans. If that got out to the media we all would have been crucified. In the end, we split up." I can't believe what he just told me.

"If the band split up three years ago, why aren't you and your father reconciled yet?"

He smiles, but it is a sad one. "With everything I had going on, I decided to keep my family in the dark and started ignoring their phone calls. When I finally got back to D.C. after trying to get my head straight, I was ready to move on, put the next foot forward in my life since I no longer had the band. I wanted to hash things out with my Dad." He closes his eyes, his head shakes gently back and forth. "I was so self-absorbed that I never listened to their messages. My father had passed away three days before I got there from a heart attack in his office." He looks at me with tormented eyes.

"Despite what a horrible son I was, my mother embraced me after giving me the news. I'm still not sure why she didn't yell at me. She should have thrown me out. I deserved it. My brothers helped me get ready for my father's funeral that day. I didn't pack funeral attire." He smiles and shakes his head again without humor.

"I never got to make things right with him. I don't even know if we ever would have worked it out." He pulls his hands back, takes a deep swig of his beer, and begins peeling at the label again. "Despite my family's support, once the funeral was done I moved to New York and put my MBA to use by starting up my own record label. There it is. So you see, when I fuck up I don't half ass that shit."

I wait for him to look at me again. I begin carefully thinking over my words. "I think your mother knows you better than you know yourself. I think she knew that you'd beat yourself up. I also think that despite not being able to clear the air, your father was proud of what you accomplished and most likely wanted to clear the air with you as well. I'm sure, regardless of everything, he loved you very much."

I got a small smile out of him, but that's just not enough. I slide from my side of the booth and invade his. I put my arms around him and kiss him.

It was meant to be comforting but turns very steamy quickly. The chemistry between us is explosive, there's no doubting that. I pull back quickly and shove a mozzarella stick into his mouth. I giggle at him as he dramatically chews like he has a full mouth.

We both relax back in the booth, ready for a subject change. I stay on his side of the bench and he tells me all about his company. How he moved back to Virginia to be near his family once his business was up and running successfully. He still has to commute a lot between the two major cities, but he says there's nothing like being home and having your family near after so many years.

We finish up the apps, well I should really say he finished the appetizers. He can really pack food away. I'm a little in awe that he finished everything.

It's almost three a.m. and the bar is starting to get pretty crowded, so we decide to leave.

We walk back to the car hand in hand, which makes me feel more excited than something so simple should. When he holds the door open for me, a flash goes off.

I look up in shock as it continues. Great, there's paparazzi taking pictures. Now there will be pictures of me in the tabloids looking like a crazed owl.

This is our first time doing something together and there's people lurking in the dark, waiting to take our pictures.

Lucas rushes around his side of the car, jumps in, and pulls away. He looks agitated and is gripping the steering wheel so tight that his knuckles are white. He stares ahead as he drives, not speaking.

We're almost to my house and I can't stand the silence in the car any longer.

"Does that happen often?" I ask softly.

Since we're not being followed, he pulls the car over and leans across the console.

The frustration he's feeling is all over his face for me to see. "It happens. I can't prevent it. Trust me, I wish I could. Unfortunately it's something I have to deal with, and whoever I am seeing will have to deal with, too." He sighs. "It takes a while to get used to. They aren't around for everything now that I'm not in the band any longer. I know that it is tough. Don't let it get inside of your head. Once the mystery surrounding you wears off, they'll move on to the next big update."

He studies my face. When I don't say anything he sits back in his seat and puts the car in drive, pulling back onto the street. Within minutes we're at The Brownstone. He gets out and walks me to the door. I waver a moment about seeing him again. I don't know if I'm comfortable being in the spotlight next to him. I do know that I don't want to let him go yet. I don't know what dating a former rock star entails, but the more I get to know him as a man, the more I want to know. I give him a hug and kiss. When he turns away, I pull him back and hug him again.

"Maybe next time we can stay here and I can cook you dinner. I make a mean spaghetti sauce and stuffed meatball." I snuggle into the hug, hiding my face and waiting for him to reject the idea.

He pulls me away from him and stares down at me.

"That'd be wonderful, and that's one of my favorite meals, too." His smile brightens and his voice deepens. "Until then I'm calling for a do over. That goodbye kiss wasn't up to our usual standard."

This is what I will call a fairy tale kiss. A real live foot popper. I press my body against his. His hands move to my hips and hold me firmly against his body. I can feel how our kiss is affecting him as his erection hardens against my lower stomach. My hands are flat on his chest, feeling the heat that is radiating from his body through his clothes.

"Invite me in.", He whispers against my lips.

I shake my head. I need a more time to process this thing we have going on. With him around, I have too hard of a time thinking.

I probably should have stopped pressing my body against his when I said no. I'm definitely giving off mixed signals. My mind and body seem to have stopped coordinating their agendas.

"You little minx," he growls at me.

Goodness that sound is so sexy.

"I better go then or I'm liable to drag you off caveman style." He reaches behind me and opens the front door.

With his other hand he shoves me inside. I watch him stride down the steps, get in his car, and drive away.

He sure loves man-handling me. Always pulling and pushing me as he pleases. I still have to talk to him about that. I'll eventually get tired of it, won't I? The quivering feeling in my stomach his behavior causes suspiciously makes me think not.

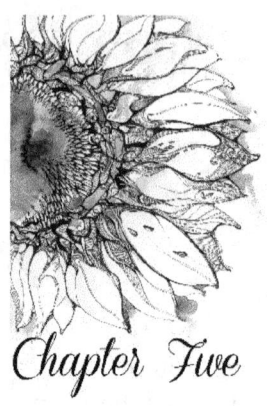

Chapter Five

"Oh my, dear lover lips, I need you badly!"

My eyes pop open and I scream.

Tara is inches from my face, caressing my cheek.

"What the heck, Tara!" I shove her away from me and sit up in bed.

"Get up, lazy bum. Someone's at the door to see you."

"Lucas?"

"Wake up with Lucas on the brain, did you? You have the female equivalent of morning wood going on, don't you?" She laughs when I toss a pillow at her head. Catching it, she throws it back at me. "No, something really strange. A girl is here asking if your dad is home."

"What? Crap. Let me throw some clothes on and brush my teeth. Is she waiting in the den or kitchen?" I rush to my closet and grab the first pair of jeans I find on the floor.

Yeah, I'm a little messy. Sue me.

"She's in the foyer. She didn't want to wait anywhere else. I told her I was going to get you." I pop my head out of the closet to see her by my door. "I'll go get you some coffee. You look like you need it after your late night." She winks at me and leaves. I hear her sing a

Britney Spears song, horribly out of tune, on her way down the stairs.

I rush through brushing my teeth and attempt a finger comb on my way to the foyer. I don't want to leave the girl waiting too long. When I reach the bottom of the stairs, the foyer is empty.

I open the front door just in time to see a petite blonde climb into the back a of taxi cab. As the cab pulls away, she looks back up to the Brownstone and sees me standing there. I can't see her clearly through the window of the cab, but I can tell she is looking at me. Instead of telling the cab driver to stop, she turns to face away in her seat. I continue to watch the cab drive and make a turn at the next corner.

What was that about? Why didn't she stay to talk to me? How would she have known my dad? She looks way too young to have been an acquaintance of his.

When I reach the kitchen, Tara has a delicious steaming cup of coffee waiting for me.

I should ask Tara if she noticed anything off about the girl. She's a photographer; she pays attention to things most people don't. I tend to notice things, too, but more in an artistic sense. Like I noticed that she had gorgeous, long, pale blonde hair. Not long like Hailey's down to butt length, but more of a waist length in that gorgeous shade that I have always envied. Okay so maybe that wasn't an artistic observation and more of an envious one. I never shook my childhood insecurities from my golden parents.

Tara looks up at me from her laptop she has sitting on the kitchen island. "How'd that go?" She's staring at me like she's expecting something.

"Well, when I got to the foyer, I opened the front door just in time to see her hop into a cab and take off. How did she catch a cab so quickly around here? We aren't exactly in a taxi hailing area." I run my fingertip around the rim of my mug, confused.

"The cab was how she got here. She had it idling for her when I answered the door. So you didn't get to talk to her at all? Did you see her?"

"I only saw that she's blonde and appears fairly young. Why? Did you notice anything?" It's my turn to search Tara's face, which she carefully leaves blank.

"Gen, I think if that girl comes back, you need to talk to her. I don't want to say what I think and blow smoke up your butt when I honestly don't know anything." She pats my hand, which is what she always does when she wants to soothe someone. "When you see her again, you'll know what I'm thinking. I have work to do. I'll catch you later. Oh, and Hailey is caught in the grips of her wildly fabulous horny imagination. I don't think she'll surface from her lair for a while." She picks up her laptop and pushes away from the counter.

"Now, if only her sex life was fabulous enough to keep her in a bedroom for endless hours," Tara muses as she walks out of the kitchen with her laptop tucked under one arm and a cup of coffee with a croissant, which I'm sure she's bringing to Hailey's office, in the other. If no one brought Hailey anything while she's working, she'd wither away without even noticing.

If I didn't know Hail so well, I'd never be able to figure out how sweet, angelic Hailey Trenton writes erotica with a limited knowledge of anything erotic. Everyone eats up her novels—H. Steele is a bestselling author. Maybe the few relationships she has had were just as steamy as what she writes? I wouldn't know since she's very private about her sex life unlike Tara, who shouts details at us just to get a reaction. Heck she never even told us when, or even who she lost her virginity to! Her lips are sealed tighter than my legs.

Heading back into my bedroom, I quickly shower and change. I plan on going to my favorite café to do some people watching. I'd love to go visit my Gram and Grand-Pop, but they're in New Jersey visiting my Great Aunt Gina. I grab my boots out of the coat closet and slip into my mustard yellow pea coat; one of my favorite Christmas presents from my grandparents. With a bright red beanie hat on my head, I start my five-mile walk to the café.

Tara and Hailey are always complaining when I take this walk, but seriously, how are you supposed to people watch when you're driving in your car? It's hazardous to others if I'm not keeping my eyes on the road.

I pass a park on my way. It's another one of my favorite places to people watch, but I haven't had breakfast yet and the café I'm going to serves the absolute best eggs Florentine. I might as well feed myself while I search for inspiration.

"Hey, Tammy." The usual morning hostess is there to greet me as I enter.

"Hey, Gen. How've you been?" She leads me to my booth, which is in the corner with a perfect view of most everyone dining, as well as people passing the café. There's no view into the kitchen, but I occasionally go back there too, and hang out with Ronald, the chef.

We make small talk for a few minutes, but she has to get back to the podium and seat the people that have just arrived.

"Good morning, Gen." My usual waitress brings me my favorite breakfast tea. "The same old eggs Florentine?"

I laugh at that. "Hey, Lucy. Yes, the same old eggs Florentine. My pop always says if it isn't broken don't fix it."

She leaves me to my tea. I look up to get busy, seeing what's going on around me just in time to see one of my best clients approaching my booth.

Vivian is what I'd describe as a dragon lady with a heart of gold. She is incredibly nurturing, but she can be like Attila the Hun and his invading army.

"Genni! It's so good to see you. I didn't know you frequented this establishment." Halfway through her greeting, she places one hand on my shoulder while the other brushes out my apparent hat hair. This is exactly why she's so motherly; I don't even think she realizes does it.

"Good morning, Viv. Yes, actually I come here quite a bit. The food is delicious and the people are interesting. Would you like to join me?" I throw out the awkward invite, secretly hoping she doesn't accept.

"Oh no, darling, kind of you to offer. I wish I could but I'm actually here with a few of my sons. They all slipped away to the bathroom. I'm guessing they are trying to formulate a battle plan for their breakfast with me. Silly boys don't realize mother knows all." She has a glint in her eye that tells me that's really possible "Anywho, I just got back from visiting my daughter and decided to round up as many of my boys as possible for an impromptu breakfast interrogation of their lives." She smiles beautifully when she speaks about them. It's inspiring to see someone who relishes motherhood so much. Especially after my mother's antipathy for her own child.

What I love most about Vivian is that when I am around her, I don't have to worry about speaking or having much input because she does all of the talking.

"Ooh, here come my boys now. You have to meet them. Boys!" She waves them over. "Over here! You have to meet someone special. Hurry up!"

I hear the voice first and I shiver all over. "Mother, please. Who are you pestering now?"

Lucas steps into view, dressed in a suit. He smiles down at me, but this isn't the smile that makes me feel weak in the knees. This is as if I'm a stranger. Another man is standing just beyond Lucas, but I don't pay him any mind.

"Boys, this is the very talented painter I'm always gushing about, Genni-V," Vivian introduces me.

"Well Genni, it's a pleasure to finally meet you," he silkily voices. His smile warms up a bit while he takes in my appearance today.

"That's what you're going to say? It's a pleasure to meet me?" I'm too angry to notice his look of utter confusion, or that of his mother's, and the man behind him.

Was he planning on keeping our relationship a secret from his mother? The old Gen would have meekly gone with it and asked him about it later, but not *the world-is-my-oyster-grab-life-by-the-balls* Gen!

When I hear his sexy chuckle, my head is about to explode. Then I realize the man I'm looking at isn't chuckling. Suddenly, the man standing behind him starts laughing uproariously, drawing attention from other diners.

A much more casually dressed Lucas comes into sight and steps around the man laughing, and drapes his arm across the shoulders of the first Lucas. Well, crap, not the first Lucas; obviously, his twin brother, Kaine.

I've done it again. When I'm not busy trying to blend in with wallpaper, my mouth runs away and embarrasses me. Both of my Gens need to coordinate a little better—this is getting ridiculous. Also, I really have to stop thinking about myself as two different people. I'm sure if a psychiatrist knew, I'd be diagnosed with something.

"Shut up, Micah." Lucas shoots his other brother a dirty look, then turns back to me. "Hello, beautiful. Have I told you how pretty you look when you get embarrassed? Your ears get all pink."

Now this is my Lucas. Seeing them both together, I honestly don't know how I made the mistake in the first place. He has my head all foggy if I didn't notice these differences right away.

Lucas is relaxed and has this "bad boy playing at being good" charm going on. His relaxed pose and tousled hair makes you want to run your fingers through it.

Kaine, however, is much more reserved. Starting with his smile to his completely perfect posture then ending with his clothes and hair being perfectly in order too.

I finally gather enough courage to look at Vivian. It's almost comical to see the broad smile that is lighting her face. Especially, with the way her gaze is ping ponging between myself and Lucas. I can already see the cogs turning in her head. She has me married with two point five kids, living in the suburbs with Lucas, and close to her own house so she can visit often.

Lucas seems to notice this as well and dons an adorable look of bashfulness.

The third man in their group finally steps forward.

I gasp.

"You!" I narrow my eyes and accuse.

What the H-E double hockey sticks? I just realized who he is now that the name Lucas said before penetrates my mind.

"Well, hello. It's been a long time, Genni—"

"Don't you dare think about finishing that sentence," I hiss in warning.

After thirteen years, my arch enemy from grade school is standing in front of me.

Micah Alexander.

When I was in fifth grade, after the seventh graders had the sex education discussion, he dubbed me Genni Genitals. Which was then shortened to Genni-tals.

Of course, everyone in fifth grade jumped on the childish moniker. After another year, he was off to high school and I was still Genni-tals. It only stopped when

Hailey, Tara, and I were sent to an all-girls high school, after eighth grade.

"Well, it looks like I'm really not needed for introductions. You seem to know most of my sons," Vivian says with a pointed looked.

I notice her thumb rubbing the side knuckle on her index finger. I have a feeling that she knew what Micah was going to say, and was ready to grab him by the ear.

I would have loved to seen that. Darn, I spoke up too soon.

Lucas is eyeing his brother, too.

"This is actually my first time meeting Kaine." I stand as much as the booth will allow and shake his hand. "Sorry about my earlier outburst."

He stiffly nods his head, accepting my apology.

"If your offer still stands, I think we will join you for breakfast," Vivian beams with a suspicious gleam in her eyes.

"Oh, of course." I slide further into the booth, bringing my tea with me. I have a feeling I'm going to need a lot more tea to calm my nerves during this breakfast.

Lucas slips around his brothers and mother. He swiftly kisses the latter on the cheek and slides into the booth next to me. "You might need another cup of that to get through this breakfast," he whispers to me, gesturing to the tea and affirming my earlier thought.

Everyone else slides into the opposite booth. The benches are generous enough to accommodate them comfortably. Lucy comes over after a few minutes and takes their orders. Good god they order enough to feed a dozen people.

Vivian catches my expression and sends me a look full of amusement. "Yes, that's all for them. It's a wonder they didn't eat me out of house and home while raising them," she muses.

"I'm a growing boy," all three chime at once.

Their drinks arrive along with my fresh cup of tea.

Vivian stares me down until I'm forced to give her my undivided attention. I can see where Lucas—and I guess Kaine, too—get their eyes from. They're piercing, especially when they're staring at you, directly. I want to shift nervously in my seat but squelch the urge.

"So, Genni, after two years of friendship, why haven't you told me you know my sons?"

This is where I wish I could blend in with the wallpaper.

"Well, honestly, I never really gave your last name much thought. At least not enough to realize you are the mother of someone I went to grade school with," I dip my head towards Micah, "and I only just met your son Lucas," I tell her. She seems to be thinking over my response.

Lucas's hand is at the nape of my neck, twirling loose strands of hair. It's very distracting and making it difficult to focus on his mother now. Finally, my explanation seems enough to please her since she is smiling again.

"Just met?" Micah snorts. "You can tell they're already bumping uglies. Using his worm to fish in her pond. Rubbing genitals." With a yelp, he shuts up.

There is the ear grab I was so hoping to see. It is even better than I imagined.

"Micah Nathanial! It's one thing to poke fun at one of your brothers but don't you embarrass poor Genni!" Viv scolds.

"Poor Genni?" Micah looks at me incredulously. "She's one of the trio of she-devils that almost got me expelled from sixth grade. She put a worm in my chocolate pudding in third grade. You should be taking my side. You're *my* mother!" he exclaims.

I snicker, remembering that. I have no doubt he did something rude first to deserve it.

"I don't know what you're talking about, Micah. My Genevieve is an angel." Lucas snuggles me against his side.

I sigh dreamily. He called me his. I shouldn't like him staking his claim, but who can help it? When you are plastered against this man's side, it is difficult to be in complete control of your facilities.

The food arrives and I reluctantly slide out of Lucas's embrace to help move dishes around to make room for everything they ordered. I really want to cuddle back into his side and sniff him. He smells amazing; a warm, manly scent with just a hint of something sweet to entice you into inhaling deeply. I'll need to find out what cologne he wears so I can write the company asking that they provide a warning label with their product: May cause flushed face and difficult respiration. Wear with caution around women.

I shift in my seat and notice Vivian smirk at her Belgian waffles. *Does this woman miss anything?*

"Well, as pleasant as this has been, I need to get into the office." Kaine drains his coffee in one gulp and moves to stand up.

While I was wrapped in my own thoughts, I didn't even realize that Kaine had inhaled the two plates of food he ordered.

"Already dear? It's Sunday morning, can't you stay a little longer?" Vivian is on her feet next to him. She's already smoothing down his lapels and adjusting his tie like she knows what his reply is going to be. Knowing her, I wouldn't doubt it.

"I wish I could, Mom. This looks like it is going to be an interesting meal, but I need to get into the office and prepare for the meetings I have scheduled on Monday. I need to fly to our New York location." He drops a kiss on to his mother's forehead before turning to address me. "It was very nice meeting you, Genni. I hope we'll see each other again soon."

After finishing his goodbyes, he strides through the restaurant and out of the door, paying zero attention to the women watching him leave. He really must live for the family hotel chain. Going into the office, on a Sunday morning, is sheer dedication.

My father was the same way; he was in the office or away on business far more than he was home.

Vivian watches her son go with pursed lips. "He's working more and more. I swear he never takes a break." She returns to her seat and starts in on her remaining sons. "As for you two. Micah, you better be eating healthy and getting enough sleep. With all of those ridiculous hours you work at that club of yours, you need to take better care of yourself."

I hear Micah mutter that'd he'd be getting enough sleep if she didn't wake him up so early for breakfast meetings. A grunt follows his mutterings when Vivian jams her elbow into his side.

"And you." She jabs her finger in Lucas's direction. "You need to slow down with the constant traveling. You have a continuous case of jet lag. Last evening, you were in such a hurry to get back down here from New York, you nearly left me behind. Work is not that important," she scolds gently. "Or was it even work that had you in such a hurry?" She raises her eyebrow and looks thoughtfully at me.

"No need to fish for answers. I was actually in a hurry to get back to see Genevieve." He gives her a grin, the one I'm starting to recognize as his "go to" when he wants to charm someone. "I just couldn't bear not having her in my arms for another moment. I had to see her glittering smile as I gaze down into the amber eyes of my dreams." Lucas lays it on thick.

Micah's snorts cease with a grunt.

This time I'm sure Lucas kicked him under the table since Vivian is seems so caught up in what Lucas was saying, she missed his rude behavior.

Vivian reaches over and pinches Micah's arm. I stand corrected.

"I don't know what I'm going to do with you," she scolds, clearly exasperated. She waves for Lucas to continue. "Go on Lucas, tell me how you met my dear Genni. Do not interrupt." She shoots Micah a withering look that is fierce enough to make me wary about saying anything.

This is great. I can hear what happened that night without having to confess that I was too drunk to recall anything. I grip the edge of the bench seat and lean closer so I don't miss a word.

Lucas is clearly amused by his mother and continues, "Well it was pretty typical. Guy notices girl in club and then notices her noticing him, you follow? While she's on the dance floor, I sent one of the bouncers to get her to the VIP area for me." He starts chuckling slowly. "Rather than the typical female adoration I expected, as soon as she reached the VIP section, she stormed right up to me, planted her hands on her hips, and told me—and I quote— 'That is not how you request a lady's presence. Since you are clearly misguided and don't know how to properly approach a woman, I'll stay just to inform you. Number one: don't send hired muscle to retrieve the lady like she's an item on a shopping list.' When he's done, he's laughing outright with Micah. Vivian sits back and starts to hoot with laughter as well.

I have to agree with my drunk self. I can't believe he did that.

When she sobers enough to speak again, she demands more from Lucas. "That explains that. Now tell me why she was photographed walking out of the club, wearing your shirt."

I nearly spew the tea I had just taken a sip of. Lucas leans back and crosses his arms over his chest, shooting his mother a dirty look. Crap. We were just dancing to her tune all breakfast.

She spoke true; mothers really do know all. At least this one does.

For once in his life, Micah is quietly listening to the conversation without adding his own jabs. His grin still makes me want to pick up a pancake and smother him with it.

"Oh, you don't know that already?" Lucas challenges with an eyebrow quirk.

"Pfft, I don't know every detail. Continue on," Vivian urges haughtily.

Lucas links our hands together and looks at me with guilt, as if he did something wrong. "The waitress that was serving our group 'accidentally' spilled a drink on Genevieve in an effort to force her to leave. She was hoping to end her shift and leave with me."

"The hell you say?! You didn't tell me that!" Micah pops up in his seat, looking outraged. "I won't have that poor behavior in my club."

"I forgot you were back in your office for all of that," Lucas says offhandedly. "Anyway, the entire front of her dress was drenched, making the material see through. I gave her my shirt to cover herself."

What a gentleman. I smile my appreciation.

The rest of breakfast passes with pleasant conversation. We discuss the things going on in everyone's life. It was interesting to be included like this, as if I were a member of their family.

Lucas picks up the bill for everyone and we all get up to leave.

I realize I didn't do any people watching. I'll have to stop at the park on my way home for a few minutes and give it a shot there.

"Lucas, dear, do you think you can drive me home?" Vivian inquires. "Kaine picked me up so that clearly is not an option and I don't want to take Micah out of his way."

He nods. "Sure, let me just walk Genevieve to her car first."

"Oh, that's not necessary. I walked," I add.

"*What?*" All three demand, staring at me incredulously.

They start to scold me about the dangers of a young lady walking by herself. They're sounding exasperatingly like Hailey and Tara.

"I'll drive you home. It's on my way," Micah offers.

I'm going with it being an offer rather than him telling me. I'm not above kicking him in the shin like I did in grade school. I'm also not a huge fan of being told what to do.

"No. I'm driving my woman home. You take Mom," Lucas decides.

I kiss the man a few times and he is already declaring me his woman. On one hand, hearing that makes me tingle, but on the other hand, I don't want to like his Neanderthal behavior. I sigh in my head. That's the key word, I don't want to like it, meaning that I actually do.

Everyone agrees without my input. We finish our goodbyes. As we're walking to Lucas's car, something occurs to me.

I call from across the street. "Hey, Micah? How do you know where I live since you knew that it was on your way?"

He smiles back at me, shrugging his shoulders, and keeps walking to his car in true Micah fashion. Not much has changed in thirteen years.

The drive to The Brownstone is pleasant; we joke over his mother completely hustling us and about Micah's antics over breakfast. When we arrive, he walks me to the front door and pulls me into a tight hug. "I'm going to pick you up tonight around six. I want to show you something."

"What makes you think I don't already have plans tonight?" He squeezes me tighter at my question.

"That's fine. Break them." He pulls back. His smile is very cocky. When he smiles at me like that, I would definitely break plans for him, but he doesn't need to know I'm putty over his smiles.

"You're lucky I just happen to be free of plans this evening." I return his smile.

"Good. I'm going to walk away now. I'm not going to give you a kiss goodbye because it wouldn't stop there," he utters that fact in a husky voice. "When you're ready for that, wear something red for me. It'll be our little secret code." Despite not wanting to kiss me goodbye, he still gives me a peck on my forehead and leaves.

He waits to pull away from the curb until I finally go into the house. I lean back against the door and heave a sigh. I bite my lip and grin, I'm already thinking over what red items are in my wardrobe.

Chapter Six

"What are you thinking?" Lucas asks as he studies my face, his lips curving into a smile.

"I'm thinking that I'm seriously in love," I breathe while I gaze adoringly at my dream house.

Chuckling, Lucas slides out of the car, opens my door for me, and helps me out. I can't believe he lives here. It's not in the heart of D.C. where I love being, but near Old Town Alexandria, right on the river. I have always loved English manor style houses. This one is huge.

"I'm glad you like it. I rarely get down time with work and the traveling that's required for it, but every chance I get—I'm here." He is dragging me behind him again.

The inside of the house is just as lovely as the outside from what I can see. Which isn't much. Wherever he is taking me, he wants to get there quickly. I'm running up the stairs to keep up.

Finally, we reach a door and he leads me through.

Gasping, I pull my hand out from his.

There's a bed in this room. I'm in his bedroom!

Dominating the room is one of the largest beds I've ever seen. I can't take my eyes off of it. I'm so focused on the bed I don't even realize Lucas is standing next to me until he cups my chin and turns my gaze up to his.

"I told you I wanted to show you something. It's not my bed. That'll come soon enough." His eyes are dancing with laughter, but his voice is gentle.

He grabs my hand and starts dragging me across the room.

"Of course, if you insist we can detour towards the bed for a bit," he laughingly throws over his shoulder.

That's when I see it.

I move past him to get up closer to it. It goes well with the earth tones and masculinity of the room.

I study it closely, despite intimately knowing every brushstroke that makes this hauntingly beautiful painting.

I held onto it for years, unable to part with it.

Two years ago, I let my agent talk me into putting it on display as a centerpiece for one of my shows. I sold a lot of pieces that evening, which was nice. Chelsea, my agent, was excited to have the piece displayed, regardless of my flat out refusal to have it listed for sale.

When the show was over and I went into the back and began prepping my remaining artwork for travel, Chelsea's assistant for the evening came dancing back to help me.

"I just finished the last sale of the evening. You'll be a very happy girl when you get this check. Especially after what I just sold *The Family* for," she happily chirped.

I could feel the blood drain from my face.

Chelsea came walking back. "Did I just see the—"

She broke off when she saw my look of absolute horror.

I ran to the front room of the gallery and out onto the sidewalk. The painting was nowhere in sight.

For several weeks I tried tracking down my artwork. No contact information was left. The credit card used for the purchase was for a company based out of New York. The receptionist for the company was a brick wall when it came to providing information. I was left with money I didn't want, for a painting I never wanted to sell.

I don't know how long Lucas has let me stand here and stare.

He's behind me with his hands on my shoulders, staring up at the painting as well.

"When I met you, I know you told me that you are an artist. I didn't put it together that you are Genni-V. Not until we had breakfast with my mother." His voice is soft in my ears. "When I saw this at an art show my mother forced me attend with her, I had to have it. I didn't care what I had to pay to get it." He pulls me back against his chest.

"At the end of the evening, when we were leaving, I saw it. It pulled me from across the room. In that moment, I felt connected to this painting. It held all of my pain in front of my eyes, yet also a hint of wistfulness, hope, maybe even love." His one hand comes up and he feathers the back of his finger down my cheek. "I felt a connection to the artist, as well. If she could paint this, then she was someone who understood. Tell me what it meant to you."

I can feel his lips move against my ear when he speaks. I lean back, allowing him to support more of me and revel in the feeling of his arms wrapped around me, holding me to him.

I close my eyes. "I painted it after my parents died in a car accident. I was fourteen. I was lost for a while in my feelings. I didn't know how to deal with them. This was the first time I ever picked up a paintbrush. It's all of those emotions you mentioned and so many more. Anger, fear, sadness, and regret. You're right, there is hope, as well. Hope that I'd learn from my parents' mistakes. Hope that rather than being a product of my upbringing, I'd find happiness where they could not. I don't think I realized that at the time. I would stare at it over the years. It helped me see where I was then and where I am now. I've come a long ways but still have further to go." I swallow through the lump in my throat. I look over my shoulder. "Thank you for showing me."

He drops his arms and steadies me before stepping around and reaching up to take the painting off the wall.

"What are you doing?" I place my hand on his arm to stop him.

"This painting means so much to you. After hearing your feelings towards it, I can't keep it. You should have it." We stare into each other's eyes for a few moments. I smile reassuringly at him.

"I'm almost there, Lucas. You understand what I put into each brushstroke. It is where it's supposed to be. Please leave it."

He cups my face gently between his palms and slowly lowers his lips. Before they can touch, "You are the most beautiful woman I've ever encountered. Your beauty is from the inside out. I'm in awe," he whispers.

When our lips finally touch, the kiss is slow and sweet. It's nothing like our previous kisses. We take our time exploring each other, light touches here and there. Slowly awakening our bodies to the passion rather than dousing ourselves in it. He breaks away first.

Despite the gentleness of the kiss, he is breathing heavily. My hand is against his chest, feeling his heart pounding in time with my own.

"I'm in a room with numerous surfaces I'd readily love to place you on and explore every inch of your incredibly delectable body. Yet, I'm not going to. I'm only human. Don't let me take more than you are ready to give, please." His voice is ragged when he speaks.

I pull away and walk over to the chaise lounge that's positioned in front of the fireplace. I take a deep breath to ready myself for what I've decided.

"I had a lot of time this afternoon to do some thinking. Mostly, I thought about our code. You're right, I do need things to go slowly, but I don't need them to go glacial." I start to unbutton my white blouse.

I begin to slowly reveal a red lace demi bra. "So I'm willing—" Two more buttons open. "—to take some baby steps with you."

I take the hungry look in his eyes as encouragement. My shirt slides off my shoulders and slips to the ground. Despite my bravado, I'm a ball of nerves inside. I start to slide my bra strap off my shoulder, but Lucas is suddenly there, stopping me.

"I know I said this before, my little minx, you do have me in awe. This time with your physical beauty." He traces his finger tip down the line of my throat and across my collar bone before moving on to trace the edge of my bra.

"Perfection." He backs me until my knees hit the edge of the chaise. He helps to lower me down across the lounge. Kneeling down next to me, he gently touches my hair that is spilling over the side. "I want to learn what you like." His lips graze mine. "If I do anything you are uncomfortable with, I need to know that you'll be okay with telling me no. That's all you need to say."

"I understand. Please," I beg, but I'm not exactly sure what for. I just know that I want more. His lips press more firmly against mine, yet remain gentle at the same time. I can feel him holding back, not wanting to scare me with his intensity. I want all of him. I want him just as wild as I'm feeling. I bite his lip and smile against his mouth when I hear him growl. The kiss deepens. His hand that was previously at my waist slides up to cup my breast. He moves his thumb to circle my nipple. It hardens to a point through the lace of my bra. His kisses move to my neck.

Running my fingers through his hair, I enjoy the sensation that his lips, tongue, and teeth are creating. His thumb is still grazing my nipple thru the fabric and it's driving me insane. My back arches in need of more.

"I know what you want, minx." Lowering his head, he takes my nipple into his mouth. A moan escapes from me. I can feel the pleasure shooting through my body and down between my legs. I want Lucas's mouth on me, no fabric separating us.

I sit up and, with his help, remove my bra. My breasts are eye level with him. He's staring at them like a starving man. I give him a brief kiss. Lucas's hands cup both of my breasts, testing the weight in the palm of his hands. My nipples are tight little points of sensitive nerve endings. Lowering his head, he begins to lavish attention on them. I can feel the moisture gathering between my legs. I squeeze my legs together to try and relieve the ache he is creating there.

"Lucas. Please. I need more," I pant. I know I told him slow, but my body is screaming, *Speed the heck up!*

"Do you want me to take your pants off and touch your pussy? Want me to make you feel so good you explode?" The sound of his voice is gruff with his own needs.

"*Yes!* Please. Touch me," I beg again.

"Say the words, Genevieve. Tell me where you want me to touch you." He starts unbuttoning my pants.

"I want your hands down there." His hands stop pulling down my zipper like he won't continue without the words. I concede. "I want you to touch my pussy."

Lucas grins, looking pleased with my compliance. He finishes pulling my pants down and off me. Tossing them to the side, he leans down and places kisses next to my hip bone. "I'm looking forward to the day I get to pleasure you while I taste you." I moan at the image his words stir in my mind.

My body jolts at his touch. Even through the fabric of my panties his fingers are magic. He moves the material to the side, sliding his fingers down my folds, gathering moisture, before moving back up to the tight little ball of nerves that aches for his touch.

Within minutes little waves are moving through my body. Using his other hand, he gently pinches my nipple causing pain and pleasure to mingle within me. I shatter into a million pieces. He's devouring my mouth and swallowing my cries of pleasure. He continues to stroke me through my peak and descent. He eases me from the intense heights he was able to bring my body to, and gives my soul time to rejoin it.

Lucas picks me up, ignoring my protests, and crosses to the bed, laying me on the sheets. I quietly watch as he undresses, revealing his amazing tattoo covered body, and climbs in next to me, pulling my body into his arms.

"We're going to cuddle for now. Then I'm going to tease you and play with your beautiful body all over again. If I'm a quick learner, you are going to scream my name a time or two more, before I let you leave here." I let his words wash over me and send heat through my already well-pleasured body. I have no doubt that he is a very quick study.

"Do I get to touch you, too?" His hard length presses against me, I wiggle my bottom. He places his hand on my hip to halt my movements.

Lucas kisses me behind my ear. "Not tonight, minx. You have me so worked up I wouldn't be as gentle as you need. Soon, though. My cock is going to stay rock hard, thinking about you wrapping your fingers around it."

I wake up in Lucas's bed. The spot next to me where he was is empty. The faint sound of music drifts to me. I look around the room and notice a door off to the side. I can see the light on from beneath it. Slipping out of bed, I pull his shirt over my head and pad over to the door.

Quietly so that I don't disturb him, I peek inside. The room is filled with guitars and records lining the walls. Lucas is sitting in a chair across the small room. His eyes are closed as he lets the music he is creating wash over him, I think. He moves his fingers deftly over the strings, making the instrument come alive much like he did earlier with my body. The sight of him playing is beautiful. That's not what has me mesmerized though. His voice is strong and deep with a bit of a rasp that just draws you in.

> *I didn't know it'd end, couldn't imagine how.*
> *If I knew then what I know now,*
> *I would have screamed aloud.*
> *Found a way to make you proud.*
> *Life goes by so fast.*
> *You close your eyes and then it's past.*
> *I took the long way home.*
> *Dragging my feet to make it last.*
> *Now I'm sitting here all alone.*
> *Wishing we could have talked in the past.*

I gasp when the lyrics wrap around me and finally penetrate my mind. This must be something he wrote after his father passed away. It's about losing someone, about living with regret.

When the last note rings out, he looks up at me. Judging by the look in his eyes, I can tell he has been aware of my presence the entire time. He let me see a piece of himself he hasn't shared with anyone else. The depth of emotion that brings out in me is overwhelming. I hold my hand out to him. After setting his guitar down, he crosses the room. Ignoring my hand, he picks me up and tosses me over his shoulder. Settling me back on to the bed, I know I'm about to be played as expertly as the instrument he just held.

The rest of the night he keeps his promise to me and then some. I scream his name three more times. He only relents long enough for short cuddles, naps, and for us to get a snack. This night is all about me. Exploring my body to bring me pleasure and learning my responses. He never pushes me for more or makes any demands. It couldn't be more perfect.

I finally fall asleep looking at the painting hanging above the fire place. It's perfect right here in this room.

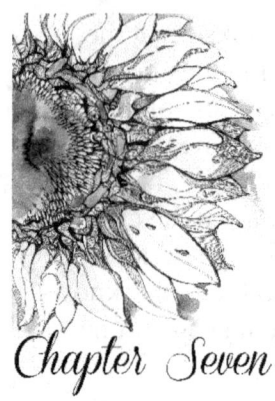

Chapter Seven

It's a novel experience, waking up in the arms of a man after a night of being thoroughly pleasured. Lucas is still sleeping. I push up on my elbow to get a better look at him. He is completely at ease; his face soft, almost boyish. I gaze at the rest of his sleeping form. I find nothing boyish in that. He is all man covered in impressive artwork I plan to take the time to admire later. His broad shoulders taper down to a lean waist. To accompany his six pack abs, he has what I love to refer to as the V to the P. Those delicious lines on each side of a man's hips. They seem to point your gaze in the direction of, well in the case of Lucas, a very impressive case of morning wood.

Holy crap on a cracker—it just twitched!

Is it supposed to do that?

I slowly reach my hand out to touch it. I want to make sure it's okay. I don't know if I should wake up Lucas and tell him about it. The second my finger grazes his flesh, it twitches again. I've watched porn before, but I don't recall twitching. I attempt to touch it again when I hear a throat clearing. If someone took a flame thrower to my face right now it couldn't possibly get any hotter. When I get the nerve up to look up, Lucas is wide awake and seems to be struggling very hard not to laugh at me.

"Good morning!" I say cheerfully. I really ought to explain the situation. "I woke up and saw it twitching and wanted to make sure it was okay. Honestly I don't think it should be doing that." My earnest rambling tips the scale and Lucas loses all control over his laughter.

I'm beyond embarrassed now. This morning after is not going that well. I get on my knees next to him, take my pillow, and try to muffle his laughing. If a jury of my peers ask, that's my story and I'm sticking to it. Before I know it, Lucas has me flipped over and pinned to the mattress, still laughing into my neck.

"Minx, you're the reason he's twitching. He likes when you look at him." At least he only chuckled a time or two during his explanation.

I want to touch him and I refuse to be told no again like last night. I pull his head down for a kiss while my other hand runs down his ribs to his hip. A little to the right and I can feel him through his underwear. He moans in the back of his throat. I take that as encouragement and slide my hand in his waist band to feel him skin to skin. My hand encounters the silken heat I've wanted to touch since last night.

"Your hand on my dick is even better than I imagined," his voice is hoarse.

I lick my lips at the sound of it. I'm impatient to learn more about what my touch can do to him. "Off." I push at his underwear. "Take them off."

At my demand, he divests himself of his last article of clothing. When he springs free, I take in the sight. He's so big and looks just as smooth as he felt in my hand. I roll us back over. I want to kneel next to him again.

I experiment by wrapping both of my hands around him, moving them up and down. Lucas shows me what he likes and helps to set a pace he enjoys. I'm really getting into it and enjoying myself, too. I want to make him scream, though.

I never found the thought of this appealing, but I want to make sure I please Lucas as thoroughly as I was last night. Rather than give him the opportunity to object, I just go for it. I lower my lips to him and take the tip into my mouth.

"Fuck!" His hips jerk and he slides further in, almost to the point of making me gag. I sit back up and look at him, anxious to know if he'll let me continue.

"Was that okay?" I stare wide-eyed at him.

He's taking deep controlled breaths. When he still doesn't say anything, I nudge his hip.

"Sorry, my brain is still trying to process your mouth on me. Did you say okay? That was way better than okay."

"Can I do it again?" I bite my lip.

"If you don't I might cry. No one wants to see a grown man cry. It is pitiful," he jokes without his normal humor.

I don't waste another moment and I take his erection back into my mouth quickly. He's right, who wants to see a grown man cry? I can't have my man crying. Well, maybe tears of joy would be okay.

I use my hands too since I can't completely fit him in my mouth. I test, swirling my tongue around the tip. That earns me a groan. I find a comfortable rhythm for my hands and mouth and before long Lucas is pulling on my hair to get my attention. Can't he see I'm busy here and thoroughly engrossed in my worked?

"Minx, you need to stop. Genevieve! I'm going to come. Minx!"

I'm familiar with the phrase "spitters are quitters". I may be some things, but I'm definitely not a quitter. I double my efforts when I feel him harden further. With a deep groan he starts pulsing into my mouth. The first spurt hits the back of my throat, surprising me. I quickly swallow.

After jerking one final time, Lucas pulls me up his body and gives me a kiss. When his hands start to roam, I break away and bound off the bed.

"Last night was me, which means this morning is your turn. So keep those hands to yourself." I thrust my hands onto my hips.

"Oh really?" He quirks his eyebrow at me.

I see his body tense and anticipate that he's going to attempt to get me back on the bed. Before he's on his feet, I'm running out of his bedroom in just a skimpy pair of panties. I don't know where I'm going yet, but I can hear him gaining on me.

I make it downstairs and head in the direction of the kitchen. I round the final corner when I hit, what has to be, a cement wall someone put up while I was sleeping. The wall makes a pained noise as it falls with me.

"Well this is turning into an interesting morning," Micah wheezes from under me.

His one arm is wrapped around me, from his attempt to keep me safe as we fell.

"Oh my god, I'm naked! Close your eyes!" I screech into his face.

Lucas finally catches up, I look over my shoulder and watch him skid to a halt when he sees my predicament.

"Damn it, Micah. What the hell?" He stands over us. "Close your eyes, asshole."

Of course he listens to *him*.

As soon as his eyes close I get up and bolt for the bedroom and my clothing. I can hear Lucas reaming him out about peeking when I was making my exit. I smile when I hear Micah's grunt of pain. Good, I hope he kicked him hard.

Once dressed, I go downstairs again. The guys' voices echo down the hall from the kitchen. They're sitting at the table drinking coffee.

"Come sit down. I poured you a cup already. I'm not sure how you take it though so I brought the sugar and creamer over." Lucas leans back in his chair and grins at me. This reminds me of the same grin he had on his face last night after he had me sit in his lap, in that same chair, and scream his name. I scoot around him and take my seat, doing my best to avoid making eye contact with him.

"So, Gen," Micah draws my attention. "I'm going to propose an end of war, cease fire, truce, if you will. One: because really—we're adults—is the hostility necessary? Two: it looks like we're going to be seeing a lot more of each other it." His eyes flit quickly to Lucas before coming back to me. "So let's start on good footing." Micah grins at me.

I must be dreaming. Is he really taking the mature adult approach?

"Uh, yeah. Sure. We can do that."

"Great. One down, one more to go," I hear him say under his breath.

"One? Don't you mean two?" I correct him.

"Sure. That's exactly what I meant." He smirks before downing his coffee. "We'll go over that list of DJs I'm interested in doing guest spots for the club another time." He pushes away from the table and stands. He gives Lucas one of those back pounding bro hugs and actually rounds the table to kiss me on the cheek. "Catch you later," he throws over his shoulder before disappearing from the kitchen.

Lucas must have put clothes on while I was upstairs. He is now wearing a pair of sweatpants and a white t-shirt. I glance over his shoulder and see what time it is. *Crap!* Eleven a.m. I have to get home to get some paintings ready to be transported before the gallery comes to pick them up. I look back at Lucas, who's watching my face.

He sighs. "I guess I have to take you home now, don't I?"

"Yes, I have to get some things done in my studio," I say apologetically.

"I really should go over some paperwork I have waiting for me in my office," he says, standing.

Lucas runs upstairs to change. I decide to keep busy by cleaning up the coffee mugs and putting the creamer away.

"That's something a man could never get tired of seeing." He comes up behind me as I'm washing the last mug. "His little woman, busy in the kitchen."

The elbow that slammed back into his stomach may or may not have been an accident. I'll never confess.

When we get back to the Brownstone, I see the same blonde woman that took off yesterday, before I could speak to her. She's at the door, poised to knock, but seems frozen in the act, like she has suddenly lost the nerve. I stop at the bottom of the steps with Lucas beside me.

"Can I help you?" I inquire hesitantly.

Her back stiffens and she turns around.

I feel like I've just been punched in the gut. Tara's behavior yesterday morning suddenly makes sense. I reach out and grip Lucas's arm.

Her eyes widen at the sight of me. "I'm sorry, I don't know what I was thinking. I shouldn't have come back." She takes off, running past me. This spurs me into action. I chase after her. I need to know who she is. Grabbing her arm, I spin her around.

"Please, wait," I plead with her.

When I look at her again, I can't help but stare. "Come inside." When she doesn't say anything. "Please?" I urge her.

She nods, finally. She stares for another moment, taking in the sight of me. We walk back together. I feel uneasy at the thoughts running through my head. When we reach Lucas, I don't know what to say. He's looking at the both of us, as well.

"Lucas this is… I'm sorry-?" I trail off. I can't believe I didn't even bother to get her name.

"Quincy. Or Quin, either is fine," she supplies.

"Right. Thanks for bringing me home, Lucas. I really need to get inside." I go on my tippy toes and give him a kiss. I hope he understands.

"Are you sure you don't want me to stay?" His gaze is full of questions I don't have the answers to yet.

"I'm sure. Go get that paperwork done. I need to handle this by myself first. I'll call you when I can." I do my best to assure him. His worry is still evident, but he gives me the space I'm requesting for this.

Once inside, we go into the den and sit across from each other on the couches. We both stare at one other. I can see that she's just as nervous as I am. I'm still in shock. It's not every day you see someone that shares your face staring back at you. Other than the obvious hair color difference, our features are nearly identical. I can tell that she's younger than I am, but not by much. Which could only mean one thing.

"I'm not sure what I should be saying or asking right now," I break the silence.

"I didn't come here to cause problems. I was hoping to speak to my father." She sits straight in her seat as if she's preparing for me to fight with her.

"Your father? John Westley?" I ask for her to clarify. I need confirmation before we could possibly move forward.

"Yes." I watch her twist side to side the ring on her ring-finger before she continues. "My mother recently passed away from cancer. Look, I don't know what I expected when I came here." She stands, her posture is rigid. "I just want to know why he never followed after us when we left or why he never tried to contact my mother about us." She glances briefly at the ring. "I think I have a pretty good guess now." She looks at the end table to the only family photo I have of myself with my parents. "If you could tell him I'm here, so I can get this over with, I'd appreciate it."

I ignore her demand. My ears are ringing over a keyword in what she just said. I need my questions answered. "You said *us*. Did your mother and my father. . . I mean, John have another child?"

"I have a younger sister, Stephanie. I wouldn't be too far off base for asking if you're his daughter too, would I?"

"Yes, I am." I stand as well, too anxious to sit any longer. "I'm sorry, this is so much to take in." My hands are clutched at my sides. "How old are you and Stephanie?" I ask in a rush.

How long did my father have a secret family? That question swirls through my mind until I'm almost dizzy from it. This is incredibly difficult to take in. Part of me is angry, another part hurt, but buried under all of that I feel the little girl I kept deep down inside of me for so many years. The little girl that yearned for family. For siblings. Another person to feel connected with and understood the difficulty of growing up in our household. After all of these years, I now have two people that are a part of my family. I have two sisters I never knew about. I grew up as an only child, yet, I wasn't.

"I'm twenty one and my . . . I guess I should say *our* sister is eighteen. We used to live here until I was eleven," she informs me.

I look up at her with shock. I'm appalled. I cannot believe that my father kept his other family so close to ours; in the home I'm living in and have come to love!

I mentally shake myself. I need to focus.

"What happened when you were eleven? Why did you stop living here?" My stomach is churning but I need to hear all of it. I need to know exactly what level of deception my father went to.

"I'm not sure what happened exactly." She, seemingly, attempts to recall for me. "I remember my parents arguing the night before we left. My mother was angry. She was screaming at Dad. Begging him to make things right. The next day she had our suitcases packed when I got home from school and we left. After that she was a ghost, just existing after we moved in with my aunts. She refused to talk about him, always saying it was too painful."

"Do you know the date of when you left?" I ask because I want to know and also because I'm stalling. She came here to speak to her father and what she's getting is a half-sister telling her he died.

"No, not the exact date. I know it was fall because on my way home from school, I walked through the park to see all of the different colors of the leaves." She crosses her arms. I know I'm out of questions unless I do a little talking of my own.

I run my fingers through my hair in frustration. I have a piece to a puzzle I didn't know existed. I now realize the reason behind my father's sudden desire to make things right with his wife. His other family left and he thought he could turn back to us.

Did my mother know about the other family? Is that why she resented me? Because this other woman was able to give him the golden haired children she so desired? Was this the reason for so much tension between them? I have so many questions swirling in my head, but I don't know where to start or how to get the answers. I'll need to talk to my grandparents.

I'm positive they don't know about Quincy or Stephanie. I may not be able to fix everything right now, but I'm sure I can provide some closure to Quincy's questions.

I take my seat again and urge her to do the same. "I'm not sure of the date you left, but I'm pretty sure it's incredibly close to the date that may help provide you some answers to your own questions. Our father died in a car accident on October twenty-eighth, ten years ago."

I watch her face as she takes in this news. I don't know if my father ever intended on following after this woman and my sisters once he reconciled with my mother, but I know that he never had the chance to.

My memories of him are taking on a Dr. Jekyll and Mr. Hyde. I honestly don't know what to think of him any longer.

I want to try and ease the ache that our father's absence and the news of his death must be causing her. I say softly, "I sure that if he lived longer, he would have been a part of your life. Even if he had to fight to be there." Whether that's true or not, we'll never know, but if it helps her, it's worth it.

I watch Quincy get up again and cross to the window overlooking the street. I understand her wanting that space and the need to reconcile what she thought she knew to what she just found out.

"I don't know where to go from here. I'm unsure of a lot of things right now. I didn't know that I had sisters. It's a lot to take in for both of us and a lot for us to think about. I hope that once the shock wears off, you'll let me get to know both of you." I step to her side to stand in her peripheral. "We didn't get to choose this situation, but we do get to choose what we do with it."

She turns to me. I don't know if I'll ever get used to seeing the same golden brown eyes staring back at me. Now that I've been in her company longer, I can see the slight difference in her face, but it's still so close to mine that I can read it like a book.

There's uncertainty there; *who wouldn't be uncertain in this situation?* I see the sadness put there with the news of Dad's death, but I also see hope, which I know is mirrored on my own face.

Other than my grandparents, I don't have much family except my mother's side, which I'd rather shoot myself in the foot than be around.

"I'd like to get to know you, too. I'm sure Stephanie will once I tell her about you. We didn't know you existed, either. I came here looking for my father. Even though he wasn't in my life, I still always thought he was there. I imagined walking up to him to demand answers and have him hug me like when I was a little girl." She sounds wistful when she says this.

She sighs. "I understand he died ten years ago from what you've said, but for me, I just lost him. Hearing this news now, and so soon after losing my mother, is so hard. It's like I have just lost both of my parents. Damn, this might not be the right time to ask, but what are you going to tell your mother about Stephanie and me?"

"My mother passed away in the same car accident as our father. We do have grandparents, though. They're wonderful people and I'd like to tell them about you two. Maybe when you're ready we can set a date to go see them."

She nods and sits down on the couch. We stay in the den for hours talking. Learning about each other.

My sisters grew up in Maryland living with their six aunts. Quin is a tattoo artist that wants to open her own shop someday. That gets me thinking that I need to speak to an attorney; other than my education, I didn't touch the money I inherited. It is only right to have what is remaining split three ways. I do well enough on my own with my painting.

Stephanie is a dancer. She's going to be heading off to college in New York this fall. Funny how our only connection is our father, who was a strict business man, but all three of his daughters are artistically bent.

After we get a little more comfortable, Quin takes off her jacket and lets me admire the beautiful ink work she has on her. She explains the traditional Japanese style work and the various meanings of the wind, water, animals, and flowers. It's a lot more fascinating with her enthusiasm.

Before it's too late, we exchange contact information. She needs to go back to her friend's house that she's been staying at for the last few days. They also let her borrow their car and she needs to get that back, as well. This reminds me of my own responsibilities. I call the art gallery and reschedule the pick-up for the artwork tomorrow morning. I'll pack up the pieces tonight.

When I slide the door open to the den, I can see Tara and Hailey in the kitchen sitting at the island. I know they're sitting there waiting to lend me support. They have the Ben and Jerry's out. I call them over to do quick introductions.

"Called it!" Tara beams. "Sorry, I occasionally like to pat my powers of observation on the back. Even though I didn't tell you what I suspected, this was totally it. So is home girl moving in and joining the sisterhood, or what?"

Leave it to Tara to use zero finesse in a delicate situation. I know this isn't Tara's version of a question, but more of her way of saying she's there for me no matter what happens or what I decide.

I can't say the idea doesn't appeal to me. "I think we'd like to see how this goes before I actually run the idea past you two and put the offer on the table."

"You know you have us behind you one hundred percent. There's no need to rush into anything, but if you want we'd love to get to know you, Quincy." Of course Hailey is thoughtful enough to bring Quincy into a conversation about her while Tara and I are rudely discussing it in front of her.

"Thanks. I have a lot to think about and I really need to talk to Stephanie about all of this, too." She gently maneuvers through the conversation without making any commitments. That's finesse.

"Stephanie? Is that your lesbian lover or something? I'm cool with the gay thing, but I don't know about two girlfriends living here. I don't want to have to break up bitch fights and throw downs because you both fall in love with me while you live here," There is zero doubt in Tara's voice that she thinks that's a real possibility.

It never gets old seeing the look that comes over someone's face when they experience the full effect of Tara for the first time. It starts off glazed, then shock sets in, and finally they aren't sure if they should laugh or be angry.

Hailey has her hand over her eyes, shaking her head.

I interject, "Actually I didn't get to that part. I have another sister named Stephanie."

"Luuuuucy, you have some 'splainin to doooo!'"
Tara uses her best Ricky Riccardo imitation. "In the
meantime, the B&J is melting and that's sacrilegious in this
house. So I'm going on a rescue mission to get it all safely
in my belly. It was nice meeting you, Quin."

"It was very lovely meeting you. Hopefully we'll
see you soon." Hailey gives her a brief hug and goes to
fight Tara for her share of the ice cream.

I walk Quincy to the door.

After an awkward moment of not knowing how to
say goodbye to each other, we finally decide to hug. I'm
transitioning easily into the older sister role; I remind her to
text me when she safely gets to where she is staying.

When I get back to the kitchen, I shoulder my way
between Hailey and Tara so I can get my share of the
goods. Understanding my need for a sugar fix, they let me
have a few before making me tell them the details. Three
spoonsful and I'm divulging the nitty gritty.

"Son of a bitch! Your dad was a fucking wanker!" I
shake my head. She took one trip to England when she was
five and she still throws out the slang whenever possible.

"Yep." My lips smack on the last syllable. "I know.
My memories of him are being twisted in my head. I'm not
sure what to think."

"I think, even though this brings up a lot of
questions, you should hold on to the reality of who he was
with you. He was a good father to you when he was around.
He was also likely a good father to your sisters or Quincy
wouldn't have come looking for him. The answers to your
questions died with your parents and with your sisters'
mother. Rather than dwell in the past, you need to look for
the silver lining and hold onto it for dear life. You now
have two more people in your life, and that's a blessing. As
far as I'm concerned, if you and your sisters can grasp it,
you have happy times in your future while you develop

these relationships. Every step won't be easy, but in the end, no matter the outcome, you'll be happy you had the opportunity to try and discover a connection with them." Hailey's voice of wisdom is slightly muffled by the spoons full of ice cream she is shoveling in, but that doesn't make it any less profound.

After we finish up the ice cream, we head back to my studio and they help me pack up the pieces for delivery. We catch up a little since we haven't really sat to talk in a few days. I keep what happened with Lucas to myself. I want it to remain between the two of us for a little longer.

We decide to order pizza in. They concede choice of toppings to me, which of course I choose my favorite: peperoni and pineapple. We end up having a small redo of the girl's night we were supposed to have two nights ago. I love that we're able to do this as often as we do. Tonight we catch a Big Bang Theory marathon. Score! I'm a BBT nerd, I laugh obnoxiously loud for 90% of the show. I can't help myself.

Around ten pm, my phone vibrates within the couch. I fish it out and find two text messages. One from Quincy, received hours earlier saying she got back fine. The latest, from my grandparents letting me know they're back from New Jersey.

Crap!

I forgot to call Lucas! The impromptu girl's night took my mind off of everything. How do you explain to a guy you just started dating that suddenly you have two sisters from your father's extramarital affair?

Tara's sleeping next to me and Hailey is across from us tapping away on her keyboard, completely lost in her story. I have a sudden desire to hop in my car and go for a drive.

I love driving past the monuments at night. Seeing them lit up and having my nation's history glowing around me never fails to stir deeper thoughts inside of my mind.

There were great men that inspired these monuments; however, they also had their share of faults.

Washington was considered a snob and looked down on the lower class. Yet he led many into battle during the revolution in their common fight for freedom.

Jefferson wrote about liberty and equality. He was a slave owner and slept with his concubine, producing seven children by her. He did "graciously" release his children from slavery upon his passing.

Abraham Lincoln was a socialist with close ties to Karl Marx. That is almost never mentioned in the history classes taught in schools.

Great men aren't perfect men. Their legacy is so great that despite their faults, they are remembered only for the good they've done.

I can try to remember my father as a great man who provided me the affection I craved as a child or I can tarnish his image with dwelling on his infidelity. Regardless, I have not really lost anything; instead, I have gained two sisters.

I don't know at what point I started to drive to Lucas's place, but I completed my thoughts about my father while staring at his dark house.

It's after midnight and I'm wondering if I should have called first when suddenly I see the front door open. A shadowy figure is standing there, waiting for me, I assume. Lucas steps out of the darkened doorway.

I'm out of the car and launching myself at him before I even realized I opened the car door. Despite the cold, he's silently holding me against his bare chest. I cling to him, absorbing his warmth. Here in the dark, it's just the two of us. I press a kiss over his heart and rest my forehead against his chest, relaxing into the rhythm of his heartbeat. When I start to shiver from the breeze against my back, he laces our fingers together and guides me into the dark house. Our first stop is the kitchen to get the tea he must've prepared for me when he saw me pull up.

We go downstairs into what I discover is his "man cave". There's a bar, pool table, and several arcade games. The back of the room is dominated by a huge flat screen television and a plush couch.

Lucas pulls me down and I sink into his side. His fingers weave into my hair, lulling me as they work their way through my curls.

"That was my sister today." Out of the corner of my eye I can see him nod his head, encouraging me to continue.

"I have another sister, too. Stephanie. I never knew about them." I turn to him, so I can look in his eyes. "He was unfaithful to my mother, to our family. I'm angry and hurt. The whole way here, and even before I left the house, I told myself every reason why I should be happy I have sisters. I've gained something precious. Underneath that is this hurt I'm angry and I can't take it out on who caused it." My eyes well with frustration.

He looks at me, thoughtfully. "You feel betrayed. That is hard for anyone to handle. Even though he's been gone for years, his actions betray the memory that you've had to hold on to and use to comfort you through your loss. You have every right to those emotions, Gen. You have every right to be angry and when you are ready, you will have every right to let that anger go," his voice is soft with a gentle caress of understanding.

We didn't speak for the rest of the night. At some point, we must have fallen asleep on the couch because I'm waking up now, in the early hours of the morning with my head on his chest and my arms wrapped around his waist.

I ease away from him, reluctantly. I'd rather stay here, like this, forever, but I have to do what I have to do, alone. If I stay longer he'll wake up and want to come with me.

I stare down at the headstone.

I feel everything building, boiling inside of me, and surging to burst forth. Finally, I rage at the cold rock that marks my parent's final resting place. I let it out, at both of them. Questioning their actions during my childhood, questioning my entire life up until I was fourteen. Why?

I'll never know and I have to live with that.

I turn and slump down against the gravestone. I hear the dead winter grass crunch a few feet in front of me. I look up.

She gracefully approaches and sits down next to me. Our shoulders rub together.

"I got my license at sixteen. I've been coming here ever since without my Mama knowing." She studies me with eyes wise beyond her young years. "I was home sick from school when Mama got the news that he died. I knew all along he was gone. I kept my silence, Quin never knew. I could not hurt Mama more than she was already hurting." I stare intently as her eyes become glassy with unshed tears and her chin quivers with emotion. "I might not have if I knew about you. I'm positive she knew he had another family; another daughter. She made the selfish decision and kept us hidden away as the only thing she had left of him." She turns her gaze in front of her. "I come here when I'm upset. It's my thinking spot, helps put things into perspective." She pats the grave. "Quincy called last night so here I am this morning."

When she's done I put my arm around her shoulders, hugging her close. I offer what little comfort I can to her—my baby sister.

Baby loosely applies; she's of a similar height to my five foot eight inches with the same inky black hair. Her eyes draw me back to memories of my childhood and sitting with my father while he read to me. They were the same sparkling green that always seemed to smile for me.

This is what I came here for. I've been trying to grasp onto this since yesterday, but finally, it grabs a hold of me. Regardless of what happened, my father loved me. I'm sure he loved all of us. I can look at my sisters, remember the good and try my best to let go of the anger. It won't be as easy as saying it, but I know I'll eventually be able to.

I look beside me and study her profile. I notice her shiver and take her hand in mine "My first act as a big sister should not be to let you get sick from sitting on the cold ground." I stand and pull her up. We walk over to our cars in silence.

"Thank you for coming when you did. Otherwise, I'd still be sitting on that cold ground waiting for an epiphany," I joke, yet I'm completely serious.

"You put on a pretty great show raving like a crazy woman at a tombstone. If you started talking back like it was replying, I was getting out of here." She smirks. "I was beginning to wonder if mental illness runs in the family so I could see about having Quin committed, but you actually seem normal. Pity."

We laugh over that.

We exchange phone numbers. If she ever needs anything I hope she uses it and doesn't doubt my sincerity.

"Listen, I'm heading to my- uh- I mean our grandparent's house now. I need to talk to them about all of this. I wish you could come. I know they will be anxious to meet you once I tell them about you and Quincy. I think it's best I do it privately, though. Plus it wouldn't be right to bring you to meet them without Quin. They raised me after my parents died. They're amazing people. I owe it to them to tell them as soon as possible." I hope she understands and doesn't think I'm trying to keep them from her.

"Genevieve. I get it. Relax. Drive safe." She leans in and kisses me on the cheek before sliding into her own car and driving away. I watch until Stephanie is out of sight before getting into my own car.

The drive to my grandparent's house was quick. When I get there they are in the kitchen sitting down for breakfast. I grab a coffee mug, fill it, and proceed to tell them about the granddaughters they never knew they had.

My grandfather is a kind, sweet, soft spoken man with few words. But after hearing the news, he is so angry that he leaves the kitchen before I can even finish. I understand that it is a difficult story to listen to. My Gram cries silently, staring out like she isn't here but can't make herself leave the room like my Grand-pop did. Neither one of them understands. I don't understand either. We never will.

After my grandfather calms down enough, he comes back and kneels next to my grandmother's chair and wraps his arms around her like he is trying to hold her together in the wake of this pain. It makes me ache all over again. They have been my biggest support system since I was a child, and after my parents death they were my rocks. Strong and steady, they held us together as a family.

When they are ready to listen again, I finish telling them everything I've found out about Quincy and Stephanie. When I am done, they are smiling again. They're now looking forward to getting to know these young women. My inner voice throws out another well-known phrase. *Better late than never*, and I could not agree more.

Chapter Eight

I walk in my front door, itching to paint what I'm feeling. I start a beeline for my studio. This may be a long session. I change direction and go towards the kitchen to grab a couple bottles of water. I stop dead in my tracks when I get to the doorway.

Lucas is leaning against the counter, eating a yogurt. *Is a man eating yogurt supposed to be sexy?* I never thought it would be but watching Lucas is giving me a new appreciation for the cold, creamy snack.

"Running off with just a text message telling me you left is not a pleasant way to wake up first thing in the morning." He doesn't even look up from his yogurt.

"I'm aware of everything you do. Don't give me that look. You're the one in trouble for leaving this morning without a word." He looks up at me, grinning and I try to smooth the wrinkle between my eyebrows from the dirty look I was giving him.

He tosses the empty yogurt cup in the garbage and puts the spoon in the sink. I move to stand next to the kitchen island to wait for him to elaborate on what he means by in trouble.

"Come here, Gen." He holds his arms out to me. I relax when he puts his arms around me. It's so easy to clear my mind and just let myself be in his arms. He slides his fingers into my hair at the back of my head and gently tugs until I'm looking up into his face.

"Don't ever do that again. I was worried when I didn't find you this morning. A text saying you needed to go do something alone did not ease that at all. Last night you were upset, I understand that you felt like you needed to be alone, but you don't have to be. I could have given you space while you did what you needed to do. You should not have gone off on your own." I hate that I made him worry. In my defense, I didn't realize he cared so much. He tugs my hair to get my attention again. "You didn't answer my calls or texts, either. I came here looking for you. Hailey was nice enough to let me in to wait for you"

I pull my phone out of my pocket and check it for the first time since sending him the text this morning. It is dead; of course it is, considering I haven't charged it in days.

I go up on my tippy toes and press my lips to his. He shakes his head at me but doesn't break the kiss. "A little better. I have other ideas for how we can make this all better." My mind flashes back to my earlier thoughts of him and yogurt. They're messier than they were before.

I bite back the grin that wants to steal across my lips at the thought of feeding him yogurt another way.

"If you'll both excuse me for a moment, I have a delivery." Hailey walks into the kitchen carrying a huge vase filled with what looks like two dozen roses.

"Oh Hail! They're beautiful! Did you make a bestsellers list again?" I'm excited for her. She really does have such a lovely agent. Then again, she is an amazing writer. She has a way with words that makes you feel like you're experiencing what her character is. Since she writes sex, she has many devoted, and very happy, readers.

"Actually my very lucky lady, these were delivered for you." She smiles at me and Lucas as she sets them down in front of us.

"Roses?" I look back at Lucas.

"Not from me. I think roses are a lazy man's flower of choice." He crosses his arms over his chest and leans against the counter. I'm momentarily distracted by the flex of his forearm muscles.

I shake my head to clear it and locate the card in the bouquet. Lucas plucks it from my fingers before I can open it. I try grabbing it back, but he holds it over his head, well out of my reach. He reads it.

"Well that's interesting," he seems to ponder while hmm-ing. "It says he's been thinking about you, and what was said when you were last together. He apologizes and would like to see you again for drinks some time."

At this point I'm climbing up his body to get the card back. If I can just get my upper body a little higher, I'll be able to get it. I'm hesitant to do that. Let's be honest. It puts my armpit level with his nose and I haven't showered yet today. I'm sure it's one of those unsaid rules of dating: Don't let men know women have body odor. Like the unspoken rule: Do not pass gas in front of men. We do not want them to know we do it, so that we can complain when they do.

So I fall back on one of the oldest tricks in the lady's rule book—guilt.

Let's do this. Eyes big and rounded, lips pouted out. Pathetic expression in place. "You're being mean to me," I whine, applying the perfect amount of inflection to my voice.

He loses his smile and suddenly looks worried. The card lowers within reach. I snatch it and run for my room. Once I reach the safety of my room, I close the door and lock it. As an added measure I go into my bathroom and lock myself in there, too.

I flip the card over and read.

Gen, I've been thinking over what you said to me at our last dinner. I was gravely wrong to mislead you. I sincerely apologize and would like to think that, although, we are not romantically involved, we may remain friends. Meet me out for drinks some time. Please? I miss our friendship. Brad.

I back up to lean against the door and scream when the door wraps its arms around me. Jumping across the bathroom, I turn to glare at Lucas. "What the heck? How did you get in here?" My voice screeches.

"You doors are remarkably easy to get into," he says, waving his credit card at me. I try projecting the pitiful look again. He quirks his eyebrow.

Darn. Think. Think!

Who wants to explain that they were too dense to notice they were being used as a beard? If Brad had been honest I might have went along with it. I had nothing else going on. Then I wouldn't be standing in this bathroom feeling like prey because the truth is too pathetic sounding. That's it! Bathroom. The light bulb flashes on.

"I have to shower now, so if you'll please excuse me." I try acting haughty, but the gleam that enters his eyes does not reassure me that I'm getting the desired results.

I back pedal. "What are you doing?"

He's slowly shedding his clothes and my brain function is shutting down with every enticing inch he uncovers.

"You said you needed a shower, I agree." He looks me up and down. "You're starting to look a little flushed. For safety purposes, you should not shower alone."

Stepping around me, he turns on the spray for the shower, adjusting the temperature. He picks me up as if I weigh nothing at all and places me under the spray, fully clothed. His mouth is on mine before I can yell my protests. The protests die a swift death against his lips. My wet denim is heavy and constricts my movements when I try and hike my leg over his hip to press myself closer.

"Clothes. Off. Now," he growls between kisses.

My shirt and bra are off within seconds. The jeans are another story; they become a frantic team effort.

When he bends down to help get my feet out, I accidently knee him in the shoulder. Knocked off balance on the wet tile, he slips flat onto his back. Lucas's feet then knock me off of mine. I land on top of him hard enough to jolt my teeth.

I peel myself away enough to look at him. His silver eyes dance with laughter. I crack first and let my laughter ring out and soon, he joins in. I push up and still feel my pants twisted around my ankles. He helps me into a sitting position, cradled into his body, and we finish removing my clothing.

The fall didn't affect his ardor. I can still feel him pressed against my back. With me leaning against his chest, he has full access to my body. Lucas's hands are freely roaming my curves, heating me more than the spray of the shower above us.

I'm very glad that when I remodeled the bathroom I splurged on this custom built shower stall. Closed off behind the fogged glass doors, the noise from the shower head drowns out everything but us. It's as if we're the only two people in the world at this point in time. His hands are driving me crazy, not staying in any one spot for more than a few moments.

"Touch yourself." He nips my ear. I look over my shoulder at him. "I want to see you drive yourself wild before I make you lose control."

The heat in his gaze emboldens me. I slide my hands from their position on his knees, up my thighs, and to my already wet folds. I part my lips and glide my finger over my clit, falling into a familiar movement.

I have touched myself since I became aware of my body's desires. It's never felt like this before. Lucas's intense gaze gives me a wild sense of excitement that I didn't realize I'd find so thrilling. His lips at my neck and hands cupping my breasts add another dimension to my already overwhelmed senses. I can feel the need, building until my body is strung so tight, too tight. Lucas finally pushes me over the edge, pinching my nipples and biting my neck. I fall from the precipice, loudly moaning my pleasure. It echoes throughout the bathroom. My moans turn to whimpers as my body falls limp, yet luxuriously blissful.

Lucas, I feel, is not done with me. He lays me back on the wet tile floor. "You drive me crazy. As hot as that was, it's not enough. I want to bring you to the same heights you push me when you get that look in your eyes and I know you are thinking about me." He nips my hip. "Lean up on your elbows, minx." The stubble on his cheek scratches against my sensitive thigh when he nuzzles me. "I want you to watch what I do to you."

Is he really going to …? My last coherent thought trails off.

His tongue delves between my pussy lips, finding my clitoris with mind blowing accuracy. Lucas is not gentle with easing me into oral. His mouth is direct and confident as it works my delicate flesh into a fever so soon after my last orgasm. When I feel like I'm going to combust, his mouth eases and gentles the assault. I drive my fingers through his hair and pull in frustration, trying to force his mouth back into its brutal rhythm.

Lucas looks up at me and runs his tongue across his bottom lip, tasting me on his mouth. "Are you crazy already?" He resumes, gently swiping my pulsing clit.

"Do you really have to ask?" I nearly scream my frustration at him. I tighten my fingers in his hair again. He chuckles while kissing a path up my body. No! This is not at all the direction I want him moving in. Go down! My mind is screaming.

His hands cup each side of my head, drawing me into a deep kiss. I can taste myself as my tongue dances with his. My pelvis rocks up, begging to be touched. Lucas makes me whimper when he lowers his body between my legs.

"Relax for me, minx. You're going to come again before I'm done." He begins gliding his length against my center, the moisture from my arousal aiding his smooth movements. I instinctively begin shifting my hips to tilt up. I yearn to feel him ease inside of me.

He kisses a path down my jaw to my ear, pausing for a moment to nibble my lobe. "You're killing me. Let me do all of the work." His hands still my hips' movement, not giving me any other option. "We aren't going to make love for the first time on a shower floor. Your first will be special."

Everything is feeling pretty darn special to me right now. I won't argue, though. I can see on Lucas's face that he's not willing to bend on what he thinks I need him to give me.

He pulls his lips back from my ear to kiss me and watches the tear slip from the corner of my eye. The feelings he stirs in me are those that I'm not even sure I can describe. His kisses remain tender. I wrap my legs around his hips opening myself up more to him as he continues his unhurried thrusts. The sensation he creates is exquisite. A slow burn is building; he plays my body like a slow song building towards a crescendo. The sounds of our heavy breathing mingling together is our music. Lucas makes love to my senses, overwhelming me, filling every need in a way I never dreamed existed. The sparks suddenly ignite, flashing through my body like electricity, causing my body to tremble like sound waves of thunder after a lighting strike.

Lucas's pace increases, with one, two, three final strokes. Groans fill my ear, serenading me with his deep husky voice. His hot release splashes onto my pelvis, forming a warm pool with rivulets running from my belly button and down between my legs. There are specks of light dancing around my vision and my feet are numb, except for a tingle in the tips of my toes. I'm not sure if I am breathing again yet.

"I want you to know that if I had a choice, we'd stay like this for the next twenty four hours, but I don't know how big your hot water tank is. I don't think it'll stay warm for that long." Lucas rolls to my side. "Cold water is not beneficial for a man who wants to stay impressively manly looking in front of his woman." He gestures between his legs. "You know, when you take into account shrinkage."

I laugh at him and he joins in. I love a man that can laugh at himself. One minute, he can make me feel like my body is shattering into a billion pieces, and being scattered in the wind while riding the waves of a mind blowing orgasm. And then the next minute, we're laughing together like we're sitting on the couch, watching a funny movie rather than soaking wet and naked in the shower, covered in sweat and semen.

I love that he worries about me and wants to be there when I need someone. I love that he doesn't mind and finds it endearing that I'm not the most graceful conversationalist.

I met a man three days ago that I don't remember meeting and I think I'm falling in love with him at the speed of light. I look at him and on the surface, he's the mind-numbingly handsome ex-rock star, but I see deeper; I see the man inside of him. Lucas is the loving family man that adores his mother and is best friends with his siblings. And despite differences, the man that idolized his father. He's the ambitious businessman that instead of pining for what he lost, decided to use his resources to build a new future for himself.

I see the first man to look at me and know that he sees all of me, too. I should be frightened. I should be running away. Instead, I'm going to run towards it. I rarely take risks, but when I do, I have always jumped in feet first and figured it out as I went. It's the rare confidence I have hiding inside of me, waiting for certain moments to give me what I need and take what I want.

I want him.

"Let's get cleaned up and grab some lunch." Lucas helps pull me to my feet, making sure I keep my balance when my weak legs wobble under me, at first.

"I make a pretty good grilled chicken salad if you want to stay here?" I want to spend time with him. Here in my home, away from paparazzi, away from people.

"If you want to cook for your man who am I to stop my little woman." His cocky grin earns him a nip on the shoulder. "Hey now, tiger, watch those teeth. No leaving scars on my tattoos."

That draws my attention to the ink on his arms and chest. I recognize the style from what Quincy showed me. There's a samurai on his arm protecting a geisha. There's black wind around them with cherry blossoms swirling in the wind. Going to his chest and onto his shoulder is a tiger swiping the samurai's raised sword. The geisha looks as if she's standing on the edge of a cliff with black water flowing below her.

The other side is just as beautiful. On his chest is what, Quin explained to me, is called a foo dog. It's sitting tall and proud on a pedestal; its eyes appear like it's gazing over at the scene on the other side of his chest. A dragon is on his bicep, wrapping up with his head coming up over his shoulder like he's going to attack the foo dog from behind. The forearm has the same black water as the left side and the cherry blossoms are swirled into the water, flowing with the tide.

It's not just a tattoo; it's a piece of art telling a story. I can't imagine how many hours he sat to have this done. The detailing in it is impeccable.

We wash quickly, so we can hurry and eat. After getting dressed, we manage to make it to the kitchen without stripping naked and mauling each other again. Though, barely. Lucas has a problem with keeping his hands to himself, but I'm impressed with the confidence he has in his stamina.

After I get all of the ingredients, Lucas surprises me by getting a knife and beginning to chop the veggies. I take out my grill pan for the chicken. The actual grill is so much better, but this is quicker and I don't have to stand in the cold.

We finish putting the salad together and sit down to eat. I usually make too much and have leftovers, but with Lucas's appetite, I'm more worried that this is just a snack for him.

When we finish eating and clean up the mess, he asks to see my studio since the first night he was in it he was more focused on me and didn't get a chance to look around.

I sit on the couch I have set up in the little alcove on the side of the studio and wait a little nervously for him to say something. He's taking his time, studying each painting. I shift nervously in my seat.

"Stop being nervous" He doesn't even have to look at me to be aware of my emotions. "You are incredibly talented. There are no adjectives to adequately describe just how talented your work is." He spends more time looking at each one like he's trying to figure out every emotion I've put into them; looking at every object or person I've found inspiration in.

On his way to where I'm seated, he notices the sunflowers he bought me, near my work area. Smirking, he settles down next to me, draping his arm over my shoulder, and pulls me into his side.

"Tell me about Brad." Darn it, I thought he forgot about that. Of course he has me trapped against him so I can't avoid him this time.

"Brad is a guy I dated, very casually. We talked and decided it wouldn't work. We wanted different things." Yeah, that sounded good. Accurate without all the nitty gritty details.

"He said he wants to be friends and get together sometime. Guys *never* want to be just friends and just get together with a woman," he points out.

"You're a guy and I'm a girl. You mean we aren't friends?" I ask innocently.

"*Hell no, we aren't friends!*" He jumps in his seat and turns me to face him. He ignores my grin. "You are mine. You have been from the first second I laid eyes on you. Get comfortable with that fact." He's glaring down at me now like he thinks I'm going to argue. He might not realize it yet, but as much as I'm his, he's mine, too.

"Okay." I drag out the ay sound. It dawns on me that he's acting a little jealous; he all but beat on his chest while claiming me. As much as I'd like the revel in him being jealous, it doesn't seem right considering the truth. I climb on his lap and bury my face in his shoulder. "Brad is gay," I mumble against him, trying my best to hide my face.

"Good." He sounds positively cheerful now.

"Good? What do you mean good?" I sit up to look at his face.

"Good. Now I won't have to have a talk with Brad about keeping his hands to himself. I won't stop you from seeing someone you consider a friend, but I can make sure they understand that every delicious inch of you is mine."

"You just peed on me!" I exclaim.

He appears shocked, looking at me like I'm crazy.

"Like a dog, Lucas. Focus. You are trying to mark your territory." I smack his chest with the palm of my hand. He chuckles at me.

"I'm fine with that. I'm a dog and I'm definitely peeing on you; figuratively, not literally." He's still laughing at me.

"Well then I'm peeing on you, too. This works both ways." I cross my arms over my chest, trying to look stern.

"Female dogs pee on things to mark territory?"

I sigh in exasperation. "Forget the dogs and peeing. I'm saying you're mine too, buddy." I poke his chest. "So you can get comfortable with that fact." I emphasize my point with a few more finger pokes to the chest. He grabs me finger and pulls me closer. Wrapping his arms around my waist, he brings his lips close to mine but not touching.

"Good. That's all I want to be." The declaration thrills me more than the kiss, though, the kiss is pretty darn exciting, too.

I pull away and thoughtfully take a look around me. I'm in my studio, which is my place, the place I love and do what I love in. I'm on Lucas's lap and we just decided in a very "Genevieve like" fashion that we're each other's. I know back in the shower I decided I want him; it's time I take him.

I climb off his lap and pull my shirt up and over my head. More gracefully than the previous time, I take my pants off and kick them to the side with my toe.

There's no room for nerves with everything that I'm feeling. This boldness is due solely to the fact that this is me with him. His calm focused demeanor calls to me and makes me feel at ease.

I cup my breast through the black lace of my bra, using the tip of my finger to tease my nipples into hard straining points. With his attention fixated on my nipples, I ease the straps down my arms and undo the clasp. I step towards him and drop the bra into his lap, atop the evidence of his arousal. He sounds strangled as his breaths quicken. Nothing he could say would make me feel as beautiful as his reactions do. I've heard the phrase actions speak louder than words and his scream to me. I want to be the minx that he calls me.

I climb back on his lap, placing my finger against his lips before he can speak. I move his hands to the side so he can't distract me with his touch. He remains quiet and lets me stay in control. I have no illusions that a man of his size and strength is doing anything but allowing me to have my way. In a battle of wills, we're evenly matched; we'll both be bending for each other at some point. Right now is his first bend.

I push my bra—which is in his lap—to the side, making sure my hand brushes against his hardness. I smile when I hear his breath catch in his throat. Next I ease his shirt up his sides and, with his help, over his head. I brush my thumb across his nipple and watch the muscles in his abs jump. I wonder if his nipples are as sensitive as mine. I'll explore that later. Now I want him naked and at my mercy, for as long as he lets me. With his assistance again, I get his pants and boxer briefs off of him. *He's so helpful.*

Kneeling in front of him after I finish pulling his pants off, I take a moment to admire. A few rays of sunshine come through the window landing across his stomach. I itch to paint him like this. Fully aroused in a relaxed pose, his gaze steadily meeting mine, patiently waiting for my next move.

I'm a little unsure of where to start; my gaze lands back on his erection. I move closer. Grabbing him, I bring him to my lips and rub the smooth head against them, feeling the silky softness. I suck the head into my mouth and pull it back out with a pop as it clears my lips and breaks the suction. I watch his hands dig into the couch and need no other signs to know what Lucas wants. I plunge him back into my mouth quickly, taking him as deeply as I can. I do this a few more times. I can feel the moisture gathering between my legs and reach down to touch myself. I continue to tease his head with my tongue while I play with myself. My other hand moves down his shaft and cups his balls. I feel his body tense. His patience is at an end and he's going to lunge for me.

I stand up and back away, out of reach. My hand is still in my panties, tracing the wet slit between my legs. By the wild look in his eye, I know he's had enough of my teasing. I move my panties down my hips and let them slide to the floor. I enact my version of what I hope looks like a sexy cat walk strut and slide myself back into his lap, devouring his mouth when I get there.

I rub my wet pussy against his spit slick cock, making us both moan. I move up again and tilt my hips into position so when I move my hips back down he'll slide inside of me. The head of his cock barely grazes my entrance before he's grabbing my hips to stop my motion. I want to ball my hands into fists and beat on his shoulders for stopping me. I am actually surprised he let me stay in control this long and get as far as I did.

"I want your first time to be the stuff of dreams, Genevieve." He stares into my eyes. "You deserve silk sheets, candlelight, and wild flower petals." Lucas surprises a quick laugh out of me over the wild flower petals. That is so him.

I can see the sincerity there. It reinforces that I made the right decision to give all of myself to this man. I touch my finger tips to his face and gently place a kiss against his lips.

"This right now. This is what *my* dreams are made of." I move my palm down his chest to rest over his heart. With our gazes still locked, I say with my eyes what I'm not ready to let my lips utter. I can feel his heartbeat quicken against the palm of my hand.

Lucas captures my lips in a kiss that, I hope I am not imagining, is filled with intense emotions on both sides. He turns us and gently lays me down on the cushions. His touches are sweet and gentle, starting with my lips and neck. I arch my back, wanting him to touch me. He doesn't feel my sense of urgency and continues his slow progress down my body. Lucas spends a little longer at my breasts, giving each one just enough attention to leave them wanting more. The trail of kisses descends down my stomach. I shiver in anticipation. Finally kneeling between my legs, he parts my thighs wider to make room for his broad shoulders. He kisses each thigh first and then focuses his attentions at the center of my needs.

"You have the most beautiful pussy I've ever seen." He slides his finger tip to trace along my lips and gathering my arousal on its tip. "Rose blushed petals." He takes his finger and licks it, tasting my excitement. "Sweet like nectar." He leans forward, giving a gentle flick of his tongue and inhaling. "A heady musk that I'm already addicted to." He's barely touched me and I'm already quivering.

"I need you, please," my voice comes out shaky.

"Your wish is most definitely my shared desire." When he finally takes me into his mouth, I moan, low and slow, awash in the magic he weaves around me. Sliding one finger inside of me while he pays special attention to my clitoris, he then adds a second finger, working it into me, stretching me, and preparing my body for when he enters me. The two sensations send me over. I come, biting my lip to control my moan of pleasure. He slowly continues to lick me, sending small shock waves throughout my body. Pulling his fingers out, he licks the moisture off of them again. Moving back up my body as slowly as he descended, he allows my body to relax from the thrall of the orgasm he gave me.

Once Lucas is on top of me again, I wrap my arms around him and rub myself against his hard length, making him close his eyes in pleasure.

He pops them back open quickly.

"I don't have a condom." He pulls back from me, looking panicked. "I haven't been carrying them around with me, lately. I never have sex without a condom. I figured if I didn't carry one I wouldn't be tempted to rush you before you were ready."

"I'm on birth control to help regulate my periods. If you're okay with it, I trust you," I assure him. I laugh at his expression. "You look like a kid in a candy store with that smile right now. You must really want me?"

He presses his erection against me. "I'm going to steal your line from earlier. You really have to ask that? Yes, I want you. Badly. That's not what I'm smiling about, though. You said you trust me. That means something. I know you must, but hearing you say it humbles me." He leans down and kisses me. "I'm going to try and make this everything you'd hope it'd be."

Our kisses are even more intense, if that's imaginable. Lucas's hands are all over me, leaving goose bumps in their wake. They move down my side to my thigh, wrapping it around his hip. I feel his blunt tip press against me. He takes himself in his hand and slides himself against my folds, gathering moisture to help with his entrance. His now slick tip slips through my lips, pushing into me.

He only has the tip in and already I feel myself needing to stretch around him to accommodate his size. He pushes in about halfway and pauses. Gathering me closer, he kisses me and pushes through my barrier until he's fully sheathed inside me. I whimper when I feel the pain of my body accepting him. I am impossibly full now. Lucas holds still over me allowing me to adjust to him.

My body relaxes. The pain is already fading and is now mixing with the sensation of this new experience. Overwhelmed by the newfound pleasure, I take a moment to enjoy the feel of him filling my body so intimately, but I need more. I shift my hips and gasp as he suddenly slides a little deeper. The gasp turns into a moan and mingles with his own. Lucas slides out slowly. Pressing forward again, he elicits another moan from me. My eyes close, wanting to focus on what he is making me feel.

"Look at me," he urges. "Keep your eyes open. I want your eyes on me, watching me make love to you." Lucas's voice is gruff at first but gentles. I nod, unable to speak with the emotion he stirred clogging my throat. He gently makes love to my body, taking care not to hurt me.

I can feel him holding back with his movements, but I want all of him. I want the wild excitement he makes me feel when he's just as wild for me. I test moving my hips with his, matching his movements.

The rumbling in his throat encourages me.

I dig my nails into his back while I look into his eyes. "More. Lucas, give me all of it. All of you." I move my hands to his hips to spur him on. He needs no further prompting. His thrusts pick up the pace. I learn quickly and match him movement for movement. We're wild in each other's arms. Lips meeting briefly then moving to everywhere else in reach; jaw, neck, ears, and collarbones. My nails are scratching down his back asking for all that he can give me. The pressure builds and builds. I want to bite, scratch, and pull his hair until he gives me what I want.

I think he senses I need something more because he finds my nipple and pinches just hard enough to send sensations spiraling through me, straight to where our bodies a connected.

I come apart in his arms. Feeling my body clench around Lucas drives my orgasm to dizzying heights. I cry out "Lucas" and clutch at his shoulders. His mouth finds mine and I swallow his groans of ecstasy. With the intensity of my orgasm triggering his own, he pushes deep inside of me and shudders with his release.

Lucas is pressing small kisses all over my face. Between kisses, I realize he's singing to me. Not a Lucas Alexander original or even a Scarlet Anarchy song, but a classic "Maybe I'm Amazed". Thank you, Mr. McCartney.

"This is absolutely perfect. Better than anything I could have dreamed." I sigh against his face and let a few tears slide from the corner of my eyes. Not breaking the haze of euphoria around us, Lucas shifts us on the couch so that we're spooning. He pulls the throw blanket I keep on the back of the couch over us. His lips press a kiss just below my ear and he starts singing again. I doze off wrapped in his arms and soothed by his voice.

Chapter Nine

Click. Click. Click.

I wake up slowly, a little disoriented. What the heck is that clicking? I blink my eyes open to see the dark lens of a camera clicking in my face. Hailey is silently pulling the back of Tara's shirt to get her out of the room.

Tara perks up from behind the camera. "Oh good, you're awake. I just got called for an assignment. I'm leaving tomorrow night. We were wondering if you wanted to go out to McKinney's Pub for some food and drinks tonight." She smiles cheerfully down at me.

I make a grab for the camera. She quickly snatches it out of reach. Before I can fall off the couch, Lucas grabs me and pulls me back against his chest.

His voice is heavy from sleep. "As much as I'd love for you to get your hands on those pictures, I really need you and the blanket to stay where you are so that I'm not bared completely to your pervert friend with a camera."

I'm not sure when Lucas woke up, but he's glaring over my shoulder at Tara who's grinning back, broadly.

"I tried to tell her it could wait but you know how she is. The second she saw you, she grabbed her camera before I could stop her." Hailey sighs and looks, almost too sweetly, at me.

Tara snorts next to her.

"Oh please. You didn't stop me because you were enjoying the sight. You are already writing the next sex scene to your novel in that pretty little head of yours. Don't deny it! As soon as we walk out, you are going to rush to your office to start typing." Tara sends a dirty look to Hailey, who is now blushing.

Lucas lays his head on my shoulder, shaking it in disbelief, I'm sure. Who can blame him when he is woken up like this?

"Can we have some privacy please? We'll be right out and can talk then," I plead.

They shuffle out, arguing with each other. Each taking a turn to look back in case they miss something. Do they think he's going to throw me down and maul my body while they're still present?

When they finally close the door behind them, still bickering, I collapse back against Lucas. Turning to face him, I throw my arm over his waist and mumble into his chest. "Sorry about that. I *usually* have more privacy than this. They're both a little off in their own ways."

Lucas pulls my face way from his chest. "Don't apologize. Trust me. It could have been worse, like running naked into my brother." He laughs again when my cheeks heat. "I like your friends. They actually remind me a lot of being with my siblings. It's never a dull moment." He kisses my forehead. "Speaking of siblings, my brother, Aryan, is back home from an assignment. I told him we would meet up tonight. If you don't mind, I was thinking we could tag along to McKinney's?"

I grin at him. "If you think you can handle the three of us girls together, sure." My tone sounds a little more ominous than intended.

McKinney's is fairly busy tonight; every pool table is being used. All of the stools at the bar are occupied and it looks like our little group took the last remaining bar height table to stand around.

Tara dated the owner's son for a while. We always get special treatment when we come in since they're still great friends. Thank goodness she didn't shatter this one's heart since this is one of our favorite places to hang out.

We arrive before Lucas's brother and order some appetizers and pitchers of beer. I decide to treat myself to a nice glass of Moscato; it's like an alcoholic dessert.

We're by the back wall of the bar and Lucas stands with his back to the crowd. He does that a lot in public; he is always making sure he's facing away from people or in a corner, so he's not as easily noticeable and drawing attention to himself. His band broke up three years ago, but the fan base must still be going strong. That or it's become more instinctive after doing it for so long.

"Someone stop me before I tear my panties off and throw them at that walking orgasm donor," Tara breathes out, staring past Lucas's shoulder.

Hailey and I both follow her gaze. Pre-Lucas I would have been struck dumb like Tara. This man is definitely something to look at. Lucas is looking at me, I think to gauge my reaction, his lips curve into an amused smirk when he looks at the girls. As he walks further into the bar, I can guess who he is. His height matches Lucas's, but has a more heavily muscled build. The most telling feature is that they both have the same unusual silver eyes. On this man, it's even more striking; his skin tone is a dark caramel, strongly indicating he's mixed race.

I can see that Tara's fingers are twitching on the table, wanting her camera in hand to put his face to film. I've been watching men react to Tara my whole life. I have never seen Tara react this way to seeing a man. My suspicions of the man's identity are confirmed when he's halfway thru the bar and locks in on our table. He strides towards us, the crowd parting for him in a Moses like fashion.

Tonight just got much more interesting.

I lean into Tara to attempt damage control. "Do not throw your panties at Lucas's brother, Tara. I don't want you scaring him away my first time meeting him."

I hear Hailey mumble something that sounded like she'd be getting a lot more books written if Lucas and his brothers keep coming around. Silently, I agree with her. I haven't told Lucas yet, but I have a plan for a new series of paintings taking on a new level of sensuality. I've never done anything like this before and it's purely inspired by him. I can't believe I went looking for inspiration the other day when it was staring me in the face.

The brothers greet each other with that manly show of back pounding. Introductions are made and I mentally sigh in relief when Tara doesn't hop on the table and ask him to let her have his babies. I never put anything past Tara, even something as outrageous as that. We let them catch up and form a quick girl huddle.

"Hurry up and let it all out, Tara. You look like you're going to burst from exercising a little self-control." I urge her to do it in the relative privacy of the huddle.

"I don't know what you mean. I don't have anything to say." This is directed over the rim of her beer glass as she takes a long drink, still eyeing Aryan.

Hailey is looking at Tara like she has two heads. At least I'm not the only one. Not sure what to make of this, I break the huddle and turn back to the guys.

"So Aryan, Lucas was telling me you were on a trip?"

"Yes, I was in India, working." Despite his strong looks, his tone is open and friendly.

"What do you do for work?" Hailey jumps on the question train with me.

"I own a company that provides private protection for traveling diplomats and people of means." It comes out sounding like a practiced job description.

"Is that dangerous?" I wonder aloud.

"It could be, but I'm trained." His smirk is cocky.

"Trained how?" Goodness Hailey is putting him through an inquisition.

"I was a SEAL prior to retiring and starting Elite Force Protection Services. Every man under my employ was also a part of an elite task force of various origins."

Something tells me that despite his good looks and so far easy-going manner, he is not the guy you mess with. I thought he looked strong before. Now knowing his training, I can more accurately describe him as possessing a lethal reserve hidden beneath an affable personality.

"So you're used to dealing with difficult people and situations?"

Aryan crosses his arms over his chest and stares at Hailey, trying to figure out where she's going with her line of questioning. I know where it's going. I know *exactly* where it's going. I catch her gaze and we exchange a smile.

"Yes," he says carefully. "You could say that."

"Good. That's very good to know" She smiles at him with angelic innocence that doesn't fool me. Lucas looks at me, suspiciously. I give him a shoulder shrug.

"Tara does a lot of traveling for work as well, actually she's leaving tomorrow which is why were out tonight." Hailey is going for broke with this pointed statement.

"Really? My line of work is a little different. I don't go to touristy areas." I don't need to be a genius to know Aryan's comment is not going to go over well with Tara. He turns his gaze to her, finally addressing her for the first time this evening. "So what do you do?"

"I'm a photographer." I can see the fire flare up behind her eyes. She kept her job purposely vague so that he can make another judgmental comment.

"Really? A face as beautiful as yours should be in front of the camera, not behind it." He flashes her a devastating grin.

It's wasted on her at this moment.

"Oh, I don't do fashion photography." This is said in a sugary sweet tone. "I travel to more exotic locations and capture whatever my assignment is. Not exactly *tourist hot spots*." The last words drip with venom. They both glare at each other. I can feel the heat from the glares even where I'm standing

I see this turning into head butting.

I better intercede.

"Did anyone else think it was cold outside?"

I'm completely ignored.

"It's dangerous to travel by yourself, princess." I can see a tick start in Aryan's jaw.

"Listen here—" Tara doesn't get a chance to finish before Hailey has her hand over her mouth and is leading her away.

I know why Tara hated that entire exchange. There were so many things wrong with it. The somewhat sexist comment about her being in front of the camera; I know it was meant as a compliment, but it can be insulting to a female photographer. Calling her princess was definitely an insult. And on top of that, he flat out insinuated she couldn't handle herself with the job she's been doing for years. I hope Lucas doesn't get too mad, but I can't just let him insult her like that.

"Look, Aryan, I bet you are perfectly capable of doing your job and no one questions that. However, Tara has been doing her job for years now and is also perfectly capable of handling herself in tough situations. She's not a 'princess.' She has teeth and quite frankly you're lucky she didn't take a bite out of your ass just now. If she were a man you would never have made those shitty comments. So, you're going to have to apologize." My hands land on my hips to punctuate my point.

I just realize that I cursed twice. Hanging out with Lucas has me cursing like a rock star. Gram would have washed my mouth out if she heard me.

Aryan lifts an eyebrow at me then grins.

"I agree, if your friend was a man, I wouldn't have said any of that. Most likely because I wouldn't have been too busy thinking she was one of the most beautiful women I've ever seen. And, I may have been able to think about what I was saying." His eyes wander over to where Hailey is calming Tara down. I see his eyes soften for a moment before he gets a genuine shit-eating grin. "I'm going to go apologize and if I'm lucky maybe I can sweet talk her into letting me kiss it all better." He shoots me a wink and slips through the crowd.

"So does he come back with that kiss or with his balls in his throat?" Lucas wraps his arms around me. Before I would have automatically answered balls in throat, but I'm not too sure with this one.

Hailey joins us back at the table after a few minutes, leaving Tara with Aryan leaning against the wall by the bar talking. Well he's talking and she is silent, which is unusual for Tara in any situation.

"Did the temperature rise for anyone else when those two nearly had their show down?" Hailey says laughingly.

We all start discussing what we're all currently working on while keeping an eye on the other two people in our group. The conversation we're having isn't sterling. We wait to see if there's fireworks or an all-out explosion. That is where my focus was until Lucas slips his hand under my shirt and up my back, rubbing in a soothing motion yet, fiddling with the clasp on my bra on his upstroke.

I steal a peek at him, but he's not even looking at me. He's still having the pretense of a conversation with Hailey, who's pretending to not be paying more attention to Tara and Aryan. She's completely unaware of my current crisis.

All I can think about now, is wanting his mouth on my breasts. My nipples harden at the thought and I feel my cheeks redden. Closing my eyes, I take a deep breath. I hope no one else notices that he has me aroused just by touching my freaking bra. I feel almost like a drug addict jonesing for my next fix right here in this flipping bar! I was worried about Tara's behavior and I'm the one having hormone control issues.

Tara and Aryan rejoining the group pulls me back from my thoughts. Darn it! I missed what happened. He doesn't look like his balls were relocated. Her mouth is still glossy. Darn, nothing happened. At least they don't look ready to kill each other anymore.

The rest of the evening passes without any drama. The guys order a lot more food, then regal us with stories of their misspent youth. Their stories explain basically how they drove their mother beautifully gray by the time they reached high school. The girls and I keep laughing at their antics and their enthusiasm for the storytelling. You can see just how close the brothers are.

I hope someday I can be close to Quin and Steph like that. I laugh harder when Aryan recounts the story about Lucas losing his virginity in the backseat of his car and his brothers interrupting by sneaking up and shaking the car during the deed. Lucas gets what suspiciously looks like a blush and is trying to shut his brother up. I lean up and give him pecking kisses while trying to contain my laughter.

"It's okay, we both have funny virginity losing stories. Your brothers thought they'd help you get the motion right. I had the afterglow recorded by my best friends," I whisper.

He smiles against my lips "You're a gem, minx."

I was a diamond in the rough, but he makes me feel polished and shiny.

"And don't you forget it, Luc." I smile back.

"Luc? You haven't called me that since the first night. I like that you're using it again." He drops a kiss on my head.

Damn, I never told him I don't remember that night. Now isn't the right time; soon but not right now. I'm not sure how he'll react, but I don't want to potentially ruin tonight.

"Come with me to New York?" He's giving me that same look his mother uses when she wants something and isn't going to take no for an answer. It makes me squirm. "I have to go there for business early tomorrow morning for a few days. I can lie and say I want to take you so I can show you the sights, but the honest answer is, I just don't want to be away from you for that long."

I have commissions to paint and pieces to prepare for my next showing. I've already barely been working as it is, lately. I can't just go to New York. It would be irresponsible. I'm never irresponsible.

"I'll go," I say excitedly.

What? Where did that come from? Did I not just hear my own inner monologue? It couldn't have gone in one ear and out the other because it was already in my head! *Crap on a cracker*, I'm going to New York.

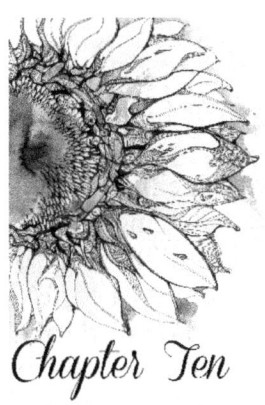

Chapter Ten

I stop painting and take a moment to reflect on my trip with Lucas to New York.

A few days in NYC turned into a week.

Luc was a lot busier than he expected with work. He didn't tell me much, but from what I gathered, one of his artists is spiraling out of control and causing bad publicity and contractual issues. I spent time during the days, wandering around museums and little shops I could find. At night, Luc and I would stay in, order food, and talk. Talking always turned in to touching and touching led to hungry sex on every available surface.

Crack an innocent joke about a man's stamina and enjoy yourself as they prove you wrong. Whew.

I met his sister, Lilah. We went out to lunch and shopping a few times. She's very refreshing. Still so young and filled with bright dreams. She reminds me of Stephanie; they are both around the same height with long dark hair, and ironically, Lilah is also a dancer. I'd love to introduce them. I think they'd hit it off, but first I need to get to know my sisters myself.

On our last evening in the city, Luc took me out to a fondue restaurant. The whole atmosphere was intimate with a dimly lit interior and small, half circle booths that encourage cuddling.

We got sucked into the romantic environment and were that disgustingly cute couple that had fun feeding each other. The feeling of romance clung to us for the remainder of the night. We held hands and debated the pros and cons of a moonlit horse drawn carriage ride through Central Park. Thankfully, we both agreed that being pulled by a horse that essentially pulled a tarp that held its poop, was not either of our idea of romantic. We went to a coffee shop and walked the city sidewalks, enjoying the hustle and bustle around us. It was a perfect date.

At some point, Luc convinced *me* that *I* convinced *him* to stay a few more days to see the sights. I didn't know I had this super power to convince people to do things I didn't know I wanted to do. I'll need to be careful with this new development, or maybe wise up to Lucas talking circles around me to get his way.

We went everywhere: the Empire State Building, Statue of Liberty, Ground Zero, and the UN. He took me to a basketball game and to hang out backstage, at a concert, in The Garden. We even went and played laser tag, which I dominated to both of our surprise. There were a few run-ins with the paparazzi; they kept their distance and Lucas made sure I was more focused on him than the camera flashes.

Now that we're back home, I miss being with him. It's been three days since he dropped me off, our separation self-imposed on my part. I haven't stopped painting since. Tara is home already. She and Hailey know how it is to get consumed by work. They have been leaving me food and drinks to keep me alive. I came up once for air to let Luc know I was going to be out of touch. Since he's the muse for my new series, he may be out of sight, but he is definitely on my mind. I also texted my sisters, at one point, to see if they'd like to come over in a few days for a girl's night. And I mentioned that they could spend the night or a few nights if they wanted. I didn't realize I was holding my breath until they texted me back to say they're coming.

I finally decide to put my paintbrush down. I look around me. My studio is a mess. I was so consumed with inspiration, I never stopped to clean anything more than the paint supplies I needed. I have never produced so many finished paintings in such a short period of time.

I rush around, performing a quick clean. I have twenty minutes to try and appear human again before my sisters arrive. Sub-human post work-a-thon grunge is not a good look for entertaining.

Dashing to my room, I grab jeans and a t-shirt. After a quick scrub in the shower, I feel alive again. I move to shut off the faucet when it stops on its own. What the heck? I play with the nobs a bit, but nothing happens. Weird.

When I get downstairs, the girls are all here and the pizza boxes are just being opened. Perfect timing. I hug my sisters real quick. "I'm so glad you two came." I squeeze each of them.

"It's a good thing you planned this late or I wouldn't have been able to make it out of the shop in time," Quin says.

"It's our thing, chickadee. We're all working women besides the runt over there." Tara affectionately tips her head at Stephanie. "Work all day and at night we play. None of those five pm early bird dinners for us."

"I may be the runt of this group, but that just means I have age on my side and will still have perky boobs when yours are sagging." Stephanie smiles sweetly at Tara. We all howl with laughter.

The easy chatter continues while we eat. My close group seamlessly expands to include my sisters. An outside observer would think we've been doing this for years. Quin holds back a little at first. I think she wants to get the lay of the land. However, Stephanie jumps right in and gives Tara a run for her money with the rapid quips and banter, keeping us all highly entertained.

"Have you even hit puberty and grown pubic hair yet, Pip-squeak?"

"Oh I have hair. It is definitely less than what you have though. You're still wearing the 'fro you grew back in the nineteen seventies, aren't you, Granny?"

"That's it!" Tara slams her hands down on the table and stands up, startling all of us. "I'm keeping her." She moves around the table to wrap her arms around a giggling Stephanie.

Tara shoots me a fierce look. "Hailey has brothers and sisters. You just got two. I don't have any so you just have to give me this one and no one gets hurt. Also I'd like to state for the record that I wasn't even a twinkle in my parent's eyes or a tingle in their loins, in the seventies." Tara ends her remark with a noogie for Stephanie.

"Anyone want tea?" I need my tea fix. I haven't had any in days. After the unanimous vote for tea, I take five mugs from the cabinet and grab my teapot from the stove. When I turn the water on to fill the pot, nothing comes out. What is going on?

"Ladies, did anyone else notice that we do not have running water?" I question. Darn it, I should have followed up on this after my shower.

Hailey jumps into action. "Tara, you call the water company. Stephanie, you go in the laundry room and get bottles of water from the shelf. Quincy, if you could grab the serving tray from the butler's pantry. Gen, you get everything else we need for the tea out. We'll move this party to the den and see what's going on. While all of you are doing that, I am going to check the water heater and pipes in the basement to see if anything is going on there."

Hailey corrals us like troops and sets us to our duties with efficiency.

"I'm on hold with the water company now," Tara announces, holding the phone to her ear.

The doorbell chimes as I'm setting the tea condiments on the tray Quincy got for me. I didn't think we were expecting anyone else to join us for girl's night. Tara leaves to get whoever is at the door.

"I didn't see anything wrong down there. Was that the doorbell I heard?" Hailey comes back into the kitchen from her trip to the basement. She joins Quin and Steph at the island.

"Yes, Tara went to get the door. You didn't invite one of your sisters, did you?" I remember the nightmare from last time vividly.

"God no! Felicity actually just moved back in with my parents. She's decided to divorce Daniel because he hasn't been giving her access to his credit cards. Sawyer told me the other day that Erica has been catting around town more than usual, bringing disgrace to the Trenton name. Trust me, they are the last two people I'd ever invite to girls night again. I still cringe over the last time they came over." She shudders delicately.

Hailey is so different from her sisters. Their father spoiled her older sisters completely rotten and made them into the worst sort of "Daddy's girls". Hailey is the youngest out of the five and has both her brothers in the middle. From what I have seen, the girls loved their position in Daddy's affections. They never got along with their younger brothers. When Hailey came, they did not like the idea of sharing even more of their daddy's lavish attention. They never grew out of their childhood obsession with being Daddy's only girls and still take every opportunity to bully Hailey. To top it all off, putting them in the same room as Tara is like putting three cats in a box, dumping water on them, and closing the lid. The Trenton's are a large close family, but not everyone is civil.

We all hear Tara's stomping before she gets to the kitchen.

"I cannot fucking believe it! You will not fucking believe it!" She enters the kitchen and her arms start flying in emphasis of her words.

"What's going on?"

"Fucktards out there were doing," she pauses to do air quotes, "'Routine maintenance' and somehow broke the main water line. Now no one on this street has water and they want us to leave our homes."

"Did they say why? When it would be fixed? What are we supposed to do?" Hailey demands

"They need to shut off the electricity and gas to the houses to make sure the water did not cause damage to those lines as well. They aren't sure how the pipe broke and need to inspect it further. So they don't know when it will be fixed, but we can call the water company to check when we can come home." Tara's hands are clenched in anger. I'm surprised she did not strangle one of the workers. "We're supposed to stay with family or find a hotel room," she finishes, shaking her head in disgust.

"We can go home tonight. We can sleep over another time," Quin offers

Damn, this is the worst possible night for this to happen. I was hoping to have Steph and Quin stay over and segue into discussing signing over assets from our father's will and partial ownership of the Brownstone. This was their childhood home. I don't want to take that from them. Hailey's parents' house is out of the question with the hot mess set living with them again. Tara's mom is definitely out of the question. We could go to my grandparents, but it's late for them and I'm sure they're already in bed. Plus I don't want their first meeting with their granddaughters to be because of an emergency.

"I'll start calling hotels," Hailey volunteers.

"Wait!" The light bulb in my head, flickers before clicking on. "I know where we can go and it has plenty of room, so you two don't have to drive back home tonight. Let's pack up and lock up."

"We'll stay here and clean up the kitchen while you all pack since we're already packed." Stephanie starts putting the items I arranged on the tray away.

I run up to my room to get my cell phone. Packing quickly, I run back down to meet the girls. I pull my phone from my sweatshirt pocket. It's dead. Darn. I hope I'm not over stepping the bounds of a girlfriend, and that Lucas is up for company tonight.

We pull up to Lucas's house before midnight. His car is in the driveway along with a few I don't recognize. I hope I'm not disturbing him and company. I didn't think about that.

It's chilly out but the night sky is clear with a beautiful, bright moon. After ringing the doorbell a few times, no one answers.

"Someone come help me up so I can see in the window." Tara is in the bushes on her tippy toes.

"Tara, what are you doing? Get away from that window. If Lucas sees us he's going to think we're psychotic," I whisper at her.

"Actually, Gen, it's not a bad idea. He'll only think she's crazy since he'd see her head and not ours." Hailey must have lost her mind, too.

Quin steps up to the window and looks up at it. "I'm smaller and this isn't my first rodeo. I spent my teen years climbing in and out of my bedroom window. Give me a boost up. I don't see a foot hold."

Great, now my sister is losing it. Maybe I can blame this all on Tara when Lucas finds us? She's usually the bad influence.

"There are lights on towards the back of the house," Quin whispers down to us from atop Tara's shoulders. "Maybe he didn't hear the doorbell back there?"

"If you want I can go around back and scope it out. Check if I can see him," Stephanie offers, seemingly wanting to do her part.

I sigh long and loud.

This is my boyfriend's house. I can't let them do this crazy crap all on their own. "We'll all go around the back and see if we can find Lucas or someone else to let us in." I join the crazies.

We all quietly make our way around the house. It's dark back here. The only light available is from the moon, peeking through the trees. I wish it was daytime and we weren't sneaking around. I'd love to take the time to admire his beautiful backyard and view of the river.

"Here are some windows." The three windows are side by side so we can all look in together. It looks like they lead to the kitchen.

"Wow. That's some stove. It makes me want to cook something," Tara whispers from my right.

"I know what you mean. I have the sudden urge to bake some cookies or maybe some muffins," Hailey whispers from behind and to the left of me.

"If you are baking or cooking then I'm eating. I suck at both, but I get what you're saying; it's a woman thing. See an awesome kitchen and you envision yourself as June Cleaver, Betty Crocker, and Martha Stewart all rolled into one hot package," Quincy says from my left.

"You have to get better with charging your cellphone, Gen. You constantly let it die," Hailey chastises me.

"I have a question." Stephanie finally joins in the conversation.

"What's up, chicken butt?" Tara acknowledges her first.

"Well, I have a statement and then a question. First, I don't see Lucas or anyone else in the house. Now my question is, why are we whispering like weirdoes and criminals?"

She's right; the house does look empty. Darn it all.

"We're whispering because we are all weirdoes, and peeking through someone's windows with the intention of entering the home. This can loosely be considered criminal activity despite the fact that we aren't entering unless Lucas lets us in. Do not even suggest otherwise, Tara." I throw out that warning, knowing she was going to say that next.

"Well if we aren't going to find a way in, what do you suggest doing? I'm freezing my ass off." Tara gets snippy with me.

"I probably could jimmy one of these windows open." Quin says thoughtfully.

"Sawyer taught me one summer how to pick locks. I could give the door a try." Hailey offers, as if breaking and entering is no big deal.

I stare at Quincy and Hailey like they've lost their minds. "At what point this evening were you all drinking? You are all crazy! This is crazy! You want to break into my boyfriend's house and then what happens when we find him? Should we tap him on the shoulder and say, 'Hey, we broke your windows and door locks. Can we *pretty please* stay the night?' You must be drunk!" I hiss at them.

"Only a little," Hailey admits. "We may or may not have done a little drinking on the drive over."

"What?!" I shriek back. "You were drinking and driving?"

Tara shoves me. "Oh, shush, Gen, now you're talking crazy. We had Stephanie drive while we followed behind you and the luggage I still had mini liquor bottles in my purse from my last trip, so we had a little responsibly reckless fun." Only Tara would describe something as being responsibly reckless. She must have slept through the English class explaining antonyms.

"You all suck. You could have saved me at least one for when we got here. Back to the issue at hand, you lushes," I chide. "Where could Luc be? There are more cars in the driveway than just his."

"Maybe he's upstairs having an orgy but not with chicks. You are all the woman he needs. It'd have to be an all-out dong fest."

I elbow Tara in the stomach. I wonder if she ever hears the things that come out of her mouth.

Quin frowns. "It's definitely not a dong fest. It would be a crime against women for a man, that damn good looking, to want cock so much, that he needs more than one at a time. We'd have to call the police on him and have him arrested for hate crimes against women or something. Is that something that could be done?" Quincy chews her bottom lip and looks as if she's thinking about her question.

"Will you all stop thinking about my boyfriend having an all-male orgy? No, you cannot call the police on him for that."

"Actually, Gen, I think she could. Virginia is one of those states with the no anal law."

We all turn to gape at Stephanie.

"What? I read it somewhere," she says defensively.

"That's assuming it is anal. Maybe they are law abiding and it's oral."

"Hailey!" This conversation is getting out of hand.

Suddenly the light from the moon is being blocked out, shrouding us in darkness.

"Uh guys, did anyone else notice the, um, sudden lack of light out here?"

"I think someone is standing behind me and blocking the moonlight. I hear breathing," Hailey whispers to us.

"Tara, turn around and see if Hailey is right," I order.

"Fuck that shit. I'll turn around when you turn around." Tara snorts like I'm crazy for saying that.

I concede. "We'll all turn around at the same time. At the count of three we turn. One…two…three!"

Behind us is a wall of large, dark figures. Their faces are masked in shadows. I don't know who screamed first, but it triggers the reaction for all of us to start screaming.

"Run!"

We take off, past the shadowy figures, and run like we're in a horror movie.

"Game on."

I hear a deep voice I don't recognize from behind us.

The adrenaline is pumping through my veins. I can hear the blood rushing in my ears. I don't know how long I have been running for. I slow to a walk and look around me. We all became separated at some point, in our escape through the woods. I don't see anyone else. I'm all alone.

I hear leaves crunching in the distance ahead of me and to the left. A crunch behind me alerts me to someone else's presence. I do the stupid horror movie mistake number one, and turn to look.

Instinctively, I swing when I realize how close he is. He ducks and tackles me to the ground. I thrash around, struggling to get free, when I hear the chuckling in my ear. I stiffen under him.

"You scared the life out of me! You...you asshole!" I glare at Lucas, putting as much heat into the look as I can manage.

I can't move my arms enough to hit him, so I do the next best thing. I bite his shoulder. Hard.

"Fuck. Damn. Ow! Watch it, minx. I think you drew blood," he hisses painfully.

"Good, you deserve it for scaring ten years off of my life." I glare. I don't care if it's dark out and he probably can't see it.

"I'm sorry. I didn't mean to scare you, but I also wasn't the one sneaking around my backyard in the middle of the night, discussing fictional orgies." He sounds like he's suppressing laughter.

I gasp. "You heard that?" I thank the darkness now. Luc can't see how mortified I am. I think my toes are beet red, too.

"I heard everything. We were walking back up from the carriage house when we spotted you and your tribe of Amazons sneaking around the side of the house." His teeth are a flash of white in the darkness when he grins.

Luc starts peppering kisses down my throat, distracting me from my mortification. The hand sneaking under my sweatshirt obliterates all other thoughts.

"Tara did have something right."

"Hmm?" What is he talking about now? *Dear god move your hand up further.* My boobs are practically panting to be touched and he's taking his sweet time.

"Your wish is my command."

Crap on a cracker, I said that out loud. He has scrambled my brain.

"As I was saying, before I was ordered to fondle your lovely breasts. Tara was right; you are all the woman I need." His voice ends on a sensual note.

He swoops in and kisses me, silencing anything I may have said. I most likely wouldn't have been able to say anything that made much sense. There is something about his kisses that anchors my soul, but shatters my mind. If I could bottle his saliva and find a way to pour it into the water supply of war torn countries, I guarantee that the next day, they would all sign peace treaties. Then again, I don't want to share; not even for world peace.

Lucas kneels above me and whips his sweatshirt over his head. Pulling my upper body up, he arranges the sweatshirt under me.

"You're going to get cold," I breathe.

"Not possible. Around you I swear I always have a fever," he whispers back.

My sweatshirt gets unzipped and spread open, giving him easy access. His mouth finds my nipple through my bra. My tank top is bunched up under my armpits from when he touched me before, I want it off but can't with my sweatshirt still on and I do not want to stop Lucas long enough to have my clothes removed. His hand moves to touch me through my yoga pants. I can tell the fabric between my legs is already wet.

"I love the yoga pants. Your ass in them is mind blowing. I can't tell you how many times I tripped chasing after you because I couldn't take my eyes off your ass long enough to watch where I was going." He palms my cheek and gives it a quick squeeze before moving back to rub me.

"I'll take that as a compliment," I laugh quietly.

He grins. "You should! I'm considering buying stock in a company that manufactures yoga pants. That or finding the person that invented them and begin worshipping him like a deity."

"I only have one thing to say."

"What's that?" He looks at me.

"Are you going to take these damn yoga pants off me and fuck me already?" I grin up at him.

I can't believe I just said that, but really there's only so much light petting I can take before I want the good stuff. Scratch that— *great stuff.*

"Oh, you're in for a treat, my little foul-mouthed hussy. I'm going to give you exactly what you are asking for," he growls.

Lucas flips me onto my stomach and pulls my hips into the air. I know what he has in mind; a thrill shoots through me. I shake my hips to taunt him. In one smooth move he nudges my legs apart, yanks my pants down, and slams into me. There's none of the usual finesse, just raw need. All of the air leaves my lungs with his invasion. His fingers weave into my hair. Squeezing at my scalp, he pulls my head back, giving him better access to my neck.

He whispers into my ear, "Is this what you wanted—a nice, hard, down, and dirty fuck?"

Pushing my hips back into him, wanting him to move, I moan, "Yes."

"Good, I want to give you exactly what you want." He gently kisses my neck; a sweet contradiction to what he's promising me.

His hands move to grip my hips. His movements are fast and hard, not like every other time we've made love where he was fluid and almost rhythmic. This tempo is harsh and animalistic. It's a coupling meant to bring to surface our basic instincts. I push my hips back, meeting him thrust for thrust. I want to give as good as I get. I want to hear the guttural moan when he comes.

He snakes one hand around my hip, finding my sweet spot.

"I'm so close, but I'm not letting go without you," his voice is hoarse.

The excitement of having sex in the woods and his magical hands playing me, coupled with his raw words, sends me over the edge. I slam my hips back into him, wanting all of him as my body grips his. We roar out together in release. Our bodies perfectly in time with each other's. We collapse to the ground and Luc rolls us to our sides.

"I'm a cave man," Lucas gasps out between breaths. "Chasing my woman through the woods and getting turned on doing it. That's as cave man as it gets. When I get my breath back I'll beat on my chest and you can call me Unga."

"After that, I might be okay with you dragging me back to your cave by my hair."

We laugh together and start to get dressed again. Everyone else is probably at the house already wondering where we are… or not. We were *really* loud at the end.

"Are you ready to face the village?" He pulls me to my feet.

"Lead the way, Unga."

Lucas takes my hand and leads us carefully out of the woods.

Chapter Eleven

The scene that greets us back at the house is similar to a seeing a circus for the first time. I sneak a peek at Lucas. His eyes are wide like he's taking it all in.

I don't see Stephanie, but everyone else is here.

I guess you could say they have not settled down while waiting for us to join them. I do really need to work on keeping my cell phone charged because this is internet video material. I don't even know where to begin to process what is going on right now.

In the kitchen to our right, Kaine is chasing Quincy around the island. His glare is full of malevolence and his right cheek is reddened in the shape of a hand. His threats of a spanking when he finally catches her, ring loudly throughout the kitchen and fuel Quin's next dash around the island to elude capture. She is glaring just as strongly back at him, calling him a lying, disgusting pig. I didn't think we were in the woods that long? Apparently, long enough.

There's a little more action in the sitting room off the kitchen. Aryan is leaning back against the wall, looking bored while observing the show in front of him. Hailey is standing in front of Tara with her hands braced against her chest, holding Tara back from Micah, who is grinning and taunting Tara over Hailey's shoulder.

"*What is going on in here?*" I yell in order to be heard over the noise.

Quincy's gaze breaks from Kaine's and looks up at us, standing in the doorway. Stopping mid run, her head whips back and forth between Lucas standing next to me and Kaine behind her.

"Oh damn," she breathes.

With her distracted, Kaine takes advantage and grabs Quin before she can get away. He barely breaks stride as he tosses her over his shoulders in a fireman's hold and exits the room.

We can hear Quincy's pleas that she 'didn't know' fade as they move further through the house.

"He's not actually going to spank her, is he?" I turn to Lucas and demand.

He takes a step away from me, putting his hands up.

"I'm not sure how to answer that question. I'd like to say *no* to keep you happy. That is very un-Kaine-like behavior, so I can't definitively say. I can assure you he won't hurt her, though." His assurance doesn't make me feel better, but it will have to do.

"Okay, I'll accept that answer, for now. What should we do about that?" I wave my hand at the other group that didn't even pause to take a breath when I yelled.

"I guess making popcorn and sitting down to enjoy the show is out of the question?" He grins when I glare at him.

Aryan finally takes care of the situation for us. Being careful not to jostle Hailey around, he reaches past her to Tara. He picks her up and places her on the loveseat before sitting on top of her, effectively stopping all struggles and turning her outrage towards him. I can't complain; his method produced the desired result.

"What is going on in here? I thought we had a truce?" I demand from Micah

That's when the gasp, heard 'round the world, happened.

"You called a truce with this ass hat? Let me up!" Tara yells from behind Aryans back. When her pushing and shoving him gets her nowhere, she resorts to old faithful.

"Ouch! You bit me!" Aryan jumps and rubs the side of his back. He glares down at her over his shoulder like she's a wild animal.

"What is it with you women and your biting?" Lucas is glaring down at me as well, rubbing his shoulder now as if he just remembered that I bit him.

I shrug my shoulders. "It works."

"You get off of her right now or else." Hailey marches up to Aryan with her hands fisted on her hips. Her small stature makes the threatening stance comical.

"Whoa there killer, no one wants the Chihuahua to bite. He's just giving her a minute to calm down." Micah throws his arm around Hailey's shoulders which she does not shrug off until she sees Tara and me noticing.

As if this night could not get any more bizarre, Stephanie has finally rejoined the group. She is thrown over the shoulder of a moving mountain. The mountain limps over to the freezer and grabs a bag of frozen peas, not even struggling with the added weight he's balancing. Everyone quiets when we notice him limp over to place a bound and gagged Stephanie gently on the couch. There are black zip ties around her ankles and wrists. A black bandana is tied around her mouth, keeping her silent. When he sits on the opposite end of the couch as far away from Steph as he can get, I realize what the frozen peas are for. He places them in his lap and closes his eyes, letting his head fall back against the couch. I guess he doesn't normally walk with a limp.

I run into the kitchen and grab the shears from the cutting block to get the zip ties off of my baby sister. When

I get back to the sitting area, Hailey and Tara are already around her, working on unknotting the bandana. We finally get her untied and she starts rubbing at her wrists where the zip ties were. We collectively turn our fury on the mountain.

"Who do you think you are?"

"How dare you do that to her!"

"You have some nerve doing that to our baby girl!"

"Why don't you pick on someone your own size?"

"I ought to kick your ass, you venereal disease toting cock muncher!"

"I'm tiny, but I'll kick your huge ass if you don't apologize."

"That's my baby sister you just hog tied! I'll go seven different kinds of crazy on your ass!"

We're all yelling at him at the same time. Quincy and Kaine rejoin the group. When Quin pieces together what's going on, she joins us.

"That's my little sister, you motherfucker!"

Dropping the peas on the couch, the mountain stands to tower over all of us, glaring. "I'm the one that came back with my balls in my stomach while she's unharmed and I have to apologize?" He looks over our heads at the other guys in the room. Not getting assistance from them, he moves to excuse himself from being cornered.

We jump him.

It was purely spontaneous. We work well so as a team that you would think this was ordinary behavior for us. Tara jumping on his back determined which way we all fell when we went down in a tangle of limbs. With the four of us wrapped around him, he can't move. Once we get him down we don't know what to do. He doesn't struggle at all; I get the sense that he doesn't want to hurt any of us despite our attack.

Stephanie stands over us, trying to get our attention. "Hey! It's okay. He didn't hurt me. When he came up behind me in the woods, I turned and instinctively kneed him." She looks sheepish. "If he wasn't so freaking huge I would have got him in the stomach but on him my aim was a little lower. Even after that, when I was struggling to get away, he was gentle." She bites her lip. "By the way, I'm sorry about the knee incident and my crazy family attacking you."

Tara squeals. "Awe! She called us family! Did you hear that, Hailey? We were included!" She gets sappy. "The pipsqueak is going to make me tear up."

We all get up slowly, easing away with caution—just in case. The guys are hysterically laughing at us. They aren't even trying to hide the fact to spare our feelings. That's men for you; they also didn't even attempt to help their friend.

I'm not ashamed to say I ran once I was up and hid behind Lucas. That's what boyfriends are for, aren't they? I think my boyfriend is defective and needs to be returned to the store; he keeps trying to tug me out from behind him.

When the mountain is back on his feet, Lucas clears his throat. "I guess some introductions are in order now that everyone has become acquainted. Most of you know this is my girlfriend, Genevieve. She brought her band of Amazons: Tara, Hailey, Quincy, and Stephanie. I have not had the pleasure to meet you yet, Stephanie, but so far, it's been a pleasure." He winks at her, laying the charm on thick. "Over there is Kaine, obviously my twin." He glances at Quincy grinning. "Then most of you know my brothers, Aryan and Micah. Last, we have commando, or professional abductor because really who else carries zip ties and a bandana on them? Dexter, or Dex as we call him."

"He's big enough to climb and swing from like a jungle gym." Tara says, eyeing him. Her assessment isn't far off.

Micah glares at Hailey when she nods her agreement. Dexter looks embarrassed under the weight of the female scrutiny he's receiving. I shake my head at Tara.

"What? I know I'm not the only one that was thinking it. I was just the one to voice it." She shrugs. Tara was born with holes in her filter. I pity the man that decides he wants to tame her and that mouth of hers.

"I told you your friends and my siblings were a lot alike. They're hitting it off great." Lucas wraps me in his arms and rests his chin on my head, which I bump when I turn to look at him like he's crazy.

"This is hitting it off great? I think your brother hit on my sister without introducing himself, so she thought he was you and she slapped him. I'm pretty sure he spanked her." I send Kaine a dirty look. "Tara is still at Micah's throat. I don't know what for this time. Aryan manhandled her and she bit him. Hailey then threatened Aryan. My baby sister was abused, albeit gently, by your friend that we then screamed at, forced to the ground, and embarrassed. Did I miss anything?"

"Oh yeah, you missed a lot." He smiles while looking around us.

My eyebrows come together. "What'd I miss?"

"The big picture, Genevieve. The big picture." Luc grabs my hand and drags me behind him and down to the comforts of the basement. Everyone follows behind much more sedately than the group has been since me and the girls arrived.

Once drinks are poured, we stand at the bar and around the pool table to watch Kaine kick Micah's butt.

"Not that I'm not thrilled about you being here, because I am, but may I ask why the surprise visit, or should I say reconnaissance mission?" Lucas asks.

"I don't know if I'd call it a recon mission. They were about as stealthy as a herd of water buffalo." Aryan smiles at all of us from behind the bar.

Tara grabs her hips. "We weren't trying to spy. We were trying to get inside."

Micah looks up after taking his shot. "You know that's called breaking and entering. Lucas, call the cops and see if they'll come arrest this one." He points the pool stick at Tara.

Aryan tries to redirect Tara's focus. "Before you go shoving that pool stick up his ass, why don't you come tell me how your last trip went? I didn't think I'd be seeing you again so soon, princess."

I'm not sure if he really loves Micah that much to keep saving him or if he keeps doing it to interact with Tara since she has been making an obvious point to try and ignore him.

"*Pizza delivery!*" a loud voice booms from the top of the stairs before stomping down. "I thought guy's night was in the carriage house tonight?" When the guy finally reaches the bottom of the stairs, he pauses at seeing that guy's night has been invaded by girl's night.

Guy's night must be a secret. If word ever got out that this much testosterone was meeting up under one roof there'd be riots in the streets. Condom and diaphragm-waving, estrogen mobs.

Luc has an impressive looking group of brothers and friends and I'm getting the tingle. The matchmaking tingle.

"If I had known we'd have females in our company this evening I would have dressed a little nicer, ladies." Newcomer flashes a set of perfectly pearly whites at us.

"You look good to me," is chorused back by the girls.

I don't join in with the other girls. I have a little more class than that. But I can appreciate the fine figure this man has with his washboard abs, defined even through his shirt, and his odd choice of shorts that ride low on his narrow hips despite the chilly temperatures outside.

Newcomer's dark hair is short, a tad longer than a buzz cut, and eyes so dark that they appear obsidian. I'm staring because I have this nagging feeling that I have seen him somewhere before. I know I have never met him because even I would not forget meeting a man like him. I give up.

I turn to Lucas to discreetly ask. "Who is that? I know I've seen him somewhere before." I add the last part so I don't give the wrong idea.

"A close friend of mine, Maddox Grant."

Ding! Ding! Ding! The bell in my head rings!

Google is my friend. I'm glad that I looked Lucas's band up after meeting him. Maddox was the drummer.

I remember what Lucas told me about his band and need to double check his health status since his smile is currently charming my girls out of their panties.

"Alcoholic, drug addict, or H.I.V spreader?" I discreetly ask.

"Neither. I was simply the drummer." Maddox grins when I whip around in shock. Apparently, I wasn't discreet enough since unbeknownst to me, he was standing right behind me. "My sisters always complain that as a toddler, once I discovered hitting pots and pans with spoons, I never stopped banging shit. Years later, I added women to that repertoire. I've been S.T.D free since '83, which is pretty awesome since I was born in '85. See, pretty boy next to you isn't the only one that wrote our songs. I've got

- 135 -

rhyming skills." He winks at me and then sets the stack of pizza boxes down on the bar.

"I can see that." I blink at him sweetly. "I'm very impressed and I'm sure most three year olds would be, too. Have you thought about writing children's books?" I innocently, yet sarcastically, inquire.

He grins over my shoulder to Lucas. "Hey, Lucky, I like this one." Grabbing my hand, he raises it to his lips. "If Lucky ever fucks up, even the slightest bit, let me know. I have this cousin that owns a horse farm. I'll grab a white stallion and be right over." His lips graze my knuckles. "In the meantime, if you could point out the single ladies in the room I'll forever be your servant."

I lean in. "All of them are single. See the slender girl with the long black hair over there?"

His eyes land on Stephanie. "Oh yeah, I'm seeing "legs" over there."

"She's my eighteen year old little sister. Hands off," I threaten. "Otherwise, happy hunting." I feel like I have just unleashed a real life Lothario amongst the maidens.

After making his rounds greeting the guys, Maddox sits on the couch and, like bait, the hens flock to the wolf. With my matchmaking senses tingling, I wonder who would best match him. Quin would be the obvious choice. Hailey could handle him regardless of Tara constantly trying to baby her like she can't handle herself. Then again Tara has potential, too.

Unintentionally, I sigh aloud. Lucas frowns at me. "Wishing you were over there, too?" I jab him in the ribs as hard as I can manage.

"No, I don't wish to be over there. I'm trying to play match maker but can't figure out which one to match. It sounds easier when you read about it in books."

Lucas shakes his head at me. "Stop playing match maker and just enjoy the show with your own match." He pulls me to his side, cuddling me against him.

"He calls you Lucky. Why?"

"During one of our tours, when we started playing the really big shows, I fell off stage."

"Were you hurt and lucky to be alive or something?"

He shifts next to me like he's uncomfortable explaining. "Not exactly. The front was usually filled with women. By the time security got me back on stage I was only wearing my boots and holding what was left of my boxers to cover myself. We stopped the show so I could finish with some clothes on. When I got back on stage from dressing, the women pretty much shredded my clothes into tiny little pieces and passed them around. When they saw me again they waved the pieces in the air, screaming 'We got lucky!' Ever since, the guys in the band call me Lucky and crack jokes."

"Maybe later I can get my own little piece of Lucky." I flutter my eyes at him.

He tucks a loose curl behind my ear. "You already have all of Lucky." He gently kisses the shell of my ear. I stare at him. The night I met him I certainly lucked out. I look around the room at our family and friends. I think I see what Luc saw earlier. They are one crazy group, but they make for a good time and actually get along great once you look past the off-humor jokes, snide comments, and threats of physical abuse. Or maybe they get along great because of that.

"You still need to tell me how girl's night got moved into my backyard." Lucas pulls me from my thoughts.

"Darn it, I forgot." I glare up at him. "Why are you laughing at me?"

"Because you are cute. You switch back and forth from your sweet, cute 'darn it' and 'crap on a cracker' to cursing with the best of them."

"I never used to curse, so I'm blaming you. You're a bad influence and I plan on telling my Gram just that if she ever finds outs I cussed."

"Hey now, no muddying my image before I even get to meet the illustrious Gram."

I bet even with his cursing my Gram will be wishing she was a younger woman when I finally introduce him to my grandparents.

"Stop distracting me! I still have to tell you about how the girls and I need to spend the night."

Micah is the closest to us, standing with the main group. His head perks up when I say that and whips around. "You're all spending the night?"

The other guys all turn and stare at me as well, probably waiting for me to confirm what Micah just asked.

"If Lucas will let us. There was an issue with the water main on our street and we were asked to leave for a few days while they repair it. So rather than go to a hotel, I had the girls follow me here."

I don't go into details, like us peeking in the front window. We already look crazy and I don't want to add another offense to the list.

"Of course you're all staying here. I have more than enough room. The guys usually stay after guy's night since we drink a lot. I still have enough bedrooms for everyone to have their own." He leans down and whispers in my ear, "We'll be sharing, of course. I've missed you the past few days."

"Stop putting your tongue in Gen's ear and let's get co-ed night started." Micah rudely tosses one of the couch pillows at our heads.

"How do you ladies feel about Guitar Hero?"

We split into teams: guys versus girls. Stephanie voluntarily sits out when we make up rules that turn it into a shot game and make a high stakes bet. She gets to referee and enforce the rules. Since she is a team girl at heart, she helps keep the game to our advantage, and the fact that Dex, Maddox, and Kaine are really terrible helps, too. Aryan and Micah are pretty good, and of course Lucas is great. They don't have what we have, though. Our secret weapon: Hailey. She's a Guitar Hero goddess. She had writers block a few years ago and played nonstop for months until she finally had something to write. At the end, the very drunk girls triumphed over the extremely intoxicated guys; not even the pizza could help with the amount of alcohol that's been consumed.

Standing outside, freezing by the patio, we watch the guys make good on the bet. They strip while we cheer them on and take off running for the river, yelling the entire way like an Indian war party. Before they can get back out, we run down and grab all of their clothes and high tail it back inside. Hailey, always the provider, leaves some towels she discovered folded in the laundry room just outside of the door for them to find.

When we hear the angry bellows behind us, we dump their clothes on the island and run, screaming up the stairs. With all of this yelling I hope the neighbors don't call the police.

"Where are we running to?" Hailey asks a very good question.

"I don't know. I haven't gotten to see much of Luc's house. We need to find a room to lay low in and formulate a plan of defense for their retaliation." Plus I'm getting winded from running around.

Stephanie stops running, gasping to catch her breath. "Whose bright idea was it to go upstairs where there's no options for escape?"

I feel the weight when their gazes land on me. So I led the pack— *sue me*.

"With all of these rooms, there has to be somewhere to lay low. Pick one and let us get gone before they are done getting dressed and come after us. I bet money bags down there has a walk in closet larger than my bedroom in every one of these rooms." Quin finishes walking the length of the hallway and picks the only door down this wing.

"This is a million times better than a walk in closet."

We step onto the balcony. I walk to the railing to look over. A colossal desk holding a computer and papers scattered across it dominates the lower level. This must be Lucas's office. It's so him. I can easily picture him sitting comfortably behind that imposing piece of furniture and using his charm to sway people to have things his way. On this level, the walls are bookshelves, filled from top to bottom. I could imagine spending hours, browsing through his collection. Scanning the shelves, something catches my focus. Walking towards it I can see that the bookshelves are staggered to form an optical illusion, hiding a staircase from obvious view of the doorway and the office downstairs.

"Over here! I think I found our hide out."

Tara bumps into me from behind when I stop short. "This is awesome!"

"He has a reading nook? This is nirvana. I need you to do me a favor and marry Lucas so I can have free access to this little slice of heaven, got that? I won't take no for an answer or I'll pummel you with my fists of fury." Hailey puts up her little fists to show me she means business.

"I'll see what I can do. If we break up I'll petition the courts for visitation rights. Is that a wine cooler cabinet?"

Tara crosses to it and swings the door open. "That's what I'm talking about." She pulls bottles out and starts tossing them to us. "Best hide out ever. Wine, comfortable seating, and huge pillows thrown everywhere."

I pretend not to notice when Tara slips Stephanie a bottle. I had my first taste of wine at fifteen. I am certain she's had alcohol before. We all grab cushions from the couches and chaise lounge and arrange them on the floor with the big pillows from around the room. Vivian had to have decorated this room for her son because I don't see a man choosing this many pillows and throw blankets for his reading area. Wrapped in the blankets and drinking wine right from the bottle, we relax to enjoy the silence for a few minutes.

"You and Lucas host the best slumber parties ever. I haven't had this much fun since we went to Amy Whitcomb's sleep over in eighth grade," Tara whispers into the silence.

I chuckle at the memory. "Remember that, Hail?"

She smiles over at me. "How could I forget that night? I finally got my period for the first time and Amy's older brother and all of his friends barged into the bathroom while I was trying to figure out how to use the mattress of a maxi pad my mother packed for me just in case."

"I forgot about that. Micah was there that night. He punched Robert Whitcomb in the nose for making you cry. Then Tara went after him since he beat her to doing it." I nudge Tara with my foot. "Are you ever going to like him? I think we're old enough to bury the hatchet."

"I like him just fine. It's just fun still. We've always been passionate about our rivalry. Since you are with Lucas, I suppose I can start having normal *adult* interactions with him." She wags her eyebrows suggestively.

Gross. I can't imagine Tara and Micah sleeping together.

"I just want you two to get along, not sleep together. Hail has been trying to get along with him and she does it without jumping his bones." I purse my lips in thought. If we didn't have such a long history with Micah he'd probably be a good catch for Tara; they only butt heads because they're so much alike.

I roll my head to the side to look at my sisters. "You still awake over there, Quincy?"

She opens her eyes and smiles at me. "Yeah, just enjoying the moment. This is nice. Sitting around, drinking wine, and talking. Besides waiting to be ambushed, I think this is a perfect moment. I propose a toast." She lifts her wine bottle in the air. "You can lift yours, too, Steph. I saw it already. To many more dinners, many more bottles of wine, and many more long talks about everything and nothing. To many more moments like this and finally to us! Our little Amazon tribe."

A murmured "Hear. Hear" goes around. We take deep swigs of our wine.

"You slapped Kaine pretty good. How did that come about?" When I ask Quin, the other girls sit up a little straighter to hear the story as well.

"I'll have to start from the beginning. I have this new older sister that is not great at passing on information and therefore, did not mention that her boyfriend has an identical twin brother."

I throw one of the smaller pillows at her head.

"Enough of that. Looks like I'll have to be the adult here and put my foot down before you start a pillow fight." Stephanie puts her arms up just in time to defend herself from the barrage of pillows we fling at her.

"Geez, you old biddies can't take a joke."

Quincy holds her hand in the air for everyone's attention. "I have two things to say. Maddox. Grant."

"I'd like to add a few more words. Orgasm, yes, and please." We laugh at Tara's contribution.

Hailey sighs happily. "I don't think I'm ever going to get writer's block again."

"That's what I like about you, Hailey." Quincy smiles at her. "Tara is an in your face kind of pervert. However, you may be worse than she is. You're the secret pervert. You look like a sugary sweet treat, but I'd bet you're a freaky freak in the sack."

"I don't kiss and tell, but I can say your imagination only gets you so far when you write erotica for a living." She winks at Quin, who laughs back.

"You B-I-T-C-H! Gen and I have been joined to your hip for forever and we've never been able to get even that much out of you! This is a girl code violation." Tara angrily wags her finger at Hailey.

"So I like to be spanked every once in a while. I didn't think it was news worthy."

"I'm charging you with treason to the girl code!" I slam my fisted hand into my other palm to imitate a gavel. "I've read your work. Your imagination could handle the spanking scenes without help. Some of the other things you've written about make more sense now."

"I can't help it if I want to make sure my readers are getting their money's worth and provide accurate accountings."

"What the hell, Hail! You never let me read any of your books. Gen, I'm stealing your copies when we go home. It's time to uncover the freak in sheep's wool I've known my entire life. Does Aunt Carol read what you've been writing?" Tara hits Hailey with a pillow.

Hailey hits her right back. "Don't you dare involve my mother. I'll tell Mom-Mom you broke her grandfather clock when we were eleven."

"You can't still use that one against me. There has to be an expiration date on the tattle." Tara glares at Hailey in challenge.

"As long as Mom-Mom still gets upset about it, I'll always have that one in my back pocket," Hailey snickers.

I'm used to their bickering. I lean over to Quin and Steph and stage whisper to them. "Don't worry, they're like this all the time. If it starts to get out of hand, you just give them a quick spank on the bottom and put them in time out."

We only last another half hour before we start to fall asleep. I outlast the other girls long enough to see each of them pass out from the combination of staying up late, drinking alcohol, and getting enough exercise to last us a year. I cannot stay up too much longer after they fall asleep since I have no one to talk to, to keep me going. I stop struggling to keep my eyes open and let them drop closed.

My last thought before finally letting sleep take over drifts through my mind.

Where are the guys? I should not have closed my eyes! Now no one is going to be the look out.

Chapter Twelve

My last thoughts from the night before drift back across my mind, snapping me awake and to full blown awareness, which I immediately regret when my head starts to jackhammer and my stomach rolls. I chance taking a look around me when I hear more miserable groans beside me. All of the girls are lined up beside me in a bed I don't recognize.

"How did we get in here?" Hailey is next to notice the change of rooms.

"Fuck me, we're only on the brink of our mid-twenties. A night of drinking should not hurt this much at our age," Tara rasps.

Quincy looks like she's in just as bad of shape as us. "Shush, please my head is crumbling off my shoulders."

Stephanie doesn't have any input to add since she's still passed out softly snoring while clinging to the edge of the mattress.

"I think the guys brought us in here." I point out the only thing that makes sense.

"I repeat, fuck me."

Hailey starts looking through the sheets and blankets.

"What are you doing?" I ask.

She doesn't stop her search. "Checking for scorpions or snakes or something. If they put us in here, we should be very afraid." At her words we all start looking through the bedding for anything that moves. With our full attention on the bed, we are taken by surprise when they attack.

They storm the room, clanging pots and pans together while singing an incredibly off key bar tune about drunkenness. The racket makes my stomach pitch. I think I am going to lose its contents right here on the bedding. I grab a pillow and shove it over my head to muffle the sounds. I am willing to suffocate myself to escape the misery. When the noise finally stops, Lucas pulls the pillow away from my face and grins down at me.

"I'm dying," I croak at him.

"It probably feels that way." His eyes twinkle with amusement.

On the other side of the bed Aryan is checking out a bump on Stephanie's head. I'm not sure if she fell out of bed when they came in or if we knocked her off the bed trying to hide our heads. Other than the bump on the head, she doesn't look as if she's hung over at all. Oh, to be eighteen again.

Micah hands me a bottle of aspirin. "Take one and pass it down to the other little monkeys." He must have seen my confusion. He hooks his thumb at Steph. "You know, five little monkeys jumping on the bed one fell off and bumped her head."

"Oh, ha. Ha. Ha."

"Here are some bottles of water to wash those down." Maddox passes the waters out to us, pouting his lips in mock sympathy as he asks each of the girls if they want him to kiss it and make it all better.

After I take the two little heavenly tablets, Lucas lifts me from the bed into his arms.

Kaine looks at us, shaking his head. "I guess you're going to want breakfast in bed?" He turns to the other girls still in bed. "When your highnesses are ready to rise, Dex is downstairs whipping up breakfast."

Lucas starts to carry me out of the room.

"Lucky bitch gets breakfast in bed while we're eating with the goof troop. Ow!"

"Quit bitching, Tara. If that was you, we'd be getting the finger from over his shoulder," Quincy says.

"You're damn right you would."

I don't get to hear if anything else is said. Lucas picked up his pace and power walks us into his bedroom that was just a few doors down from the room we just left. Striding to the bed, Lucas tosses me onto the middle of it, causing me to bounce a few times.

"You are trying to kill me this morning. The aspirin is not working yet. You are being mean!" I roll onto my stomach to bury my face into his pillows.

Lucas climbs on the bed and lays on top of me, nuzzling his face into my neck.

"Au contraire, you are the one that has been mean to me. Last night I thought I was going to get to cuddle in bed with my beautiful girl. Instead she passes out drunk and I had to sleep alone."

I turn my head to the side to face him. "What happened to you guys last night? We expected immediate retaliation."

"We decided to let you girls quake in fear for a while longer and went back down to the basement and played a couple rounds of pool." He feathers kisses down my jaw line.

"Jerks. I knew it would not have taken you that long to find us," I mumble with less heat than intended, but seriously I'm not sure I can stay mad when he's near me, let alone laying on top of me.

"Nope, we knew where you were the whole time."

I try to turn to get a better look at him. "How did you know where we were?"

He stops kissing me and gives me a very boyish grin. "The library is a part of my office and I have private documents in my office. So there is a security system in that room with motion detectors at each door that notifies me by text when someone's entered the room. Also a hidden camera sends me a quick snapshot of whoever is entering."

I turn fully around in his arms so that we're chest to chest and give him the fiercest frown I can muster. "That's cheating."

Luc cradles my head in his palms and starts massaging my scalp. The dull throbbing finally relaxes. "It's not cheating. It's called using your resources. You ladies did not stand a chance. Just like that wine cabinet didn't stand a chance once you ladies found it."

"I wouldn't have pegged you for a wine drinker."

"I'm not. My mother stocked it for me. She insisted that I needed wine for when I have guests."

I can only imagine what I look like this morning. My curls are most likely forming a rat's nest around my head, my eyes are probably bloodshot from the hang over, and my mascara must be smeared around my eyes in a raccoon mask. Still that does not stop Lucas from looking at me like I'm a princess making her debut at a ball. That "ah" moment where the fairy tale princess is at the top of the grand staircase about to descend in all of her finery and everyone stares, unable to look away from her beauty. Every little girl fantasizes about having a moment like that. Usually it's your wedding day, but he makes me feel like that every time he looks at me.

"Our breakfast better get here soon. I want you naked and in my arms. Cuddling is the best that way; your body fits to mine like a puzzle piece."

Someone knocks on the door.

"Speak of the devil. That's our breakfast. Come in!" Luc yells at the door.

Dexter walks in carrying a big tray of food. Behind him, the other guys parade past, carrying more food trays. He sets the tray down on the nightstand for a minute, goes to get the small table by the sitting area to place right next to the bed, and then transfers the tray to there.

"Make sure you eat plenty, Gen, and drink another bottle of water so that you properly rehydrate." Dexter essentially clucks at me like a mother hen.

"Thank you. Where are the guys going with the other trays?"

"Well, the princesses in there decided to elevate themselves to queens and demand breakfast in bed." We start to hear yelling from the room the girls are in. "I don't think they counted on us deciding to join them in bed. I better go before there's no room or food left for me." He winks and quickly leaves to join the others.

Lucas shakes his head and chuckles quietly. "You know, your little group of Amazons are a really bad influence on my brothers and friends."

He starts arranging the plates on the bed in front of us. It all looks delicious. The scrambled eggs make my stomach rumble in anticipation. They look cheesy and have crumbled bacon in them. Food orgasm—foodgasm.

"I am not even going to argue with that statement, but I will say that you know the guys are loving it." I'm feeling pretty cocky on that point. Those guys do not seem the type to take crap from anyone, yet they're taking it and giving as good as they get with the girls.

"I'll cede that point. I would say that we should all go out sometime but visions of mayhem flash before me. I'm too pretty to go to jail."

I laugh at him and elbow him in the side. I don't know if I can think about all of us going out together yet. I'm still recovering from the rowdiness of last night's impromptu gathering of family and friends. He probably isn't far off; going to jail would be a likely possibility of a public outing together. I nod my head in agreement and dig into the food.

"Mmm, don't take this the wrong way, but I need Dexter to make these for me every morning." I moan some more. It can't be helped; these eggs require a moan of appreciation with every bite.

"You'd think he was a chef, not an ex SEAL." Lucas says while forking in another bite.

"He was a SEAL? I could see that." I nod.

"Aryan was one of his commanding officers in their platoon. When Aryan retired and started Elite, Dex wasn't far behind." Lucas is already finishing his breakfast by the time he's done with his explanation.

The man cooks, is like a mother hen, and an ex SEAL. Maybe I can see if Hailey would be interested in going on a date with Dexter.

"Is Dexter single?"

Luc quirks his brow at me. "How am I not supposed to take it the wrong way when you're moaning and asking questions like that?"

"Not for me, silly. I'm thinking Hailey."

"Leave it alone, Genevieve. They can handle their love lives on their own. They're adults; they can work it out for themselves."

"I just want to help a little. Do you know something I don't?" I examine his face for a tell. His poker face gives nothing away.

"What would make you think that?" He removes the empty plates from the bed, turning his back towards me. "What I do know is that by the time I'm done with these plates, you better be naked and ready to cuddle with me naked or there will be a spanking in your future."

I start to giggle.

Lucas looks at me from over his shoulder. "You think that's funny?"

"I giggled because Hailey told us last night that she likes to be spanked." I cock my head to the side and look at him, thoughtfully. "I've never been spanked before, but it seems kind of kinky. I'm not sure if I would like it."

Lucas finishes with the plates and stands to strip out of his clothes. "Does the thought of being spanked turn you on?"

"It's not something I've given much thought to before. I guess I could say it never used to, but the thought of you doing it does."

"You're killing me, minx. Get naked."

I get on my knees and quickly undress. I don't care if my movements are sexy or not. Anticipation is racing through my veins. Is he going to spank me now? Later?

Lucas climbs on the bed and lays back against the pillows, pulling me down with him and into his arms. I press myself against him and wait for him to make his move. After a minute passes he still hasn't done anything more than play with one of my curls.

I crane my head back to look up at him. I take the time to really look at him. He looks exhausted. There are dark circles under his eyes that I did not notice before.

"You look tired."

He gives me a small smile. "I am. I couldn't sleep last night, knowing you were so close but not in my arms. I got up a few times to get you but had to stop myself. We had Dexter stand guard at the door in case one of you woke up and tried to leave. That's the cover story, I think we more likely decided that to keep Maddox from sneaking in and starting that orgy Tara was fantasizing about."

I give him a kiss on his chin. "You should take a nap."

"I plan on it. I had to wait for you last night, so now you are going to have to wait for me and wonder when I'm going to do it." His hand slips down to rub my butt.

I cuddle in closer to him. After a few minutes his breaths even out and he relaxes into sleep. The rest of the house is quiet. I hope everyone didn't kill each other. It'd be really expensive to replace the carpets from the carnage. I smile to myself at my thoughts and fall asleep.

Lucas shifts underneath me, pulling me from my sleep. I hear the soft ringing of his cellphone on the nightstand. I sit up so that he can reach for it.

"Sorry, I didn't mean to wake you." He grabs the phone and frowns at the screen when he sees whose calling before answering. "Hello."

I climb out of bed, still a little groggy from our nap. I get Lucas's attention briefly and signal to him that I'm going to jump in the shower. When he nods back to acknowledge me, I locate my suitcase by the walk in closet and bring it in to the bathroom with me. Luckily my hair doesn't take that long to get the knots out of it, so I am able to get in and out of the shower quickly. I put jeans and nicer top on. I'm always wearing jeans or yoga pants and a t-shirt when I see Luc. I want to look a little nicer for him, so I add a touch of makeup, as well.

I'm just finishing zipping up my suitcase when Lucas pokes his head in, holding the cellphone to his chest.

"I have to finish this call in my office. I'll be done as soon as possible."

"Don't worry about me, take your time. I'll just head down and find everyone else." I smile and walk out of the bathroom behind him.

This call must be very important because he seems really distracted. I was hoping to get a compliment when he saw me but I don't think his head was with me when he was talking to me. Not that I need a compliment but when a girl puts a little extra effort into it, it would be nice.

I tense as Lucas closes the bedroom door behind him. Did I just overhear him say Lissandria's name? Ex-girlfriend Lissandria? Is she who is on the phone? I gnaw on my bottom lip. No, Lucas wouldn't be talking to his ex while he's with me. He's in the music business, she's in the music business, and he said he was going into his office which means it's about work. Her name is just a coincidence, something work related. Maybe she beat out a competing artist that works for Luc in record sales or something and that's why she was mentioned. I shake the thoughts from my head and go downstairs to find the others.

I head for the kitchen. I want some tea to calm my nerves. Dex is leaning against the counter eating a mammoth sandwich. I look at the time. We didn't eat breakfast that long ago.

"That is a huge sandwich for someone that ate breakfast just two hours ago."

He looks up from the plate and smiles at my greeting. "You know what they say about big men." My eyes widen at his insinuation. His smile broadens even more. "Big man, big appetite."

My cheeks flame. My mind was in the gutter and he knows it. "Where's everyone else?" I ask to change the subject.

"Kaine left right after breakfast for the office and you just missed Micah; he had to head to the club to do some paperwork. Aryan and Maddox took Hailey, Tara, and Steph to grab groceries for dinner tonight. Quin is on the back patio enjoying the view and this warmer than normal mid-March day."

Dex is a total alpha-male but I can see him knitting me a sweater to wear outside too. He would be both talented and deadly with a knitting needle.

"Thanks." I decide to skip the tea and head out to talk to Quin.

I am so ready for winter to be over. It is not my favorite season. Dex was right, it is a lot warmer than normal. It's almost sweater weather. The chair scrapes against the patio when I sit down next to Quin. We look at each other for a few moments. This is our first time alone together since that first day. I still can't believe I have sisters. What's more shocking is how we fell into this familial relationship with ease. I'm sure there will be some bumps in our future, but right now, I think we all need the family connection.

"I have an appointment next week with my attorney who used to be Dad's attorney to have what is left of what I inherited from Dad to be split between the three of us."

She looks at me sharply. "That's not what this is about. We don't need anything."

I grab her hand and hold onto it when she tries to pull it away.

"Trust me, I know that. That doesn't change the fact that it's the right thing to do. The thing that should have been done from the very beginning."

The tension seems to leave her body and her shoulders droop. "Why didn't he?"

I know she's not asking because she wants the money; she wants to know why our father didn't make plans to care for his two children in case of his demise. They should have each been added to his will right after their births. His heartlessness angers me because I know it hurts my sister.

"He was a coward wrapped up in too many lies of his own making." I squeeze her hand to offer what little comfort I can. I can't fix all of his wrongs but meeting with the attorney is the first step to righting some of them.

We make plans to go see our grandparents tomorrow. That is my second step to fixing things. Together we are building a bridge over waters our father left muddy. I just hope those waters never rise to meet our bridge. Next step is to get them to move in. I want my sisters near me, at least until Stephanie has to leave for college this fall. I appreciate the time I do get to have with her right now. I just wish it were under different circumstances than putting off going to college to mourn her mother. I'm going to need a little more time to work on that before I bring it up to both of them.

The rest of the group comes back with their arms full with bags. Actually, I should say Aryan and Maddox are carrying a mountain of bags in their arms. The girls are "supervising". Stephanie comes and sits with Quin and I. Hailey and Tara lead the guys inside to put away the groceries and give us some privacy.

For a moment we sit quietly staring across the lawn and down to the river. I've been alone with each of them since discovering that I had sisters but this is the first time the three of us are together by ourselves. I feel as if I need to say something significant but nothing comes to mind.

"Yesterday I thought that I would walk into the house and it would be like walking into any other house for the first time. I was so young when we left that the flood of memories took me by surprise," Stephanie continues to stare at the river as she speaks. "I remembered sitting on the bottom step waiting for Dad to come home so that I could show him what I learned at ballet. Mom would be in the kitchen humming while she prepared dinner and Quincy would be sitting at the island doodling. Then I thought what would it have been like with Gen there?" Her voice carries undertones of guilt as if she feels bad for having that memory.

Quin clears her throat before speaking. "I've thought about it over and over again trying to figure out how he could have had another family. The more I think about it the more I realize how much time he spent with us. He spent so much time with us, being a great father, I don't see how he could have spent much time with you. I hate the idea of that."

I meet her gaze and hold it. "I love both of you already," I turn my head to meet Steph's eyes when she turns to look at me. "I spent so many years wanting to feel connected to a family. Its true our father didn't spend much time with me but the time that he did, I cherish. I'm angry with him for this situation but I'm glad the time he wasn't with me was spent with the two of you. A few weeks ago I decided to push myself out of my comfort zone because I craved more than the life I was living. Just days later you two walked into my life. I can't ignore that."

I reach my hands out, resting them palms up on the table, waiting for them each to hold one. I link our fingers together. "We're all connected and these are our first steps. We have every right to be angry just like, when we're ready, we have every right to let that anger go." I borrow Luc's words. "I am not the most emotional woman, it just isn't me to sit here and cry over something I cannot change. I'd rather pick up the pieces given to me and make something from it. It's not going to be this easy all of the time, but I'm not going to turn away from you when you're what I've wanted for as long as I can remember." I give their hands a squeeze. "Please don't feel guilty or be sad for having happy memories, you deserve them and I do not want to take that from you."

I notice both of their eyes are bright with unshed tears. I stand, pulling them up with me. When I unlink our fingers and open my arms, we share our first sisterly group hug. Hopefully, the first of many.

Stephanie lifts up on her toes a little to see over my shoulder and begins to chuckle. "Maddox is standing at the door with his hands on his hips and tapping his toe. I think he wants us to come in." Steph informs us. I look over my shoulder and laugh, as well. That is exactly what he's doing. Any minute now he'll start tapping his forefinger against his wrist.

"We better go in. There's no telling what he'll do if we don't." Quin says with a smile. With one last squeeze we break apart.

When we join everyone else inside to help prepare the food, everything is already laid out in work stations for each dish we're making. I'm not surprised when the guys volunteer to help with cooking dinner; my Gram would say their Mama's raised them right. We send them out to the grill with a pile of steaks and get to work on the sides and salad. Maddox stays inside and starts cleaning the potatoes for dinner; the girls and I gape at him.

Noticing our inactivity, he glances up briefly before continuing his work. "You know you can get on with the girl talk. I won't think it's rude if you want to talk about me while I'm standing right here."

Tara shrugs her shoulders. "I had a dream last night that Gen sucked Maddox's cock."

I start to choke. Stephanie pounds on my back to assist me all the while her shoulders are shaking from suppressing her laughter.

"It's going to take a lot more than that to scare me into leaving. All you've done is confirm for me that you have my cock on your mind." He winks at her. "Are you ladies going to get this show on the road or am I going to do all of the work? I mean I'm cool with you wanting to think about me for a few more minutes but don't take too long because this dinner won't prepare itself."

Hailey walks behind him to go to the fridge.

"Good job." She congratulates him for beating Tara at her own game.

"Give me a chance and you'll soon find out I do a great job." Maddox takes that opportunity and runs with it.

At the stove I'm sautéing mushrooms and onions to go with the steaks. "You are incorrigible." I shake my head. I've been doing that a lot lately.

He finishes cleaning the potatoes and dries his hands. "I'm actually very en-corrigible, at least for all these other ladies. *I will not sleep with you and show you how it is when it's done right, Genevieve!*" He yells the last part at me.

I whip around, holding the spatula I was using to stir the mushrooms and onions up in defense. He's lost his mind. If he takes one step towards me I have the right to defend myself.

He turns towards the doorway of the kitchen. "Lucky, you have to put this one on a leash, man, or learn some better moves already. I can't keep worrying about my virtue around your women because you don't know what you're doing."

His outburst makes sense now; he must have seen Luc leaning in the doorway. He's still crazy, I'm not going to lower my spatula, yet, just in case.

"You are the lucky one this time, Maddox. If she was holding a knife, instead of a spatula, you might be bleeding right now. Stop scaring my woman." Lucas crosses the room to me and gives me a quick kiss. I feel a shadow of apprehension again when I think about his phone call, but I stamp it down.

"Everything okay?" he asks.

"Yeah, everything is fine. I just keep feeling like we're forgetting something for dinner." I make a point to look at what everyone is preparing to play it off. "Salad dressing! We don't have salad dressing." I push away and fling open the fridge door. "Just as I suspected. No salad dressing."

"Calm down, Gen." Stephanie looks up from what she's doing. "It's nothing to freak over. My mom used to make this simple dressing from scratch that I can whip up quickly."

"Thanks." I start rubbing my forehead.

Lucas looks at me, his brows furrowed with concern. "Are you sure you're fine? Is your headache coming back?"

"I'm good, just a minor freak out. We just started dating and since I'm technically cooking for you I want everything to be good. You know, typical girl wanting to impress her guy type of thing." I smile weakly.

Lucas wraps his arms around my waist and stares into my eyes. "You could burn all of the food and set my kitchen on fire and I wouldn't be any less enthralled by you." He presses a kiss to my lips. "I'm going to head outside with the guys. Don't worry about everything. Regardless of how it turns out, I'm going to love it."

I stay, standing there as he passes me to grab beer for himself and the guys. When he passes me on his way back he lean in near my ear. "Your mushrooms and onions are burning," he whispers. My eyes fly to the stove. I never turned the flame off when I turned to defend myself from Maddox's mental instability.

"Darn it." I use the spatula to stir them around. They're beyond recovery. I toss them in the trash and start over again.

"You know, sugar pea, I don't know you well, yet, but even I could see that something upset you when Lucky came in. Tell Daddy Maddox all about it." He wraps his arm around my shoulder.

The girls drop what they're doing and come over, too.

"It was nothing. Really guys. I just thought I heard Luc talking to an ex-girlfriend on the phone earlier. I'm not even sure if he was so I'm not going to make a big deal about it."

"I don't know if he was or wasn't. Whatever the call was about, I do know it was harmless for him. He's different with you. You're good for him. For a few years now, he's been walking around with a black cloud on his shoulders regardless of the success he's had. You made that cloud go away. Now huddle in ladies. Let's hug it out and get shit done. I'm starving." Maddox holds his other arm out for the girls to move into the hug.

The girls and Maddox surround me, squeezing me with their hug. I always know their support is there, but right now, it's nice to feel it, too.

"Alone with the ladies for five minutes and you're already trying to wrap yourself around all of them. One of these days you're going to catch an S.T.D." Aryan comes into the kitchen with the plate of cooked steaks. "Of course your part of the dinner isn't done yet. The princesses are taking their time."

"Shut your trap. We'll be done in five minutes tops. Cover those steaks with foil so the juices can redistribute. By the time that's done, we'll have this finished and the table set." Tara sticks her tongue out at Aryan.

"You know, Aryan," Hailey starts, looking at him thoughtfully. "You said Maddox was trying to wrap himself around all of us and one day he's going to catch an S.T.D. Are you saying that one or more of us have something?" Hailey does it so rarely, but when she does, she really knows how to stir the pot. We all turn to look at him menacingly.

"That is not what I was saying at all, especially when four out of five of you are currently holding knives. I was talking more along the lines of his proclivity to take home strippers with questionable morals."

"Oh come on! That was one time! I didn't even touch her. When she started discussing prices I sobered enough to realize my error in judgment," Maddox whined. We all laugh at him.

"Gross. Now I need a shower just to be sure since you touched me." Hailey bumps shoulders with him jokingly.

"Who touched you?"

We turn to see Micah standing at the back door.

"What is it with everyone skulking around my backyard? I need to install a fence," Lucas grumbles while helping Quin set the table.

Micah strolls in taking off his coat. "I could smell the steaks all the way in my office at the club and decided to swing by for dinner."

"Ditto, but I used the front door like most civilized people would." Kaine comes into the kitchen from the front of the house already divested of his coat.

The guys start looking at their watches and the ones not wearing a watch check the time on the microwave.

"It's five-thirty," Lucas says.

"How observant you are. I'm glad you mastered time telling in second grade like the rest of us." Kaine gets snarky.

"You're not working. You're here and in my house for dinner— *at five-thirty*," Lucas stresses.

"Haven't you been telling me I need to come over, have dinner, and hang out more often? So here I am." Annoyance flashes across Kaine's face. I've seen that look a time or two cross Luc's features.

"Yes, definitely. But it's five-thirty."

For twins, their communication skills with each other suck.

"I think what Lucas is getting at, from what I understand, is that you are somewhat of a workaholic and leaving work this early is unusual for you." I try to clear things up for them.

"Well today, I went in late and left early. People and habits can change sometimes." Kaine shrugs his shoulders nonchalantly and goes into the fridge to grab a beer, tossing one to Micah as well.

"So what's for dinner?" His question snaps us back into motion and we finish putting everything on the table and add the settings for our surprise company.

Dinner went smoothly. The food was good, conversation flowed, and no one threw anything. Sitting at the table surrounded by boisterous conversations, everyone yelling to be heard over the others, reminds me of a traditional Italian family gathering. When we're all done and everyone does their part to clean the mess, I think something I never in a million years would have thought possible. Micah has to go back to the club and I'm going to miss him. A feather could have knocked me off my feet when he came up to give me a hug and kiss on the cheek telling me, "Night, Sis." Aryan started it and now all of Lucas's brothers are calling me "Sis". Only a few weeks have passed and my family is growing in leaps and bounds.

My thoughts drift back to hearing that name. Lissandria. My stomach turns. Life would be cruel to give me so much then snatch it back as quickly as it was all given. Life has been cruel to me before, giving me childish hopes then having them dashed across the rock at the bottom of the proverbial cliff. At fourteen, I became jaded. I can look at the last ten years and realize I was just waiting for the other shoe to drop. Now that I finally want something, I want something just for me. I can feel the shoe right above my head.

I walk out of the room, leaving everyone chatting behind me, not offering an explanation and avoiding the possibility of meeting anyone's gaze. I don't know where I'm going, just that I need to be alone right now. My emotions are churning, becoming raw, the closer they rise to the surface. I need to get myself under control. I wish I could paint. I need that right now. Painting is my therapy even more so than it is my career.

I close the door behind me and flick on the light switch when I reach my destination. I can't go into my own little haven so the next best thing is Luc's music room. This room is his music career, lined with his achievements and mementos. There's so much more in here than I noticed the first night. A little table with picture frames catches my eye. The photos are of a younger Lucas and other musicians. I close my eyes briefly. I can't even escape in here, I don't know why I thought I could. I open my eyes to look at the picture of Luc and Lissandria. It looks like they're at Disney Land judging by the mouse ears they are wearing.

She's so beautiful it makes me sick. I know I'm green with jealousy. What if she's trying to get my man back? The keyword in that sentence has me clawing my way out of the black hole that my jealousy thrust me into. *My* man. If she wants him, guess what Goldilocks, you can't have him. I've never fought for anything in my life because I've never had anything I wanted to fight for. Now I do, and I'll come out swinging if need be.

I sit down in Lucas's chair and lay his guitar across my lap. I've never played a guitar before so I'm not even going to try. Just sitting here plucking one string at a time while watching and listening to the vibration of the string relaxes the tension I've been holding inside of me since earlier today.

I look up when Luc walks in. I knew he'd eventually find me and I'd need to explain why I nearly ran out of the kitchen like there was a fire.

"I let your lie to me slide, earlier. Telling me nothing is wrong isn't going to work a second time. You can talk to me about anything." He pauses as if to gauge my reaction. I don't give him one. He takes a deep breath and takes a few steps into the room. "If I have done something to upset you, I need you to tell me because I can't fix it otherwise, and I want more than anything to fix whatever is going on."

I lower my face into my hands. I don't even know where to start. There's still so much in my head I need to process, and I'm not used to having to discuss things.

Lucas pulls my hands away from my face. Kneeling in front of me, his eyes plead for me to talk to him. Those beautiful silver eyes make it impossible for me to deny their silent request. "It's just a lot all at once. I started to feel overwhelmed and wanted to be alone." My voice is barely a whisper. He moves closer to hear me better.

"Are you saying to me that this is moving too fast between us? I know things went faster than I planned, but I was letting you set the pace, or I thought I was." The uncertainty in his voice kills me. Especially, since he jumped to the wrong conclusion.

"I didn't mean us, Luc. It's just that after my parents died, I never allowed myself to want anything. Ever. I want this, all of this. The friends and family. The dinners and rowdy gatherings. A month ago, I painted. Occasionally, I went out with someone I dated who always spoke at me, never *with me*, and then I went back home and painted some more. That was my existence. Now I have a boyfriend, my sisters, my best friends, your family and friends. It's more than I ever allowed myself to want and now that I have it, I want to keep it so badly. And I'm terrified something will happen and I'll lose it all." I don't know when I started to cry but tears silently roll down my cheek. Cupping my cheeks in his palms, Luc dashes the tears away with his thumbs.

Setting his guitar to the side, he takes my hand in his, rubbing the lines of my palms with his thumb, before leaning down and pressing his lips to the center. Pulling back, he nods at my hand like he's satisfied or has come to a conclusion. He holds the palm of my hand against his heart; I can feel it racing. When he doesn't speak I return my attention to his face.

"The night I first met you changed everything. The first time you smiled at me, my whole world shook. The axis shifted beneath my feet and never went back to normal. I never wanted it to go back because it shifted for the better. After I got you home that night and tucked you into bed, I watched you sleep. Meeting you that night was like looking up at the sky and seeing a comet soar past. Once in a lifetime. You are my reality. Every night since meeting you I fight sleep because you are better than any dream. I love you."

Luc is looking into my eyes. Behind is normally confident gaze I can see a hint of uncertainty as if he is worried I don't feel the same.

I kiss him with everything in me. The tears caused by the overwhelming emotions mingle with our lips. He couldn't have said it any more perfectly. Girls grow up dreaming of moments like this. He's right. Reality is better. I don't want to close my eyes even long enough to blink. I want to hold onto this moment and never let it end.

"I love you, too. I'm your reality, you are my reality, and this moment right now is *our* reality."

He picks me up and I wrap my legs around his waist. He walks us into the bedroom. Rather than taking me to bed he gently lays me down on the blankets in front of the fire place. I look around me. The fire is blazing in the hearth. A bowl of chocolate covered fruits are nearby. Candles flicker around the room casting a soft glow.

"Were you planning on seducing me, Mr. Alexander?"

He grins, looking around the room inspecting his handy work. "That was the idea but you have beaten me to it."

"I haven't done a very good job of it. We're both wearing too much clothing for it to be considered a successful seduction." I flirt shamelessly and begin taking off my own clothing.

Lucas follows suit. The fire in his eyes and look of purpose settling on his features seduces me far more than the setting he created. Undressed, I watch the glow of the flames dance across his skin, highlighting and shadowing his body in erotic play. We come together not just drawn in by our magnetism but also by love.

Each touch is slow and deliberate, savoring the feel and taste of each other. When Luc slides into me, it's electric. Our body, hands, and lips are joined in every way possible. Caught in the current of feeling, my eyes drift closed.

Lucas pulls my focus back to him, all of him. "This is our reality," he whispers across my lips. My eyes open and lock with his. Together we move, thrusting in time with each other, rising to epic heights before peaking and crashing down, shattering into millions of molecules that reform as one.

"That was—." I place my index finger against his lips, silencing his words.

"Indescribable. There is no word in any dictionary of any language that could do it justice."

He nips at my finger against his lips. "That's exactly what I was going to say, minx."

We stay by the fire, wrapped in each other's arms until the embers burn low and our body heat isn't enough to keep us warm. We climb into bed and make love again just as thoroughly as the first time. Afterwards we collapse next to each other, spooning. I idly trace patterns on his arms, not ready to fall asleep yet.

"Don't be afraid of losing all that you have that matters." He links our fingers together again. "This is never going to go away."

He loves me.

Chapter Thirteen

On our way to Gram and Pop's house, we stop at the cemetery to visit our father's grave since Quin had not been to it before. Stephanie, Lucas, and I stay by the car so that she can have some privacy. This morning when Lucas offered to come, I welcomed the support. Lucas coming with us eased some of their tension as well. I was too lost in my own thoughts of the upcoming meeting to have a conversation. He kept the conversation going with my sisters, sticking to light topics to keep their minds off their nerves. After the cemetery, we arrive at our grandparent's house. Lucas gives my hand a squeeze, silently telling me that he's there. Without him, this would have felt much more difficult. I'll always cherish what he did for my sisters and me this morning.

Gram and Pop must have been watching for our arrival because they're both on the porch, waiting for us to exit the car. Gram is nervously wringing her hands; she's probably been doing that since I called to let her know we were coming. Pop is right behind her with his hands on her shoulders to comfort and support her through her nerves.

I turn in my seat to look at my sisters. "They look like grandparents," Stephanie murmurs weakly

"Yeah, they didn't want to scare you away so they left their horns and pitch forks in the closet." I make a poor attempt at a joke. I'm nervous and it's the best attempt at humor I can do. "This is really hard for them, as well. They feel a certain measure of guilt. They aren't sure why their son did what he did and they can't help to wonder if they could have done better raising him."

"That's ridiculous. They're as much the victims as we have been. If they could have done something different with raising him we won't know, but I'm not about to go marching up there pointing fingers and assigning blame at a cute old couple that looks like a skinny Santa and Mrs. Claus." Quincy reaches around the seat and playfully punches my shoulder. "And you stop being nervous. Everything will be fine. Put your big girl panties on and let's do this. If Grandma up there gets feisty, we brought along our very own body guard."

We get out of my car and walk up the steps to the porch where our grandparents are waiting. I give them both a squeezing hug and kiss.

"Gram, Pop. This is Quincy and Stephanie." I gesture to each so that they know who is who.

Gram stares at them both for a few moments. Her eyes tear up until they begin to flow down her cheeks. She fists her hand and brings it to her mouth to try and cover her trembling lips.

"I am so sorry." Over and over Gram shakes her head, apologizing to her granddaughters. The girls move to either side of our grandmother and wrap their arms around her. They rub her back and murmur to her that "it's okay", soothing her apologies. Pop steps up in front of their huddle and places his hand on each of their shoulders

"You are two very beautiful young women, inside and out. Thank you." He is quickly included in their hug

I step back to let them comfort each other. Lucas wraps his arm around my shoulder and pushes my face into his chest, drying my cheeks that I didn't realize were wet. I send a silent prayer of thanks to their mother. Regardless of her faults and reasoning for keeping them away from our family, she raised two very open, caring, and compassionate women.

"Look at these girls, Phyllis. They're Westley's through and through," Grand-Pop booms loudly with pride. "And this one, why she's got the prettiest green eyes I've ever seen. I was looking at those same green eyes, not two hours ago, when you're Gram came and dragged these old bones out of bed." He winks at Stephanie.

"With three beautiful young granddaughters, I'm going to need to buy more shotgun rounds. Speaking of shotguns, Genni-V, get over here and introduce this young man to your Gram and I," Grand-Pop admonishes me.

I've never brought a guy home to meet my grandparents. I was so focused on my sisters that I didn't even think about having to introduce Lucas to my grandparents.

"This is my boyfriend, Lucas Alexander. Luc this is Gram and Grand-Pop or Mr. and Mrs. Westley." I chew my bottom lip nervously.

"Nice to meet you, sir." Lucas shakes Pops hand firmly. I didn't doubt that Lucas would have a strong handshake; my Pop always said he could judge a man by how he shakes and the worst is a man that tries to shake your hand with a limp noodle.

He kisses Gram on the cheek. "I can see where Genevieve gets her charm and radiance."

Gram blushes prettily at Lucas. "Look who's talking about charm. I saw you on the T.V. once, when our football team went to the big game. You and your band played the half-time show. Manners, talent, and good looks. Your mother should be very proud."

"Thank you, I'll tell her the next time we do dinner or I'll save it to use the next time I do something she doesn't approve of."

"Rascal. Help me inside, I'm not as young as I used to be for all of this standing."

"It'll be my pleasure." Lucas offers Gram his arm to assist her inside. I watch her hand sneak up to his bicep and give it a squeeze.

"Do you spend a lot of time in the gym?" Gram flirts with him, causing him to blush.

"Remember, son, I have a shotgun. Watch your hands around my women," Pop growls. Quincy and Stephanie follow behind Gram and Lucas, laughing over our grandparent's antics. I wrap my arm around Pop's waist to follow behind them.

"Don't worry, you're still my favorite man and your arms are just as boast worthy." He puffs out his chest at my praise and leads me inside strutting.

When we get inside, Gram already has Lucas seated at the table with a massive plate piled high with fresh baked cookies and a large glass of milk.

"Sir, I don't know if I can heed your threat. These are the best cookies," Lucas pauses to say between cookies.

"I know it, son. That's why I snatched her up for myself. She caught me with her eyes and kept me with her cookies." Pop winks at Quin and Steph.

I quietly take a seat next to Lucas while he eats his cookies. Gram and Pop bombard the girls with questions about their childhood and growing up. They're leaving no stone unturned, trying to get to know their granddaughters. When Quincy tells them of their mother's passing, our grandparents squeeze their hands in their own and kiss their heads with sympathy.

They are fascinated with Quin's chosen profession and Gram is enthusiastic hearing about Steph's aspirations as a dancer; she did ballet when she was younger so she had that new connection with Stephanie, as well. Each girl gets the third degree, much to my amusement. They don't mind though; they're asking questions as well, finding out family stories and history.

I nudge Luc with my knee and stand, gesturing for him to follow me. Gram catches my eye before we leave the room. She smiles and nods her approval. I lace my fingers with his and lead Lucas towards the back of the house. Despite not living here any longer, this is still my favorite place to be. The back parlor still holds all of the art supplies even though Grand-Pop has a difficult time holding the brushes with his arthritis. Everything is in the same place I remember.

Grabbing a sketch pad and pencils, I sit on one of the chairs next to the little table I know Pop takes his morning coffee at since this is his favorite room as well. Lucas takes a seat opposite of me before leaning down and removing my shoes and socks. Placing my feet in his lap, he massages my arches. I start to sketch. Sketching isn't my forte but I'm decent at it.

"This is the room I made the painting hanging in your bedroom," I say without looking up from the sketch pad.

"I love you," he plainly says.

I look at him and smile. "I love you, too. Thank you for coming with us. It actually went a lot easier than I imagined."

"Your grandparents are wonderful people. First for taking you in and continuing to raise you into the amazing woman you are today. Also for opening their hearts and arms to your sisters when they were just as nervous as you three were. Let's not forget Grams cookies, they're incredible. If you tell me you can bake those cookies, I'll get down on one knee right here."

I grin at him. "Do you have my ring, rock star?"

"Not yet." He starts tickling my feet, causing me to squeal and kick my legs. The pencil jumps across the page, destroying my sketch of Lucas. I toss the pad on the table, pull my feet away from him, and tuck them underneath me.

Lucas spins the paper to face him so he can look at the sketch of himself. "It's a good thing you're a talented painter. Your sketches would have made you a starving artist."

I throw myself at him. Knocking us and the chair to the floor. Straddling him, I start tickling his ribs for pay back. It's not long before he flips our position and lays on me to keep my wiggling fingers from his sides. He kisses me to halt my attempts to continue my attack. He brushes the hair away from my face so that he can look into my eyes.

"Tell me about little Genevieve. I got to hear about your sisters growing up. Tell me about you growing up. I bet little Gen was an incredibly charming little girl."

"Sad." I swallow around the lump in my throat.

Lucas pulls back in confusion to examine my whole face, I guess.

I elaborate. "I was a very sad kid. My parents weren't like yours. My father was rarely home and my mother was a very cold and bitter woman for a long time. She was never happy with me as her daughter. She always judged me and found me lacking. I wasn't the blonde haired golden child they wanted."

"Sometimes when people have something lacking within themselves, they target someone they perceive as weaker to tear down. Especially, when someone is young like you were and cannot defend themselves." His voice sharpens with anger that I know is not directed at me.

"I have nightmares sometimes that I'm going to be just like her. It scares me. I couldn't live with myself if I did that to a child of mine." I tell him one of my deepest fears. I've never told anyone about the nightmares I have about my mother sometimes and how they morph into me looking down at my faceless children with disgust.

"People from all walks of life handle abuse in two different ways. Some people take the bad, learn it, and follow in its footsteps. Other people learn from it and follow their own path. You're the second and don't let yourself doubt that." His tone is stern.

"Would you still say that if I told you I have this weird jealousy of blondes?" I bite my lip nervously.

"I'd still say that and tell you that we all have our own hang ups. It's how you handle them that counts. You aren't running around with scissors cutting off the hair of every blonde you see. So you're good. Don't ever doubt that." He leaves no room for argument.

So I kiss him instead. We kiss for a few moments before he pulls his lips back. "Crap, we're in your grandparent's house and I'm ready to jump you like a horny teenager." He doesn't look happy about that.

I laugh at him. "You said 'crap.' I've never heard you watch your language."

"We're in your grandmother's house. If I curse, I can already imagine your Gram burning up the carpet to get back here to drag me away by my ear and wash my mouth out." He smiles like he's imagining her doing that. "Besides, you heard her, my Mama did a good job raising me. I can't have her change her mind because I couldn't respect her house. Which means I need to get off from on top of their granddaughter while in their home." Lucas stands up and pulls me to my feet, too.

A little less than an hour here and my former rock star bad boy is watching his language and striving for sainthood by not giving in to temptation. If I was selfish, I would have left to go home already so that we could make love. I smile to myself; that plan still has some merit.

"You are right. We should get back to the others. I'm sure they're at least up to questions about high school by now." I stop and turn to Lucas. "Tell me something no one else knows. Like something you've never told anyone." It's only right that he tell me something after I revealed my mommy issues.

"Well I have this really weird thing about sodas. I only drink light colored sodas in diet and dark colors in regular. It's the weirdest thing, and I'm not sure why, either." He looks like he's really giving it thought to figure out why.

"Luc, I meant something a little more personal, not something a waitress at a restaurant you frequently visit could figure out."

He looks down at the floor deep in thought. I get the sense that he knows what he wants to tell me but is fighting saying the words.

"The day my father died, I called him." He pauses to swallow. "He couldn't even give me the time of day. He was in his office at the hotel. I remember being aggravated because he had me on speaker phone, like he couldn't bother to stop working for a minute to talk to his son he's been estranged from. I was actually scared to tell him my career ended and I was coming home. When I didn't get right to the point of the phone call he told me 'I don't have all day. I have an important meeting starting in five minutes, so you have thirty seconds to stop wasting my time.' Here I was acting like a child scared to tell his dad he was coming home and he couldn't give me the time of day. It's like after I left, he completely wrote me off. He was great while growing up, but some switch flipped for him; instead of having twins, he had only one prodigal son. I got angry and hung up on him. Ever since I found out he died that day, I always wondered what could have changed if I didn't hang up. If I stuck it out and tried to mend things. Or worse, what if my calling caused his heart attack."

The crack startles Lucas and me. I didn't think, I just did it. Hindsight clearly shows it was an overreaction.

"You slapped me."

"I know," I say weakly

"Why did you slap me?" His eyebrows pull together as he looks down at me still rubbing his cheek.

"I've seen it done in movies. The dramatic moment when the male lead says something heartbreakingly ridiculous. I was in the moment." I look at the red mark I left on his cheek. "I think it's safe to say it was a little too much. I should probably stop watching so many chick flicks."

"If that's what you get from watching chick flicks please avoid action movies. I don't want to worry about you pulling a gun on me or blowing up my house when you have a moment."

I bite my lip and redden with embarrassment.

"As long as you don't go around carrying blame for your father's heart attack on your shoulders any longer, we shouldn't have anything to worry about. Seriously, Luc, it was most likely something as stupid as him not eating the right heart healthy cereal for breakfast before going to work. You calling was a coincidence. No one blames you so you have to stop blaming yourself."

"Thanks for putting me in my place, minx. Next time do it without the hitting." He chuckles against my lips when he leans down to kiss me.

"Let's hurry back to the kitchen before Grand-Pop decides to check on us with his shot gun he's been waiting years to use."

Lucas, trying to be funny, shoves me to the door and pops his head out to see if the coast is clear. I laugh at his silly behavior and pull him through the doorway. We hold hands again and walk back through the halls bumping shoulders along the way.

When we arrive at the kitchen, the only person still at the table is Grand-Pop. "Hey. Where did everyone else go?" I ask.

"They went around back to check out your grandmother's greenhouse. Why don't you head back there and leave your young man here to talk to your old grandfather?"

I look over my shoulder to Lucas; he smiles to reassure me that it is fine and nudges me forward to get me moving.

"Okay. Don't scare him away. He's a good one." I lean down and give my pop a kiss on the cheek.

"Wouldn't dream of it, sweetheart. Now go on, he's in good hands. He should be thanking me for saving him from your grandmother's botany talk."

I wish he would have saved me, too. I understand men need to do "the talk". It's an integral part of bonding. Maybe Gram will almost be done telling the girls about all of her flowers. Hopefully, neither of them are a kiss ass and asks too many questions, otherwise, this will be painful. I walk into the greenhouse just in time to hear Quin ask a question. Groaning, I drag my feet to reach where they are standing.

It is two more hours before we finally leave our grandparent's house. We decided to stay to have lunch with them. We weren't allowed to leave until everyone exchanged contact information and promised to visit again.

The car ride back home was nice. Steph and Quin took turns telling me about what happened after Luc and I left. Our grandparents did not disappoint with their entertaining questions and stories. I'm not as subdued on the way home as I was for the ride there, but I'm still lost in thought about what Lucas told me happened with his father. I need to find a way to help him remove the mantle of guilt from his shoulders. I want to talk to his mother, but Vivian would probably mother him to death over it. I could maybe talk to one of his brothers. Yeah, that's what I'll do. I'll talk to Kaine. He worked closely with his father and he's Lucas's twin. He would be my best bet.

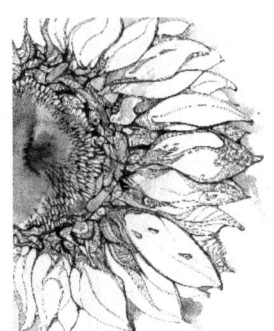

Chapter Fourteen

When we got back from our visit with Gram and Grand-Pop, Lucas excused himself to take a phone call in his office. In the meantime, I thought a bubble bath in his colossal tub would be divine. Ten minutes into my bath, I can hear Lucas moving around in the bedroom. That was a quick business call. I wonder if Lucas will join me in the tub.

Speak of the devil. Luc comes into the bathroom while I'm busy musing ways to get him into the bath with me. He's wearing a suit. "Hey?" I stare at him.

"I have to go to L.A. right away, minx. The artist I was telling you about, that is spiraling out of control, has taken a nose dive and I need to go and see what can be done," he tells me as he approaches the tub.

I feel disappointed but try to hide it. "Okay, I'll let the girls know. We should be able to find a hotel to stay at until we can go home." I try to focus on what needs to be done now that Lucas is going to be leaving, and from the looks of him in the suit, that will be soon.

"Absolutely not. I'm not kicking you and the girls out. You stay as long as you need to and don't leave a second sooner. If I didn't have to go, trust me, I'd be naked with you, exploring what is under all of those bubbles. Just seeing you like that, I might not make it through airport security. If they pat me down, they are going to think I'm carrying a concealed weapon." He wags his eyebrows at me.

I groan and lay my head back against the rim of the tub. "I can't believe you just made a penis joke about the size of your water pistol." He takes a step towards the tub like he's ready to hold my head under the water. "Just kidding! I meant bazooka!" I laugh out loud at his broad smile after being compared to the much larger weapon.

"I'd show you my bazooka if I didn't have to leave in five minutes." He kneels next to me to place a sweet kiss against my lips. "Miss me while I'm gone. I'll call as often as possible. I'm not sure how busy I'm going to be, but judging by the manager's report, I'll have my work cut out for me."

"I will miss you. I hope you have a nice flight and that things aren't as bad as they seem right now." I kiss him one last time.

I watch him, as he walks out of the bathroom to get his luggage and leave. This was unexpected but I'll deal with it. Lucas has been a great host, completely making sure we've all felt at home. I guess the girls and I can do a girl's night part two. After drying off, I go in search of the girls to see if everyone is available.

Tara is sitting at the kitchen table with her laptop. I'm sure she's going through photos from her latest assignments, that's the only thing she's ever on a computer for. "What it be, chickadee?" Tara grins at me from over the top of her screen.

"Really, Tara? You would never know you went to a private school and learned how to use proper English. Your grandparents should consider asking for a refund," I tease her.

"Remember the first time we met and you told me about alibis?" She smiles at me.

"Of course. I was suckered into all of you hair brained plans ever since." I meet her smile with one of my own.

"I remember thinking that day that you looked like someone who needed a friend. I was lucky. I've always had Hailey from day one and then you became our third musketeer. You two always made me feel needed, especially when my mother started using the heavier stuff and wouldn't come home for weeks. Now you have two sisters and Hailey has been telling me to back off. Lately, I've been feeling adrift. I haven't wanted to take assignments because if I leave, when I come back you won't need me any longer." Tara's eyes are sad. She always has her tough as nails exterior on display, but behind that is the hiding little girl whose mother was neglectful and abusive in a manner that outdid my own.

"I slapped Lucas earlier for saying something absurd, don't think I won't do it to you, too. Seriously, Tara? I can't believe you think that. Let me set you straight. We do not need you. We love you, we want you, but we do not need you. I could have an orphanage of siblings waiting to find me but that doesn't change what you have always and will always mean to me and Hailey. We're the group with mommy and daddy issues. We've made our own family regardless of being blood relatives or not. You and Hailey accepting my sisters into the group without question meant the world to me. I could stop thanking you for loving me enough to do that." I go around the table and hug her.

She squeezes me back. "Don't give me too much credit. They aren't hard to like. I plan on corrupting them as soon as possible. Stephanie scares me though; I have a suspicion she could show me a thing or two."

"Yeah? You got that impression, too? I want to lock her away. She's my brand new baby sister. She's like the doll I don't want to take out of the pretty box because I'm scared I'll get it dirty."

"I know what you mean. Did you see the fucking legs on that broad? When she turns twenty-one, I pity every woman who goes out with her man when she's out because their boys will be too busy staring at our baby girl. She's a stunner." She worries her bottom lip thinking about Stephanie, which is funny because even though Tara always protective of Hailey and I, she never actually worried about us like she clearly does with Steph.

I lean my hip against the table. "Lucas had to go to L.A., so I was thinking we could do girl's night part two. Are you in?"

Tara jumps up and does a little booty dance. "Hellz to the yeah, biznitch."

I shake my head at her behavior. "You round up the rest of the girls and meet me downstairs. We'll contaminate the man cave with a girl's night tonight."

We split off to get started. I run down to the basement to check out our options for tonight. Some things catch my eye and I formulate a plan to add a twist to our usual girl's night. I finish getting everything set up right before the girls come down the stairs. I step back and check my layout.

The girls come down and see what I have planned and start to whoop with excitement.

"This is fan-fucking-tastic!" Tara hollers in excitement.

"Well take a seat and let's get this going." I notice Hailey giving me a smirking look. "What?"

"You have this naughty aura lately. You wear it well. Lucas has been very good for you. I think the guys would have a cow if they saw what we're about to do." We fist bump as she goes past. We're girls playing at guy's night; fist bumping equals totally appropriate.

"I tried ordering pizza, but I'm not sure what happened. I pressed the speed dial labeled "pizza" and when the guy answered I asked for delivery, he said okay and hung up. I don't know if he's not bringing anything or if he recognized Luc's number and is bringing his usual order. If it is okay with everyone else, I'd like to wait a bit to see if he shows up and if not, we'll look up a pizza place." Everyone agrees and we settle in.

Twenty minutes later I'm staring at the hand of cards Quincy dealt me. I have a pair of jacks. I've only played poker one other time so I'm not that skilled, but I'm sure a pair of jacks isn't something to fold over. I take a big puff on my Cuban cigar and chase it with Lucas's best whiskey, just how Tara showed us to do when I poured the drinks from the snifter and passed out the cigars.

"I'm going to put this in my next book. This is great. Girl's night but in guy style. Normally I'd say not for me, but I can see why guys choose to relax like this." Hailey folds her hand and leans back in her seat, puffing on her cigar.

"Ding dong, delivery." We turn towards the stairs. "Well I can't say that this is what I was expecting when I got the call for pizza." Maddox swaggers towards us.

"How exactly did you get our pizza order?" I ask

"I'm the number on speed dial. My sister and brother in law own a local pizza joint so I always bring the pies when I come over." He pulls a chair over and straddles it. "So ladies, looks like you're dipping your toes in to the forbidden. I'm insulted you didn't intentionally call me. I thought you loved Daddy Maddox." He pouts his lip.

We just stare at him.

"You are all ruthless. Cut a guy a break. My girlfriend just broke up with me, my friends are all busy, and even my family throws me out when I try to hang with them."

"Aw, really? You had a girlfriend?" Stephanie looks at him sadly.

"Well, not exactly a girlfriend. I slept with her here and there when things were slow, but for me, that's the closest I've had to an actually girlfriend since high school. She seriously told me I had commitment issues. Can you believe that load?"

We throw pretzels at him.

"This is girl's night. You dish out the real emotional crap and let us offer mind blowing advice you would normally need to pay big bucks to get, or you get out because you have the wrong equipment for girls' night." Tara crosses her arms over her chest and stares him down.

"Alright." He leans back, knitting his hands together and placing them behind his head for support. "I come from an upper middle class family. My being a drummer was supported as a hobby but never a career choice. I didn't have it as bad as Lucas, but my parent's always let me see their disapproval with my choices. My mom had a best friend who had a daughter the same age as me. We grew up typical, always knew we'd be together and get married when we became adults and would have the two point five kids and a dog together. We were devoted to each other. We had the plan forever. When the band got the big contract and opportunity, I went running to her first to give her the news. We got our signing bonus a few days before we were supposed to leave. I bought her this diamond ring. I knew she was it for me and I wanted to have my rock on her before I had to leave. I went to her house to surprise her and there was my dear cousin, Stanley, humping my girl, Mindy, like a dog in heat. Long story short, she agreed with my parents about my hobby being a poor choice to put all of my eggs in that basket and felt that she was better off with Stan the man, who planned on becoming an accountant. Now they have the two point five kids and the dog I wanted for my family." He leans forward in his seat, folding his arms and resting them on the table to look closely at each of us. "I held up my end of the deal so now it's your turn to give me some sterling advice."

Tara jumps from her seat and goes to Maddox, grabbing his face. She lays a big smacking kiss right on him. "Screw that whore ten ways to Sunday." She goes back to her seat.

"Anyone else want to offer sympathy?" Maddox flirts.

The rest of us take turns hugging him and kissing him on the cheek.

"Now that I've bared my tattered soul to you, ya think I can get a drink and maybe dealt into the game? When you get to the pillow fight portion of the evening I'll sit that one out if you don't mind. I would prefer to just observe." He winks at us and Quincy deals him in.

"I'd like to add for the record that no one here is ever going to call you Daddy Maddox," I toss at him.

"It's all good, I'll just learn to live with King Maddox," he quips. We snort at him and get on with the game.

It's a good thing we weren't playing with real money. Maddox wiped the floor with us. He's been an interesting addition to our group. He's actually very intelligent even though he tries to hide it behind his laid back, man-whore image.

Getting back on track with the regular girl's night tradition, we gather round and put on the gossip channel. Maddox groans his complaints. He's clearly outnumbered, though.

We yell at the television over the latest celebrity screw-ups and "ah" over the birth announcements.

A picture of Lucas and I pops up on the screen. It was taken the morning we had breakfast with his mother and brothers. They're cropped out of the picture and you can just see Lucas with his arm across the back off the bench behind me. I should have been more prepared to see something about me and Lucas, but I thought it wouldn't be big enough news to still be appearing on the gossip channel. The text 'East Coast' appears across the top of the photo and the screen splits in two when a picture labeled 'West Coast' shows up next to it. The picture shows Lucas eating with Lissandria in Los Angeles. I don't need the show host to tell me that this was only taken a couple hours ago after Lucas landed in L.A. He's still wearing the same suit he left here in. The host speculates that Lucas has maintained a relationship with girlfriend, Lissandria, while establishing a new relationship with an unknown woman at home.

No one is speaking. The bubble around our good time has burst. I take a deep breath and put on a brave front. "You can't believe everything you see on these shows. I'm sure there's a logical business explanation for their meeting and Lucas will tell me about it when he gets home." I look around the couch at each of them. "No one kicked a puppy, so stop looking so glum. Ready to start the movie?"

"Good girl, don't let the paparazzi create drama in the middle of your happiness. It's their job to make up stories to try and stir up some real drama." Maddox gives me a high five as I pass him to turn down the lights for the movie.

I try to focus on the movie but all of my concentration is being used to stop myself from texting Lucas to check on him. Or call him and question him. I know Maddox is right. I need to breathe through this and believe in Lucas. It's easier said than done, but I'm going to trust him.

After the movie ends, we clean up everything and repeat the number one girl code rule. What happens here, stays here. What is said here is never repeated to other ears. Maddox is amused by our rules but repeats the promise to the group.

"Hailey, do you think tomorrow you'll be able to call the water company and find out what's going on with the pipe? I'm really behind on my deadlines for some commissions." I've never been good at talking to people about things. Hailey has a way of finding out what she wants and getting her way.

"Sure. I'll do it first thing in the morning."

When I get to Lucas's room I'm exhausted. I take my clothes off before collapsing into bed. My phone vibrates on the nightstand. Lucas's name flashes on the screen. I can't tonight. I do plan on having faith in our relationship, but I need to decompress from the shock of seeing that tonight. I flop on to my back. I'll let him think I'm already sleeping. My phone vibrates again on the nightstand. This time with a text message.

I love you. L.

I smile sadly at the screen and give it a kiss. We'll figure this out. I'll just let him tell me what's going on when he comes back.

The next morning Hailey, Tara, and I see my sisters off. Unfortunately they have to go back to their lives. Quin is needed in the shop she works at and Stephanie has a new dance program starting. She is fortunate to find this to keep her in shape before she goes to school this fall. I understand, but I am still sad over seeing them drive away.

"I called the water company. We can go back today. They fixed the pipe yesterday. I thought you called them yesterday, Tara?" Hailey casts a look at Tara.

She makes a face. "Oops."

"Well that was fast. Let's get our stuff and go. I really need to get some work done. You two are lucky that a lot of your work can be done on laptops and anywhere." I run inside.

I'm aching to get to work again. I need to refocus.

On the drive home, Hailey's mom calls and demands she make an appearance home so that she can see that she's eating enough and nag her to death about getting married and having babies, I'm sure. Hail's mom is fabulous and extremely nosey. After we get home and put our bags in our rooms, I meet Tara and Hailey in the foyer. They're both going to see Hailey's mom. I opt out and tell them to give her a hug, kiss, and my love.

In my studio, the light is flashing on my answering machine. My agent doesn't have my cell phone number. Call it eccentric but I like not having to worry about her hounding me wherever I am. I skip checking the message and decide to get my supplies setup. I'd rather have something new to tell her about than tell her I've been slacking off. I shoot Lucas a quick text. My first since his call and text last night.

We're home now. The pipe was fixed yesterday. Your house is locked up. I'm going to be painting. I'll see you when you get home. Gen.

I press send and stare at the text. The fact that I didn't acknowledge his I love you or send one of my own screams at me. I'm sure it's not going to slip his notice either. I can't do it. I cave and send him a second text message.

I love you.

Does that make me strong or weak? Smart or stupid? Right or wrong? Last night hurt me, but is it okay to hurt Lucas before I know anything for certain? Pushing him away while he's with her if it is truly work related doesn't seem wise; the thought hurts more than seeing them together in that photo yesterday.

A vision pops into my head of my emotions that I need to put to canvas. The image I have in mind has shades of two colors meeting at points and blending into an even more beautiful shade. In other parts the colors are completely divided; a line is clearly drawn between them and they will never meet. I pick up my paintbrush and start to layer and blend the colors to create what I will call *The Struggle*.

Chapter Fifteen

The door being wrenched open alarms me. I look up from my work to see a very pissed off Lucas charging towards me. Half way to me he changes course and goes to my supply table. Picking up my cell phone, he checks it, then he moves towards me again.

"It's dead again." He shoves the phone at me. "I've been calling and texting you for two days without a single word back!"

I quickly try to think of something to say but every excuse seems paltry and better left unvoiced.

"Do you have any idea how worried I've been? I left what I needed to do for work early again for you," he bites out.

"I didn't tell you to leave anything the first time or this time." I tell him with more heat in my voice than intended.

"No? What was I supposed to do? You are the woman I love, yet the closer we're getting the more I can feel you pulling away. You told me that you love me, too. Do you honestly mean that if you can go two days without me, no problem?" Lucas softly asks me as his anger is replaced with dejection.

I move away from my stool, leaving him standing there. At the back wall I start to remove covering after covering. Each time I've gone days without him, I paint to the point of desperation. My sole focus is trying to make my emotions and thoughts a physical entity. It's like a beast is on my back demanding everything I have and then pushing for more. Away from him I border on obsession, trying to objectify and analyze something more complex than fathomable.

"I haven't been without you for a second. You are in my head constantly. Everything I've done since coming home has been about you!" I make a sweeping gesture with my arm.

There, it is all laid out in front of us. The highs and the lows of my emotional roller coaster.

Lucas steps beside me, watching my face. "Tell me what you see when you look at what you've created," he murmurs, keeping his gaze locked on my features.

I swallow, unsure what he's asking of me.

"Step back from where you are emotionally right now and tell me what you see. Tell me what your paintings means for us."

I close my eyes to clear my head. When I open them and stare at the paintings again, my eyes well up with tears. I can't do what he asks and detach my emotions; what I'm staring at is my emotions.

I turn to face him full on.

"I love you. Yes, there is fear and jealousy, but the love is worth putting myself out there for."

On some level I didn't realize that I was feeling like a failure. How many days ago was I saying I was going to fight for my man? For us? When the first punch was thrown I ducked and ran.

"Jealousy?" Lucas sounds confused.

It's time I put the cards on the table so he can see where I'm coming from. Deep down I know I can trust him, but the young girl in me is still feeling insecure.

"I guess you didn't watch much TV while in L.A. I saw the picture of you having dinner with Lissandria," I plainly state for him.

"That was a work meeting. I told you I have an artist in crisis. Her manager and other executives from my company were there as well." He grabs my hands in his. "I can't tell the paparazzi what they can and cannot report. I know that experiencing the havoc they can wreak is new for you. I also know that it's a lot to ask for you to trust me when you are seeing that and with the fear you are experiencing." His hands slide up my arms to my shoulders. "I'm a bastard for wanting you to put yourself through this but I can't let you go. I would regret it for the rest of my life and I don't want to live with anymore regrets." He cups my chin between his palms.

I close my eyes to block him out for a moment. I believe that it was a work meeting. I knew that I would. I whisper with my eyes still closed, "Promise not to hurt me."

"I promise. From that first night, I have only ever wanted to cherish you." His thumbs caress my cheek bones. I sway into him. He grabs my arms again to steady me. "Are you okay?"

I open my eyes again and my vision wavers. "I forgot to eat. I'm feeling a little woozy." My words come out garbled.

Lucas leans down and sweeps me off of my feet. "You little idiot. I need to hire a keeper for you. Someone to follow you around with a fully charged cellphone and make sure that you eat." He looks so serious. I attempt a joke.

"That's not the kind of talk for carrying your beloved across the threshold." My tease only earns me a thunderous look.

"I'm not carrying you across any threshold. You are going to sit right here on this couch until I get back." He gently sets me downs even though his tones says he wishes he was dropping me *none* too gently onto the couch. "After you have something in your stomach and are feeling better, I'll give you a spanking you'll always remember, so you never forget to take care of yourself again."

He leaves me sitting there, staring after him.

"I'll call my mother and tell her we aren't going to be coming to dinner tonight," he says coming back into my studio, carrying a plate with a sandwich on it.

"What? We were supposed to have dinner with your mother tonight?" I say alarmed. "I thought you weren't supposed to be home yet how do we have dinner plans for tonight?"

He shoves the plate with the sandwich at me. "If you answered your phone some time you would know. Lilah is home from school for spring break this week. Mom wants all of us at the house tonight for dinner. When she told me about it the first time I let her know we couldn't make it because I was working. When I landed today she called me to see if I was okay with her inviting you to dinner tonight even though I couldn't make it. Since I was back in the area, I told her to tell the cook to plan for us, as well. If you would have had your phone charged, you would know this." He gives me a narrow eyed look.

I turn my gaze to the sandwich on the plate. "What is this?" I ask dubiously.

"Peanut butter, banana, and honey. It's my go to. Now stop looking at it like it is about to jump at you and take a bite already. You aren't going to feel better until you do." He sits on the couch next to me and leans back, resting his hands behind his head.

I admire the flex of his muscled arms before taking my first bite. My mouth begins to water and it's not at the thought of eating the sandwich. I haven't seen him work out once, yet his arms make me want to rub myself against him.

Lucas takes the uneaten sandwich out of my hand and puts it up to my lips. "Bite."

I take a bite, but the taste is lost to me as my mind is consumed with thoughts of rubbing against him, and even better, him rubbing against me.

"Bite again. Hurry up and finish this sandwich. If you don't stop looking at me like that, I'm going to rip your clothes off and throw you down before ravaging your insanely sexy body, but I refuse to do that until you've eaten first," Lucas growls at me.

I take bigger bites to try and finish the sandwich quickly, which is difficult due to its sticky quality. I finish the sandwich in record time with my lady parts hoping Lucas will make good on his words.

I swallow the last bite and meet his eyes.

We fly at each other with rabid hands and lips. Tearing clothes and nipping skin. Our clothes are tossed every which way. When we are finally naked, Lucas shoves me to my back. My mind squeals with glee. This is exactly what I want, him deep inside of me. I cup my own breast and pinch my nipples. I close my eyes in anticipation of Lucas plundering my body with his own.

"Open your eyes, Genevieve. I want you to see me take you." His voice sounds husky to my ears and much further down my body.

I look at him in confusion only to see him kneeling between my legs, watching me. Once I am looking, he lowers his mouth to allow his tongue to sweep across my clitoris with sure strokes. It's not what I wanted, but I'd be certifiably crazy to complain. I moan aloud as his tongue brings me higher and higher. He lacks zero confidence in his abilities to drive me out of my mind. He adds a finger to the action, pushing me to the brink then driving me over, giving me a mind-altering orgasm.

"That's one," he murmurs against my vagina, still gently stroking me and sending aftershock tremors through my body.

I place my heels against his shoulders and push him back. I'm all about give and take. When he falls back, I crawl over to him.

"My turn," I purr at him, causing his dick to jump for my attention. I take him in both hands, enjoying the feel of his hot length against my palms and knowing that soon enough, I'll have him exactly where he should have been ten minutes ago. I stroke him a few times while slowly lowering my mouth to him. I watch his stomach muscles clench in anticipation. My mouth curves with an unholy grin before finishing my descent and taking as much of him as I can manage. I use everything in my arsenal, tongue, and hands to be blessed by his ragged groans of appreciation. I move my head and hands, getting into a steady rhythm. I can feel him getting harder in my mouth and move my hand down to cup him, feeling his balls tightening as well. I pull back and bite my lip to contain my grin. I love that, with very little effort, I can drive him to this state.

I crawl on top of him, straddling his hips. I rub against his hardness a few times before rising above his tip poised in position to take all of him inside of me. He grabs my hips to steady me. Holding onto his biceps for support, I shift my hips and his shaft slides home. I arch my back in pleasure, placing my chest level with Luc's mouth. He greedily takes my nipple between his teeth before sucking. I whimper with pleasure. Still gripping my hips, he begins to show me how to move atop him. I learn quickly and rock with enthusiasm, taking back the control I wanted from this position.

He slowly starts to rub my hips and thighs, caressing me before moving his hands backside. *Slap!* I gasp in shock. My butt cheek stings from his hand.

"I told you that you earned yourself a spanking." He squeezes my cheek again before pulling his hand back. *Slap!*

"Oh my god!" my gasp turns into a moan as he moves inside me again from beneath me. He rubs where he smacked me, soothingly easing the delicious burn he caused.

Rub. Squeeze. *Slap!* And repeat Rub. Squeeze. *Slap!* All while continuing his upward thrust. I am unbelievably turned on by this. As he continues to repeat the process I reach down and rub my throbbing clitoris between my two fingers, rolling it back and forth. My breaths are increasingly becoming more ragged by the second and my other hand clenches Lucas's shoulder to support me from falling forward. I watch the pleasure crossing Luc's feature: his pupils are dilated, his nostrils flare with his heavy breathing, and his cheeks are flushed with color. The pleasure builds at my core before bursting free and rippling over my body. I squeeze Lucas hard, screaming my pleasure. I drop my head to his shoulder, still rocking with him. His fingers tighten on my hips when he peaks, groaning into my neck and flooding me with his pleasure.

Still breathing heavily, I pull back from his shoulder enough to kiss him. He grabs my face and prolongs the kiss, taking control once again and making me dizzy with his very skilled lips.

"This is my favorite," Lucas says so softly I almost believe I imagined the words.

"Hmm? What's your favorite?" I question.

"Our scents mixed together. Sometimes when I'm working, in the middle of a conference call or meeting, I close my eyes and think of our scent." He presses kisses to my neck, inhaling deeply.

I smile to myself. When he's like this, I wonder what the world would think if they could see him. Badass rock star and music mogul that is a shark in the boardroom being gentle, patient, and loving with me. He melts me every time he's near.

"You actually spanked me." I blush at the memory.

He laughs deep in his throat. "Yes I did, and you liked it. A lot." I don't need to look at him to see that he is smiling. I can hear it in his voice.

"Tell me about being with the band and touring. You never talk about that."

He starts rubbing his hands up and down my back in a soothing motion. I think he's trying to soothe himself more than me. "It had its ups and downs. The beginning was like a brotherhood on the bus. Between shows the creative juices would flow to create our next album. We'd jam out in the aisle, letting the notes, beats, rhythm, and words swirl around us. We were all hungry to make it and make our marks in rock and roll history. We did it. Everything we wanted and more. We were living the dream."

"Where do you think it all went wrong?" I hate to ask and ruin the mood.

"What we didn't know was that age, naivety, and inexperience were against us. Drugs and alcohol were thrown at us left and right. We dabbled here and there, but we were still hungry so our focus was the music. Once we established ourselves, one party to celebrate turned into years of endless partying."

He hugs me closer. "I wasn't squeaky clean. I did my share of shit, but nothing compared to a couple of the other guys. Maddox's poison of choice was women of all variety and quantity. He kept his nose clean from the coke and never drank to excess. He has his reasons for that and he's always had my respect, but man could he leave a trail of angry women behind. Our bass player, Kenny, and rhythm guitarist, Pat, got sucked in quick to the darker side of the rock scene."

"Pat was added to the group when we reached L.A. by the record label. He knew how to play and was nice enough that he easily fit in with us. Pat had the makings of an alcoholic right from the start. He started drinking at breakfast every day. Add the coke and ecstasy and whatever else you could imagine to that mix and he became a full blown crack addict with an alcohol addiction. Towards the end of our last tour he wasn't even able to take the stage for some of the shows. The label we were signed to were raging at us daily."

"Kenny, I don't even know what to say about him. He was an original bandmate. He was the first guy to let me touch a guitar when I was fourteen. Without him, I wouldn't be who I am today. At the same time he's also one of my biggest regrets. I don't know at what point, but somewhere along the tour dates he contracted HIV. I couldn't tell you how he got it. He loved women and he loved heroine."

"He found out he had it and kept it from the rest of us while continuing to have unsafe sex and sharing his needles with groupies. He left women knocked up all over the country and we aren't even sure if he did it internationally. Luckily none of the children were born with HIV. That was pure luck, not by any help from the bastard. I found out that in the US, all women get tested when they're pregnant for the disease so that the children can be treated. Not every country has those regulations. I don't know what I'd do with that on my conscience.

"I feel like I should have seen it. The signs had to have been there. Here we are touring the world and living in the haze of our lifestyle, and meanwhile we've created a monster and let him out to play. The fucker died." He pulls back and looks me straight in the eyes. "He died and I'm glad. He put hundreds of people in danger and risked his children. I mourn who I knew growing up, but with the monster he became, I was relieved when I heard of his death."

I think about what he's saying. I'm not sure if I can hold that against him. I'm not sure I wouldn't feel the same way if Tara or Hailey did something so contemptible. It's sad that these boys discovered their dreams sparkled like diamonds while clean, but once dirtied, they showed that they were really made of glass. "Started off rock stars and became rock victims."

"Yeah, you could say that. Pat lives in Alaska now, and he's sober. He has a wife and four kids." He smiles. "I get the family Christmas card every year. It's cute."

"Four kids. Wow." My amazement seeps into my voice. "That's a lot."

"I guess. My mother had five. I guess I never thought of four being a lot. How many kids do you want to have?"

I stare at him.

"Don't get all crazy eyed, Gen. It's just a question, not a proposal for me to impregnate you," he chuckles.

Relaxing again, I start, "I honestly don't know. I was an only child so at the very least, one. After that, I would have to see; it's a really big decision. I don't know if I could bear to mess up one child let alone multiple."

He puts his hand over my mouth. "Don't start worrying about it now. You'll be an amazing mother. You will just have to wait and see when it happens." I nod my head with his hand still over my mouth.

"I have to call Mom and tell her we aren't making it to dinner tonight." He lifts me off of his lap and places me next to him to rummage through his pants pockets.

I grab his arm to stop him.

"We'll go."

"Are you sure? She wouldn't mind if we cancel."

"I mind. I want to go. The whole family is going to be there. I don't want to be the reason you aren't going. I won't be the reason Vivian is disappointed in us." I stand up and start dressing again so I can get in the shower. Pulling my pants up, I glance at him over my shoulder to see him watching me dress. "Hurry up and get the overnight bag I know you have packed in your trunk. We're going to be late and we still need to shower. If you're quick maybe you can shower with me." I waggle my eyebrows at him and power walk out of the room to avoid his grabby hands.

I race through my shower knowing if Lucas joined me we would never make it to dinner and we are going to be late as it stands now. By the time he makes it to my room I'm in my closet dressing already.

We pull up to Luc's childhood home. The huge structure stands regally in front of a circular drive. I smile broadly with a memory, long forgotten over the years. I can't wait to share with Lucas.

"Stop pouting already." I've gotten the silent treatment since he came upstairs and saw that I beat him out of the shower.

"You shouldn't be so happy, woman. Tempting a man with shower time and then cruelly yanking it away from him is not something to be happy about. I'll have you know, I'm considering writing my congressman and having it be proposed as a punishable crime. Next time you do it you could face the death penalty." He continues to pout.

"Alright, I'll add this to my list." I'm still smiling. I can't help it.

"What list would that be?" he petulantly asks.

"The list I'm compiling of reason why you should be committed in case the medical professionals, I may or may not be consulting, ask. Crap, you're dramatic. You should have taken up acting after singing." I blow raspberries at him. "You should be curious about why I'm smiling so much."

He turns in his seat to face me better.

"Alright, I'll bite. Why are you smiling, Genevieve? Other than the twisted torture methods you employ on me?"

"I've been here before," I gush with excitement.

"You've been here? To my house? What? When?" He's finally catching some of my excitement.

I'm bouncing in my seat. I can't wait to tell him about the time I was here when I was eleven.

"I'm not sure if you know, but Vivian and Hailey's mom are really good friends. They used to be sorority sisters."

"Yes, I knew that. I recognize little Hailey coming here from time to time with her mom."

"Exactly! We used to spend a couple weeks at each other's houses during the summers. One of the weeks we were all staying at Hailey's, her mom brought all of us with her to visit your mom!"

"Okay, that makes sense. Cool. Let's go in now," he says satisfied with my explanation.

"No!" I yell stopping him from getting out. "That's not the whole story!"

He smirks at me. "You say I'm dramatic. That was ear drum piercing."

"We came for tea. Hailey's mom insisted we all wear these really pretty dresses while here. Tara was excited about coming because Hailey's mother told us to be on our best behavior since *all* of Vivian's children were going to be at tea that afternoon. And even at eleven, all of the girls knew about the hot Alexander brothers."

I watch his eyes widen when he realizes what I'm saying. "That's amazing. I would have been seventeen then. The year before I left home. I don't even remember that tea, although, I'm sure mom forced us all to go and I was more worried about getting out of there to go hang with my band." He holds my hand, linking our fingers together. "Was I a prick?"

"I'll keep telling the story, no more interruptions, mister. When we got to tea, we were sitting on the opposite side of the long table from the older boys, much to Tara's dismay The mothers sat between us, though, I'm sure it was to keep us and Micah in line. You and your brother's were sitting together and we couldn't tell you and Kaine apart. That didn't stop Tara's prepubescent hormones. If anything she was worse."

"Once tea was done, the girls and I went for a stroll around the yard since you guys disappeared inside, thwarting our valuable stare time. We were passing the garage when water spray from the hose began to soak us. Micah took the opportunity away from the mothers to play his little prank. We started to run after him and my shoes slipped on the wet pavement and I fell on my knees. The garage door opened and one of the twins was standing there getting ready to hop into his car. I can only imagine how pitiful I looked soaking wet with scraped knees. He came over to me, unbuttoning his button down shirt, and slipped it over my shoulders to cover my wet dress. He said, 'You okay, did?' I was so confused. 'Did?' I asked. He grinned at me and said—"

"Yeah, damsel in distress, pretty girl." Lucas finishes the memory for me.

I meet his smile. "I had no idea it was you since I couldn't tell you and your brother apart. I realized now that it was you because under your shirt you were wearing a band t-shirt."

"If I knew I was rescuing my better half back then, I would have never forgotten that memory." Lucas looks bashful.

"No seventeen year old boy was looking at an eleven year old girl and thinking about a relationship, and if they were, they ended up in jail or something." I laugh. "My favorite part is history repeating itself."

He laughs out loud. "Twice now I've saved you from a wet dress with my button down shirts. I need to keep those with me around you. I think I've earned a kiss for my gallantry that time and this time."

We meet in the middle over the console between us. A kiss is never simply a kiss between us. It'd be like saying Mt. Everest is just a hill.

A knock on the window pulls us apart.

Aryan is on the driver's side. "Hey, I just got here and was heading in. I figured you'd prefer me interrupting you before Micah does." He points towards the house.

Looking out of my window, I see Micah quickly making his way to the car. When he reaches us, he pulls my door open and pops his head in. "Hey, Mom said get inside already." He looks at me. "You're looking flush, Sis. You shouldn't be walking."

I fight his hands but he undoes my seat belt and pulls me from the car, tossing me over his shoulder before running back to the house. I bounce roughly on his shoulder, nearly knocking the wind out of me. He runs right through the door that Lilah is holding open for us.

"*Hey, Ma! Look who I found outside!*" he yells, still running with me through the house.

"Micah! Put her down right now. I don't even know where to begin questioning what's wrong with you sometimes." I can hear the exasperation in Vivian's voice.

"Here I am, being a gentleman, and I'm getting chastised by my mother." He flips me off of his shoulder and onto a couch. "Gen wasn't feeling well. I found her looking very flushed and dazed. She required assistance into the house and as you can see Lucas wasn't up to the job. You should talk to him about how to take care of women properly."

I finally get my bearing enough to notice that someone else is on the couch next to me. I push my hair from my face. I don't recognize the woman next to me. She's stunning. No, not stunning—exquisite. I look like a hobo next to her, especially now that I've been tossed around by Micah.

I'm staring at her—speechless. *And* because I'm staring, I don't miss the nasty look she gives me back. Her eyes take on an assessing glint and judging by her attempt to smile at me, which is coming across as more of a sneer, I rate lower than bird shit landing on a pile of garbage at a landfill. Yes, that is exactly how nasty the look she is giving me is.

"Genni, I'm so glad you and Lucas could make it. Where is that son of mine?" I stand to embrace Viv and kiss her cheek.

"He and Aryan were following behind at a much more leisurely pace."

"Forgive me for being so rude. Genni, I'd like to introduce you to Marla." Vivian extends her hand to the ice queen on the couch. When she doesn't rise, I step a little closer and put my hand out in greeting.

"Hi Marla, nice to meet you," I say in my friendliest voice

When she touches my hand to acknowledge the greeting, it barely feathers my palm before she's pulling her hand back like I'm dirty. Well that was strike two with Miss Friendly.

Lilah bounces in to the room and gives me a squeezing hug. Her warm welcome thaws me from the glacial one I just received.

Lilah gets Vivian's attention. "I'm supposed to tell you and Gen that Luc and Aryan are going to be a few more minutes. They have some business to discuss and want to get it out of the way before dinner."

So that's what is taking so long. What kind of business would Lucas needs Aryan's security firm for?

Next I'm greeted by Kaine, who was standing by the wet bar on the opposite side of the room. He crosses to me.

"Hey, Kaine, how's breaking your habits working out for you?" I ask.

He looks at me oddly. Darn, I stuck my foot in it again. I guess he went back to being stuffier. Maybe that was a onetime thing he regrets and wants to forget happened, except, I just brought it up again. I didn't stick around that night, so I don't know what happened after I left the kitchen upset. What if he rushed back to work after dinner, immediately regretting leaving. *Darn. Darn. Darn.*

He shakes his head at me and smiles. "I can see what the attraction is. Not only are you beautiful, you are utterly refreshing, Sis."

I breathe a sigh of relief. "Oh thank goodness. I thought I said something wrong and you were thinking that

I'm weird." He throws his head back and laughs so loud that everyone in the room turns to look at us.

"Damn it, Genevieve. You have the wrong brother again. I'm your man." Lucas cracks his joke while walking into the room.

"Ha. Ha. Funny man." I slip my arm around Kaine. "Kaine here, was keeping me company while you were busy ignoring me."

"Kai."

"Huh?" I look up at Kaine.

"Call me Kai. I prefer the people that are closest to me call me Kai. Especially if you're going to yank my twin's chain about me keeping you company; Kai is more personal." He winks at me then crosses the room to greet his brothers.

I cross the room to the wet bar and join Micah. "So what do we have and what's the 411 on the ice queen over there." I lean back, resting my elbows on the bar watching everyone in the room greet the two stragglers.

"Ice queen? You're nicer than we are. Lilah and I are calling her the ice bitch."

"Okay, you don't need to convince me anymore. I like yours better. Ice bitch it is." We share a grin.

"She's one of Mom's picks," he answers the question in my eyes. "Whenever we have a get together here, Mom will invite someone she thinks is suitable to make her grandbabies and tries to set her up with one of us."

Shocked, I ask. "Who's this one for?"

"That's the kicker. We don't find out until dinner when Mom goes, 'Oh honey, let so and so sit next to you. She does this and that and you do something or other. You'll have lots to talk about'," he says in a sugary sweet female voice, trying to imitate Vivian.

I turn to the bar and lean over it, trying to hide my laughter so that no one notices. I start to snort, causing Micah to start laughing at me.

"Oh, Genni, dear!" Micah says in that voice again.

I'm in a shaking fit now. My knees quake and give out. I slide to the floor hysterically laughing, tears roll down my cheeks. god love Micah. He gets on the floor next to me, keeping me company and having a fit of hysterics of his own. I'm not facing them, but I know the rest of the dinner party is watching us.

"Looks like the life of the party is over here." Lucas slides down with two glasses in his hands, which tells me he was standing over me long enough to pour the drinks. He hands me a glass of white wine.

"Micah, do the voice for him." I pat his arm.

He does and Luc joins in on our laughter. The two of them get louder each time I snort. I finally get enough control over myself so that I can turn around and face everyone else in the room again. Lilah silently joined our group to watch Vivian at work.

Across the room Vivian is standing between Kai and Aryan talking to Marla. Marla looks a lot friendlier now as she chats with the eligible bachelors being offered to her on a platter.

Lilah leans over. "Which unlucky bastard do you think it is this time?" she whispers.

"Doesn't look like Marla cares. She'd take either one of them if it was up to her. Or probably even both if possible," I whisper back out of the side of my mouth. After I say it, I feel my ears redden. I can't believe I just said that to their little sister.

"You're right, she's practically eye banging both of them right in front of my mom," Lilah murmurs back, earning her a look from both of her older brothers sitting next to us.

"We're going to be having a discussion, young lady," Lucas tells her.

"Fuck yeah, we are. Eye banging, my ass," Micah grumbles.

"So why aren't you being corralled over there?" I ask Micah.

"I got myself out of the running the second I noticed the broad. I played up being the embarrassing son so that Mom would keep her far away from me. I have the act down to a science." He grins, proud of himself.

"No you didn't!" I whisper in my best scandalized voice. Honestly, I wouldn't really be surprised with him.

"Oh yeah, he did," Lilah confirms.

"I've noticed something. When we all get together, our maturity levels drop to that of kindergarteners. We're at a dinner party in a fancy mansion, yet we're all sitting on the floor like it is story time," I say to my floor companions.

"Tell me about it. I'm thirty, yet here I am." Lucas jokingly smiles.

"I nominate Micah for the blame." I elbow him in the ribs. Lilah laughs into her glass of soda.

"Sorry, minx. I'm going to have to say the blame is all yours. You become delightfully carefree when we're around our group." Lucas wraps his arms around my shoulders and pulls me into his side. "I'm going to say it's because you are happy and can let loose, after having to be overly mature for most of your life."

I grumble a bit about that.

"Stop that. I think it's adorable." He wraps a finger in my hair and gives it a gentle tug.

Across the room Aryan and Kai cast us pleading looks as they escort Marla to the balcony, I'm sure at their mother's urging. Which leaves us with Vivian bearing down on our little group. I now know how Simba felt when the wildebeests stampeded through the gorge.

When she reaches us, she crouches down to our level and grabs Micah's scotch out of his hand, tossing it back in one smooth motion.

"I really screwed the pooch with this one," she says aloud while looking over her shoulder at the door the party of three disappeared through. I'm stunned and don't know how to react. Lilah is giggling while he brothers are staring slack jawed at their mother.

Vivian reaches over and pats my shoulder. "Ignore my children. They're just shocked. They've lived their whole lives believing their mother is infallible."

Lucas slowly shakes his head with a dazed expression still on his face. "Nope, that's not it."

Micah chimes in, "Not even close. We're shocked you've finally realized you can make mistakes." I snicker when he gets his ear pulled.

"So, Genni, before we have to get off the floor and head in to dinner, tell me, do you have any more pieces I'd be interested in?"

I bite my lip, wondering if I should tell her about the pieces Lucas inspired. I guess I don't need to go into great detail.

"I'm working on a new collection right now for my next show. I sent a few pieces you might like to a gallery for a show I'm collaborating on with a few other local artists. Well, my agent collaborated, I just sent the pieces. I guess you would like those a lot more than the other ones. The others are very different from my usual work. I'm not sure which pieces will be going to my private showing. There are a few that may not go up for sale. I'm not certain of the details yet, but I'm getting paintings done rather quickly." I break off from my dialogue when I realize I'm rambling and everyone is staring at me.

"Alright, let's get things moving. Maybe if we finish quickly, your guest will leave early," Lucas says while helping us to our feet.

"Oh, I don't think we have to worry about that too much longer." I peer around Vivian to see Marla stomp back into the room.

Her mood doesn't seem soothed after her brief walk. It could be because she's soaking wet and shivering, or she could be shaking in rage. Both are a possibility. She storms over to us. Vivian gasps in surprise when she turns around and sees her soggy guest.

Stepping into Vivian's personal space, Marla begins to shriek at her. "Your sons are vile beasts, completely lacking in all manners! You didn't raise men, you raised animals!" The last is yelled at an almost inaudible disciple.

"I don't know who you think you are, coming here saying things like that. Clearly, you are the one with issues regarding manners. You can leave here right now on your own accord or I'll be happy—scratch that—jubilant to escort you out." I step around Vivian and narrow my eyes at my foe.

We're so close, I can see the rage building in her eyes. She's finding the idea of scratching my eyes out enticing, I'm sure, but my direct and steady calm seems to make her hesitant to act on it.

She sneers at me. Her voice is low enough that only I can hear her words. After making her point she struts out as if her expensive high heels aren't making sloshing noises with each step. I notice that the other brothers are a few feet behind where Marla was standing. They must have come in quietly during my exchange with her.

"Well this is certainly going to make spin class a little uncomfortable." Vivian closes her eyes and breathes. "Would you boys like to explain to me why that young woman came back in here wet?" She opens her eyes and stares daggers at Kai and Aryan.

Kaine clears his throat. "There are some things that a man should never say to his mother. What happened out there is one of those things. I will say that she fell completely on her own. Neither of us were the direct cause." He finishes by crossing his arms over his chest, signaling that is all he will say of the matter.

Pretty ballsy move, putting his foot down like that when he's speaking to his mother. Vivian's known in society to be about as pleasant as a sledgehammer to the head when she wants something.

"I'll take that for now. You remind me of your father when you take that tone. Let's go in to dinner before the cook comes out threatening to quit again in that accent I can barely understand when he gets all worked up because we're late." She leads the way to the dining room.

I hang back a little to hear what the brothers are talking about. *Did I just hear that right?* She tried grabbing Kaine's privates and when he side stepped her reach, she missed, teetered on her heels, and fell in. She really did have some nerve coming inside yelling about manners and animals. She lacked class and respect for herself and others. Her parting words are still in the back of my head. Pathetic and desperate to hang onto a man that's been behind my back already and not bothering to hide it from the cameras. The media sure did their job painting me as someone to be pitied by the public. Whatever, I'm shaking it off and I'm going to enjoy this dinner.

Dinner was hectic with chatter. No quiet family sit downs for the Alexander's. Vivian glows around her children; she keeps them in line. However, regardless of age, these siblings did not outgrow the antics. I can see why she is so happy. She is surrounded by love and loves them back in a completely selfless way.

After dinner Vivian asks me if I'd take a stroll with her to her greenhouse. I nearly groan, hoping she's not like Gram who has to go into detail about every plant and how she grew them. Wine glasses in hand, we companionably walk side by side in silence.

After closing the door behind us, I let my gaze wander around the greenhouse. It looks more like a tropical paradise. I can hear water running and under the light of the moon and the dark sky, it's gorgeous. I follow Vivian through the foliage I can hear that we're getting closer to the sound of water. Through the foliage, I can see a sitting area up ahead next to a pond with a waterfall. Vivian takes a seat and motions for me to do the same.

"I was talking to Kaine the other day and he mentioned meeting your sisters. Forgive me if I'm wrong, but I thought you were an only child."

I clear my throat. "Yes, I was. I only recently discovered I have two sisters."

I watch her ponder what I said. She looks at me, assessing my features as if the answer for how she'd like to proceed with this conversation will be there.

"I knew them," she finally says.

"My sisters?" I ask, confused.

She gives me the 'I can't believe you asked that' signature mom look. "Your parents." She waves her hand as if she's clearing the air. "I knew them when we were younger."

"I had no idea. Is that why you have always been so interested in my work?" I try to puzzle through her revelation.

"Heavens no. I truly do love your art; your talent is immense. To be quite honest, I couldn't stand your mother. What's worse is that she snagged your father before I could." She laughs when my mouth hangs open.

"Oh yes. Your father was very dashing in our day. Your mother and I went to the same finishing school. We never got along. I won't speak ill of the dead, but I will say, she was barely pleasant, even on her best days. I remember the night she and I both saw your father for the first time." She pauses in thought like she is remembering all of the details all over again. "You know how DC society is, everybody knows everyone. I was at a function with my parents. I had been forced to go because a good friend of the family's son was going to be there. They had been discussing merging their businesses. They felt that a marriage would strengthen the business dealings with one another. I'll never forget the moment your mother first saw your father. I was standing with my parents and the other family, doing my best to ignore them while their son stood on my other side doing the same.

"I heard a gasp and saw your mother standing nearby, mouth open and eyes wide. She looked flustered for someone that was always as put together as she was. When I followed her stunned gaze to see what finally ruffled her feathers, I could see the reason for her reaction. John was incredible in a tuxedo. Add to that his debonair features, gorgeous, clear green eyes, and perfectly windswept hair, everyone noticed when he walked in.

"For weeks after, your mom and I tried to get his attention. My parents didn't make it easy since they threw me together with their friend's son every chance they got. I wasted a few weeks, but I eventually lost the drive for the competition. It didn't hurt that I also happened to see the looks your dad was giving your mother when she wasn't looking. So, I politely bowed out of the running to be Mrs. Westley."

I can't believe Vivian's story. Just wow. I never knew how my parents met. It sounds romantic, but obviously, I know it didn't have a fairytale ending.

"Wow. Whatever happened with the other guy?"

"Well I called a meeting with the hippie geek." She chuckles richly at her description of him. "He wanted to study the environment and save the world. I wanted to marry someone that would indulge my expensive shopping habits and not get in my way."

"I guess it's a good thing you didn't marry him then. I hope your parents weren't too disappointed." I smile.

"Actually dear, they were euphoric. We made the mistake, or delight depending on how you look at it, to have drinks while we figured out ways to thwart our parents. The next morning, I woke up hung over, and snuck out of his apartment. Less than a month later we were married, and exactly nine months after that we had Kaine and Lucas. You see, sometimes parents do know best. We didn't get what either of us wanted, but we both got more than we asked for."

That strikes a chord within me.

Then the rest of her words suddenly strike me. "The hippie geek was Luc's father? Mr. Alexander?" That doesn't sound at all like the man I've heard about.

"That was my George. Single, college-aged bachelor, and ready to take care of the world. On the other hand, newly married and father of two, George buckled under the weight of his family's legacy. More so under our combined family's businesses." Her tone is bittersweet.

"Wow. I would never have guessed." I shake my head, trying to make sense of this.

"I thought Lucas might have talked to you about the issue he and my husband had. That's why I'm telling you this. I think if you know more of the story, you'll be able to help my son heal." She grabs ahold of my hand, demanding my complete attention.

"My husband was not unflawed. I know that, accepted it, and worked on it with him. When we got married and his dreams of helping improve the world ended, he threw himself completely into work. He felt that if he had to do this job instead of the dreams he had, then he'd do the job to the best of his ability so that his wife and children could be proud of him. His passion was replaced with an obsession.

"The night Lucas told us about the band, I cried and pleaded with him to stay. George was enraged, unreasonably so. After my son left and enough time passed, I was able to see past my own despair over our son leaving and think about my husband's actions that night and every day after. He loved Lucas but his soul was being eaten away at by jealousy. Here Lucas was, standing up to his father and going to live his dreams, while George gave up his own for his children under the weight of his father's demands. The jealousy ate away until he was bitter, and once he was over being bitter, he was too stubborn and proud to make the first move to mend things. Every day it tore him up inside."

She reaches under the cushion of her seat and pulls out two envelopes. "When each of our children were born, George sat next to their bassinet the night we brought them home and wrote them each a letter. The day we were informed of my sister and her husband's tragic accident he did the same with Aryan without hesitation. I never read them. He wanted to give them to the kids when they finally

- 215 -

had significant others or children on the way. After he passed away, I went through the clothing he was wearing that day and inside the suit jacket pocket I found another letter with Lucas written on the front. I don't know how long he was carrying it around with him. I didn't read this one, either. I want you to take them and when you think the time is right, and he's ready, let him see how his father was only human and made many mistakes he deeply regretted, but he always loved him. Even when he did not show it."

I nod in understanding. "I'll do whatever I can."

"I know you will, sweetheart. That's why I'm trusting you with this." She gets up and walks out of the greenhouse.

I don't know how long I've been sitting here thinking, just staring at the letters in my hand, tempted to read them, when Lucas touches my shoulder, causing me to jump in surprise. He smiles softly at me. "Hey, minx, I didn't mean to startle you. It's getting a little late. Are you ready to go?"

I nod and stand up. Wrapping my arms around him, I give him a hug. "I'm ready," I say out loud.

To myself I add, *I'm ready to go wherever you are, whenever you are, and whatever way you want to go. I'm ready to heal you the way you are healing me. You are more than I ever asked and hoped for. I will do everything I need to be the same for you. I love you. One of these days, I'll scream it to the world so that everyone is aware. Let the paparazzi and media report that, and I'll never cringe at the sight of them again.*

Chapter Sixteen

After seeing the attorney, regarding dividing assets, I go to the park near my house and sit on a bench under this big beautiful willow oak tree. It's still too soon for the leaves to begin growing back, but the branches still sway in the wind like a hula dancer without her grass skirt. During the summer, it is my favorite tree to sit under for shade while people watching. Even with the nip in the air, there are children on the playground wearing their winter coats, running around, chasing each other while their mothers sit nearby drinking coffee, discussing their children, and watching closely to see if they need to jump up to kiss a boo boo or break up a scuffle. I wonder if Linda, Quincy and Stephanie's mother, brought them here as children to play while our father was working or with me. I imagine she would since they lived so close.

I went into attorney Robert's office today, unsure how to word my requests to him about my sisters since he was a good friend of my father's and I did not want to malign his memories of his friend. He knew more than I did. He knew about my father's affair and about my sisters. He even knew about Linda leaving my father and about my father's odd behavior the day of the car accident.

I never knew that my mother was ill. She had various personality disorders, some that I never heard of before. A daughter should know about these things. That is why she was never happy with anything that she viewed as less than perfect, and was completely dependent on my father. Dad wasn't happy that day because he was finally going to fix our family. He was happy because he filed for divorce and custody of me before coming home. He planned on taking me and going after Linda and my sisters. Having my mother go for a drive with him was his way of trying to protect me from the fall out, especially since she was unstable.

I take my phone from my pocket and look at the screen, wavering a moment before dialing anyway. "Hey, minx." His deep husky voice sends shivers throughout me. Hearing his voice soothes my doubts about telling him what I'm thinking.

"I think my mother may have done something to cause the car accident that killed her and my father," I blurt without preamble. The silence on the other end is heavy.

"Where are you?" he demands.

I quickly tell him my location. When I don't get a reply, I pull my phone away from my ear to see that he's already hung up. I place my phone back in my pocket and tilt my back to stare up to the sky. Maybe something in the clouds will tell me why my very dull life has turned into one big, happy, dramatic roller coaster, taking me on the ride of my life. I sit here for some time, looking but not finding the answers. The sky doesn't seem to hold a transcendent moment of clarity for me today.

My cold hand is enveloped in a large warm palm. I slip mine free and slide my fingertips over his hand, finding comfort in the familiarity of his calloused fingers from years of guitar playing. I lazily draw random patterns over his skin, enjoying these few seconds of simple pleasure.

"Are you ready?" His voice is gentle.

I turn and admire his strong profile. His jaw has a day's worth of stubble. He didn't bother to shave before coming to me as quickly as possible. I can still see that his hair is rumpled and looks to only have been finger smoothed.

"You look like you just rolled out of bed."

The corners of his lips hike up. "I did. After I got home last night, I had to deal with some conference calls from the issue in L.A." I nod in acknowledgment.

I don't want to look at him when I tell him what I learned and my suspicions. I move myself onto his lap, wrapping my arms around his neck, and lay my head on my arm, out of view. Once he wraps his arms around me, I begin.

It flows out of me in a detached tone. My father was going to raise me with my sisters. My mother was mentally ill. The car accident may not have actually been accidental. What I thought was true love, when my mother ran back to the car, could have possibly been suicide rather than the act of selfless love I built up in my fourteen year old mind.

"My life could have been so different if he did not die that day." My voice is empty as I utter this.

"We could sit on this bench until the sun dips below the horizon and rises again asking the 'what ifs'. The 'what ifs' are nice, but they're fantasies that aren't attainable. You got dealt a shitty hand, minx. When that hand folded and you were dealt your next one, it wasn't so bad. Here is a 'what if' for you. What if your father lived and chased your sister's mother to Maryland and you eventually drifted from your friendships with Hailey and Tara because of distance and different lives? You never realize your talent, so you don't become an amazing artist. You never went out with friends after an awkward break up and you never met me." His voice dips in the end as if the thought of not meeting me is physically painful. "Nothing real in life is built on 'what ifs'. What you have now is as real as it gets."

"Thank you for making something that is so difficult to comprehend seem so insignificant compared to what I have now." My lips move against his cheek as I speak. I lost a lot that day, but I didn't lose everything, and even though I didn't grow up with my sisters, they were only delayed in coming into my life; I have them now.

Turning his head to look at me, our foreheads come to rest against each other. "I love you. Everything is trivial compared to that." He presses a kiss to my lips. "There's a food truck around that bend of the walk way. Let's grab some hot chocolate."

"I love you, too. You obviously know the way to a woman's heart, get something chocolate in her mouth." I climb off of his lap and offer my hand to help him up.

Using my hand, he stands and takes the momentum to pull me close.

"I'll pump you with enough chocolate to make you dizzy if it gets my minx back into full fighting form." We chuckle together.

"Lead the way, my dear chocolate pusher. Now I know who will be my enabler when I need my fix," I tease.

When we get back to the Brownstone, I take my time hanging our coats in the foyer closet. No need to shove it in Luc's face that I'm a slob.

"You're actually hanging the coats?" Surprise laces his voice. I look sheepishly over my shoulder.

"Oh come on, Gen, I've seen your walk in closet and your coat closet before. You're a tornado with clothing." He slaps my butt with the back of his hand. Grabbing my hand, he pulls me behind him, towards the kitchen "Relax. When we live together I'll hire a personal maid to just to pick up after you. Or maybe a personal assistant, the idea of someone being near that always has a charged phone is still very appealing."

I dig my heels into the floor to stop our forward progression, I'm stunned and it shows.

Sighing, Lucas turns to face me, giving me a look that says duh, Gen. "You're fixating on the part where I said when you move in, aren't you?"

Mutely, I nod my head. I'm not sure I've even blinked since he said those words.

"When you're ready, you are going to wake up every morning right next to me. Trust me, Gen, this is a major concession. Every fiber of my being is screaming to drag you away and tie you to my bed until you scream that you never want to leave. But I'm keeping Unga under lock and key." He grabs a fist full of my hair and wraps it around his hand like a caveman ready to drag me away. Instead of pulling my hair, he gently unwraps his hand and starts to smooth the mess of curls. Still focused on his task, he opens his mouth, "I know you have a lot of changes happening quickly that you haven't had control of and you need to feel in control of something. You have the say in this, but it won't always be like that. There's going to be times I take control and make decisions, most of the time, I hope to make decisions together." He stares into my eyes, hypnotizing me with his beautiful silver irises. "I respect the strong woman that you are so I know there will be times you will lay down the law with me, too. I just hope you do it while you're naked." His grin is infectious.

"What if I asked you to move in here instead?" I tease.

"Move into a house to be with my beautiful minx and her female posse. Sounds frighteningly appealing. It could work." He tilts his head to look up as if he's seriously pondering it. "If I could be informed of the one week of each month I should be away on business for my own safety, I'll do it."

"I can't believe you just said that!" I jab him in the stomach with my finger.

"Damn it, woman, watch those claws." He walks away into the kitchen, grumbling to himself. I'm pretty sure I just heard him say that the week must be coming. If looks could kill, there's enough heat in my gaze to burn him alive.

I catch up to Lucas, when he stops at the threshold of the kitchen. I stop next to him.

My outraged gasp gets attention. *"Is that my ice cream?"* I storm across the kitchen and turn the container around to see that it is indeed mine. "That's my break up Ben and Jerry's, how could you?" I snatch the spoon out of Maddox's hand, right before he puts it in his mouth.

"Excuse me?" Lucas stomps up to us.

"Not now, Lucas, I have to deal with this." I shoo him away, not taking my focus off my frenemy.

"A woman's BB&J is sacred," I tell Maddox sternly.

"A BBwhat?" he asks puzzled.

I roll my eyes exasperated. "Break up Ben & Jerry's, if you're going to commit a crime in my house, at least know what you're doing."

Lucas growls at me. I'm sure he's annoyed that I'm ignoring him but this is important.

"Uh, Gen." He starts looking nervously to the side.

"Shush, I'm not done yet. I would never go to your house and just drink all of your beer, especially if you had one designated for certain life events such as break ups due to its comfort factor. I'm not sure why you're sitting at my island, eating my break up ice cream but no more! I'm cutting you off!" I stomp my foot in emphasis.

"What do you mean 'break up ice cream'?" Lucas's roar is deafening.

I swing around; his face is red and the veins in his neck are popping out.

"Is there something we need to talk about, Genevieve?" His jaw snaps shut after the audible question mark.

Suddenly my moment of enlightenment comes. "Lucas, it's my ice cream from my break up with Brad. I never got to eat it." I attempt to placate him.

"Why didn't you get to eat it?"

"Well because Tara dragged me out and I met you." Is that really important at this moment? I don't say it out loud since he still looks a little red.

"Exactly. You met me."

I stay quiet and nod my head again, trying to soothe him.

"You are dating me now, aren't you?"

"Yes, I just said that."

"You aren't dating Brad any longer."

"No, hence the ice crea—."

"Are you happy with me?" He moves on before I could finish.

"Yes." What is he getting at? The look in his eyes is making me nervous.

"Were you happy with Brad?"

"I guess not." His eyes narrow. "I mean no."

"Well then there's only one thing left to do." Grabbing the two full ice cream containers and the half eaten one from my hands, he strides to the sink.

"Oh, Lucas, no! Not the ice cream!" I throw myself at his back to stop him, but he easily holds me back as he puts the hot water on full blast to wash my creamy deliciousness down the drain. I turn to Hailey and Tara who I ignored earlier, even though they're both sitting next to Maddox. "Help me!" They hide their bowls of my ice cream, in their laps under the counter, so Luc doesn't see it. They're no help.

"All done." Lucas turns back towards me with a look, daring me to say something. He threw down the gauntlet.

And I sure as hell am picking it up.

"*You mother fucking, sweet stealing, son of a whore!*"

I slap my hand over my mouth, stunned at what just came out. The silence in the room is deafening; every one's mouth is open in shock. I turn to flee the room.

"Where are you going?" Maddox yells after me.

"I have to find a church and go to confession."

"Gen, you aren't Catholic, though." Hailey yells.

"Well, I'm going to hell if I don't because saying sorry doesn't seem like it's going to cut it after that." I hear them all laughing as I run up the stairs. I'm glad the thought of my eternal damnation sounds funny to them.

I slam my door shut and lock it for good measure.

In my closet I slip out of my clothes and put on Luc's shirt. I got it back from dry cleaning weeks ago but still haven't returned it to him. He'll just have to wait now. I throw myself across my bed and hug my pillow to my chest.

The door handle rattles.

"Gen, open up." Luc's voice is muffled by the wooden door.

"Gen, if you don't open up I'm going to call my mother and tell her that last part you screamed at me."

I think for a moment to recall what I said. Oh my god. He wouldn't, would he? "No, he wouldn't do that to me," I mumble into my pillow.

"You're right, I wouldn't."

I glare over my shoulder to see him putting his credit card away. I really need to change my locks or something. The bed dips from his weight, when he sits on it.

"Did I ever tell you about the time Aryan met the President? He tried to tell him that he should appoint Mom as the Secretary of State and send her overseas to handle the conflict. Mr. President thought he was joking, especially when he told him she could have everything cleared up by dinner time. Then he met Mom. Unfortunately for world peace, she turned down his job offer."

His attempt to make me laugh is funny but not funny enough to erase the memory of my B&J being washed down the kitchen sink drain.

"I'm getting the impression that, despite you being dressed in one of my shirts like an erotic fantasy of mine, if I touched you, I'd be limping away."

I pinch my lips together to keep from answering him.

"Get dressed and meet me downstairs. I'm going to make this all better." He gets up.

"You're going to buy me my own Ben & Jerry's ice cream factory and have them make me my very own flavor?" Go big or go home.

"Very creative, but no." He turns and walks out.

I lay there a few more minutes, but curiosity gets the best of me.

Downstairs, the others are in the den gathered around the love seat. I move in between them to see what they are looking at. I stare enthralled by the image blown up and made into a canvas.

"It's beautiful, Tara. Your talent is mind blowing."

"Yeah, I was saving it to give to you and Lucas for a special occasion, but I figure saving Lucas from you murdering him is a good enough occasion," she quips.

The image is the one she took of us after Lucas and I made love for the first time, entwined around one another while sleeping. Even in sleep, the happiness on both of our faces is evident. I can't take my eyes off of Lucas in the picture. I put that look on his face. I smile smugly.

"Seriously, Tara, thank you." I had to say it again. I'm still in awe by what she captured.

"No thanks needed. I couldn't have done it if you two didn't do it." She snickers. "Now go let him do a little groveling, I'll get this up to your room."

I give the girls hugs and kisses good bye. When I turn to Maddox I raise my fist as if I'm going to hit him.

"You made my S list, buddy."

"How was I supposed to know it was your ice cream? I was invited over by that one." He points to Tara. "I was told there would be ice cream sundaes. She used my stomach to manipulate me."

"Thud, thud, thud," I hear Hailey quietly behind me.

"What was that?" I look at her.

"The sound of her being thrown under the bus." She winks.

"Time to go." He tells me but pauses to address Tara first. "Don't forget to give me that SD card. I want all of them." Lucas grabs my hand and drags me out not waiting to hear her reply.

He's back to dragging me places again.

After a short drive, we pull up to a nondescript building.

Inside is a quaint restaurant set up, the décor is Middle Eastern. The aroma of the food being prepared in the kitchen is rich with exotic scents.

A young, good-looking gentleman comes out of the kitchen with a warm greeting for Lucas and speaks rapidly in a language I cannot understand. Lucas speaks the same language almost as quickly.

"Genevieve, this is my friend, Adham. His family owns this establishment." I start to reach out to shake his hand but quickly pull back. I'm sure I heard that men of that region do not shake hands with women. I hope I did not insult him. I look to Lucas for guidance.

Adham laughs before addressing Lucas. "She is precious, my friend." His voice is lightly accented yet holds a refined quality to it. Turning back to me, he extends his hand. "I am a modern man, Genevieve. It will be a pleasure to shake the hand of the woman that has captured my friend, especially when he needs to bring her to see me so that I may satisfy her needs."

My eyes widen and I look at Luc. What the heck did he bring me here for?

"That is not what I said," Lucas tells him.

"Are you sure? Your Arabic was not without flaw."

"Your brain is flawed. You must be inhaling too much cumin when you cook again," Luc retorts.

"Too many years of loud music has damaged you, you don't have the ear for my beautiful language." He winks at me. "I will go get your treat now."

When he's back in the kitchen, I lean towards Lucas "What did you order me? It better not come with a happy ending." I whisper with a joking tone.

"You'll see. The happy ending comes later when we're home."

Adham returns with a bowl of what looks like ice cream. "Booza." He pushes the bowl towards me.

"There's liquor in here?" I look around the bowl. "I don't think I should eat this. It's a little too early for booze."

Adham shakes his head and laughs at me. "Booza is ice cream in my country." He pushes the spoon towards me.

I look from the bowl to Lucas and Adham repeatedly. They seem to be expecting something. I hope they don't have to high of hopes because I don't think anything is better than Ben & Jerry's.

I take my first spoon full.

Except this. This is multiple orgasms in my mouth. It is chocolate and hazelnut. The thick creamy goodness flavor sticks to my mouth. This is so different but not. Regardless, it's incredible.

"So do you still want a Ben & Jerry's factory?"

I cover my bowl with my hands. "Shh. Do not say things like that in front of my booza."

I was so focused on my new favorite treat and not wanting to finish it too quickly. I don't know when, but at some point, Adham went and got me a second bowl of heaven.

For the next couple hours, we stayed and talked with Luc's friend. Thankfully, they remained speaking in English so that I wasn't left out of the conversation. It was very nice, but this experience may have ruined B&J for me.

Before we left, Adham had someone bring me a tub of Booza. Thank goodness he said it'll last long enough to get home. I'll need to find the ultimate hiding place, so that the girls don't get their greedy lips around my treasure. Maybe I can have Lucas destroy a gallon of fat free lactose free ice cream and put my yumminess inside as a decoy. We make it to the car quickly since we just parked right outside the door.

"I'm forgiven?" he asks.

"Yes, but I still don't know why you washed my ice cream down the sink." I watch him from the corner of my eye.

He sighs and grips the steering wheel. "I was acting stupid. I don't want you to have anything that has to do with any other man. At first, I thought you meant you were keeping it on hand for if we break up which made me angry for the few moments I lost my senses. When you said it was because of Brad and you were upset you didn't eat it, I lost it and took that to mean, despite your relationship crashing because of something you couldn't control, you still had feelings for him." He smiles guiltily.

"I have a guilty pleasure. I don't eat sweets really, but when I do, B&J is my junk of choice. *And* I eat it when I'm happy, sad, or confused. I really wanted some to the point of being obsessed, especially after that meeting with my attorney. I feel better about everything because of you, but my ice cream would have been a cherry on top." I bite my lower lip, waiting to see if he says anything about my ice cream confession.

This wasn't the kind of confessional I was talking about needing earlier but bearing your guilty pleasures to the man you love has to be good for the soul too, right?

Crap. I didn't apologize to him. My actions did provoke his reaction. "I'm sorry. I should not have been referring to it as break up Ben and Jerry's. I was practically asking for you to blow up." If he had done something similar, I probably would have done something crazy too to be completely honest with myself.

He squeezes my hand. "We're good."

His phone rings. He pulls it from his pocket, checking the screen before answering. I can hear whoever is on the other line speaking before Lucas got to even say a greeting.

"Gen, check your phone for me," he whispers away from the receiver.

I pull my phone out of my purse. It's dead. The call must be for me. I start to feel anxious. What could have happened for someone to be calling Lucas to find me when they can't get through to me on my own phone?

I notice Lucas making turns to change directions. He's still on the phone. I can't gather any details from his side of the conversation.

"We're already on our way." He hangs up the phone and grabs my hand again.

"What's going on?" The edge of panic in my voice is discernable.

"We have to go to Maryland. We're meeting Quincy at the hospital. The others shouldn't be far behind. They're too upset to drive so Maddox is going to drive the girls over."

"What's wrong with Quincy? What happened? Is she going to be okay?" I'm trying not to panic but can't help it; the tears are already slipping down my cheeks despite my struggle to hold them back.

"It's not Quin, baby. Stephanie was attacked. We don't know the extent of the injuries or what happened yet. She had to go in for surgery. We aren't sure what the surgery is for yet. Quincy hasn't been able to get any information from the staff in the emergency room. I'm sorry. We'll find out everything possible as soon as we get there."

I break. I'm sobbing uncontrollably. I hug my knees to my chest and break down. I've been walking an emotional tight rope for weeks, swaying and fighting to keep my balance. This sends me plummeting over. I'm an hour away from my sisters, and when they need me the most they aren't able to reach me. Lucas rubs my back in a circular motion, trying his best to calm me while breaking every speed limit sign posted to get us there as quickly as possible.

We arrive in record time. My tears have dried at this point. My focus now is my sisters. Walking into the seating area, I see Quincy is quietly crying in the chair closest to the doors the doctor will come through with our news.

I crouch in front of her. "Hey. Have they told you anything yet?"

She shakes her head. "I can barely get them to look at me when I'm standing there." She points to the nurse's desk.

I give her a hug, squeezing hard. Harder than I even intended because now I'm burning up.

I walk towards the nurse filled with purpose. "Excuse me?" The nurse holds her finger up to me to wait because she is on the phone. Without remorse, I listen to the conversation. She's on the phone with a nurse from another floor making plans for their coffee break.

Click. My finger holds down the button on the receiver slot.

The nurse realizes what I did and stands up angrily.

"Good, now that I have your attention, you are going to remain quiet until I am done speaking to you. There is a young girl named Stephanie Westley under this hospital's care. She was brought in here for surgery. We have not been told anything more than that. I'm going to repeat for you that her last name is Westley and I'll wait for it to ring a bell in your head that the Westley family

- 231 -

provides large amount of funding for this and several other hospitals in the Virginia, DC, and Maryland area. We are good family friends with almost every board of directors for this and several other hospitals. Now that you are aware, if you need your job and want to continue working here, or even in the medical field in the area, I'm going to suggest you go back and find out everything you can for us, regarding Stephanie Westley. I would hate to have to call my grandfather and tell him the hospital he gives so much to isn't able to tell him what is wrong with his granddaughter." I watch the nurse pale as my threat sinks in. "You can speak now." I'm condescending and bitchy, but if it gets me answers, I don't care. This is my family.

"Y-y-yes, ma'am. I'm so sorry. I'll be right back with all the information that is available." She runs through the doors.

I stand there staring at the doors the nurse disappeared through. I feel incredibly guilty for having treated her that way, yet on the flip side of the coin, I would do it again and again if need be.

I go back to sit with Lucas and Quin. My foot taps with nervous energy. I ignore it and try to keep from going through the double doors the nurse disappeared behind.

"The nurse will be back soon with everything they will be able to tell us at this time." I try to reassure my sister.

Tearfully, Quincy looks over to me. "Thank you."

"Don't thank me. She's my sister, too," I say it harsher than I intended. The stress of the situation and not knowing anything is wearing at us already. Even Lucas is unusually quiet, just tapping his finger on the arm of the chair.

The doors we entered opens. Aryan and Dexter come through. *How did they find out?*

"Is she okay?" Dexter demands.

"We haven't found anything out yet, I just sent the nurse back. She'll have information for us this time." My tone expresses that I didn't give the nurse any other option. He nods his head and moves to the wall nearest the doors and leans back to wait for the news.

The doors open again to let Maddox through with his arm around Tara. Behind them is Hailey and… Kaine?

Tara rushes over to hug me. I think she needed it as much as I did. Hailey sits on the arm of Quin's chair and wraps her arms around her. Aryan is on the phone across the waiting room, pacing. Kai leans against the wall next to Dex. Maddox is handing out tissues and asking how they take their coffee. I guess he's going to get the sludge for our wait.

I don't understand what everyone is doing here. How did they find out what is going on.

"Why?"

"Because they all care about you and Steph. It's what family does."

I didn't realize I voiced my question until Lucas answers it. We are a hodge-podge family. It means a lot to have them show up in full force.

"I just got off the phone with the detectives investigating the attacks." Aryan comes over.

"Attacks? More than one?" I'm confused.

"There's been a string of attacks on young girls in the area. Steph is just the latest victim. I'm going to head over to the station. The detective is ex-military and is going to do me a favor and let me take a look at what they have to see if I can spot something they are missing."

I nod my agreement. "Please do. Make sure they find whoever did this to her."

"I'm going too." Dexter steps up.

"Are you sure you don't want to stay here?" Aryan asks.

"I'm sure I'll just go nuts sitting here doing nothing. If I go with you, I can at least be doing something to help her. Besides, Gen will call us as soon as they find out any little detail, won't you?"

It was worded as a question, but it came out more as a demand. For a second time I nod my head.

"Do everything you can."

"Thank you for your help," Quin speaks up from behind me. "Sorry I've been a little out of it. I need to pull myself together for her."

Dexter pulls her into a tight hug. "We'll do whatever needs to be done to catch the bastard."

Gently he pushes her towards Kaine so that he can guide her across the room to sit again.

The doctor comes through the doors.

"The family of Miss Westley?" he calls.

We all crowd him.

"That's us. We're her older sisters." Quin and I are in the front of the pack.

"Your sister made it out of surgery successfully. She suffered an open fracture to her left femur as well as a severe tear in her meniscus that needed to be repaired, too. She has several lacerations and contusions. She's not a pretty sight, but she's lucky to be alive after falling off a roof top."

"Was there anything else—" I can't bring myself to say it, to ask what I want to know.

"If you are asking if there was any other trauma found on her body, the answer is no. From the physical exam performed there wasn't any signs of abuse. However, we won't know for sure what occurred until she comes around from the anesthesia. A nurse will notify you when she is placed in her room. Someone will be able to wait with her until she wakes, which will not be for bit." He turns to leave and stops. "Also, which one of you scared the nurse at the desk into not wanting to come back up here?"

I step forward. "That would be me."

"I want to apologize for her lack of sympathy for the circumstances. In the future I'm going to recommend she not be placed at this desk to handle the families."

"Thank you, doctor."

He disappears back through the doors.

Taking a deep calming breath, I turn back towards the group.

I address the guys going to the police station first. "Find out everything you can so we know what she went through and can be prepared to help her when she wakes up. Tell the detectives they can come tomorrow if she's up to giving a statement. I do not want her to be forced to handle it before she is ready. I know you are both very busy men, and I can pay you whatever for doing this. Of course you'll be the one to sit with her, Quin. She'll find the most comfort with you being there beside her. I'm going to stay here. If anyone can't stay, don't worry about it. Just showing up means so much to us."

When I finish my little speech, I meet everyone's stare and they all start talking at the same time. Protesting loudly, they collectively yell at me for insulting them for saying I'd pay them for their help or that they can go home. Dexter storms out of the waiting room.

Hailey improves on my plan by sending Maddox and Kaine out for food and coffee. We'll all be happy eating. Tara and Hailey volunteer to go to pick up things to help Steph feel more comfortable for her stay in the hospital.

"What's going on? How is she?" Micah comes through the door. With everything going on I didn't even realize I overlooked his absence.

Hailey grabs his arm and steers him back towards the door. "You can come with us. I'll explain on the way."

"Good idea, he would have drove you all nuts, waiting here with you," Tara says before following after them.

"That was good to see," Quincy says. I'm not sure about what. She catches my confused look and waves her hand as if everyone is still standing there in front of us. "That I'm not the only one being slow on the uptake of our new family and group dynamic. I'm just so used to it being me and Steph, calling our mom or aunts. With Mom gone and our aunts on a cruise and out of reach, it is nice having someone else to count on, but it's still taking some time to get used to."

"I know there have been a lot of changes for us lately." I hold her hand. "But I think they've been great changes and we're doing pretty well with them."

"Alright you two emotionally-damaged, beautiful women that I love, let's make ourselves comfortable. We don't know how much longer our wait will be. We should try to contact your aunts and grandparents as well so that they are aware of what is going on." Lucas nudges us towards the chairs again.

"If I call the aunts they will end their cruise to get back here and raise hell," Quin groans. "This is their first group trip since Mom got sick. They need this. I'll call them after we know more and when they are almost home."

"I'll call Grand-Pop, he'll be able to tell Gram and keep her calm." I pull my cell phone out only to realize it is still dead. Lucas shoves his phone at me.

"Go do what you have to do." He kisses my forehead before I walk away.

The conversation with my grandfather was difficult. He wanted answers to his questions and I wasn't able to tell him anything more than she pulled through surgery fine. I explained the scene with the nurse. I wanted him to know I had thrown our last name around in case he heard it from someone else. He let me know he'd handle Gram and see if there's anything more he can find out about Steph's condition and prognosis.

Luc's phone starts vibrating in my hand. Checking the screen in case it's Pop calling back, I see Liss is the caller. I'm sure Liss is short for Lissandria. I'm not going there; too much else is happening that's more important.

"You got a phone call while I was on the phone." I tell Lucas, handing it back to him. The phone vibrates again, signaling a voicemail.

When he sees who the missed call is from he quickly scans my face as if for a reaction. There isn't one. She's the past and work. I'm here now, and with luck, the future.

"I'll handle it later. Whatever it is can wait until everything is okay here." He holds my hand to reassure me.

"Westley family?" A nurse calls out.

"Yes?" Quincy answers, pulling me to stand with her.

"You sister is in her room now, resting. If you are ready, I can take you all up now."

"All of us? We were told only one at a time," I question.

"Ah yes, that is the usual policy, however I've been instructed to—" she hesitates as if she doesn't know how to word the next part of her sentence without sounding rude.

"Keep us happy?" I finish for her. Grand-Pop didn't take long to make some phone calls.

She nods sheepishly.

"Thank you, we're sorry to have been trouble, but we're definitely going to take the leniency given to us. We have more people coming back soon. Can we leave their names so they can be directed to the room upon their arrival?"

"Yes, of course. I'll get you a pen and paper to make your list of approved guests." Lucas stays behind to make the list.

Quin and I follow the nurse, anxious to get to the room and see our sister. Before allowing us into the room, the nurse stops us. "In case she has woken up, temper your reactions to seeing her. Your sister fought back and has the marks proving that. They will go away, but don't let your reactions to seeing her for the first time upset her." She opens the door for us and leaves.

We step quietly into the room. She isn't awake yet. We look at each other and silently agree that now is not the time to lose it when she may wake up at any moment. We approach the bed on either side of her. I may cry later, but seeing her now enrages me. I look up to watch Quincy to see how she is handling it. From her earlier reaction I expected tears despite our silent resolve. Instead, I see the same rage I am feeling.

"She's going to be okay," I say aloud; it's more for my own benefit. I need to hear the words said out loud.

She's a mess of bruises and cuts. Her leg is elevated and immobilized. They said she fought back and fell from a roof and every inch of her black and blue skin shows that. *She is going to be okay* is my silent mantra.

"You're moving into the Brownstone," I tell Quin. I know she's going to argue, but I'm prepared.

Quincy shakes her head. "Gen, you know we can't. Our jobs are here."

"I went to see my attorney this morning. Everything is being taken care of regarding Dad's will. You'll have enough money to open the shop you want if you choose to. We have to be realistic with Stephanie, she's not going to be teaching dance classes any time soon. Hell we don't even know if she's going to be able to dance after this." I throw the harsh truth out there. "Living here she only has your elderly aunts taking care of her. In D.C., she'll have one of us home constantly to watch out for her and we can hire someone else to help. We'll find the best therapy money can buy to get her back on her feet, and it'll be easier to do that there."

"This doesn't need to be discussed now," Lucas interjects from behind us. He looks at Stephanie and a tick starts in his jaw. "There will be a time and place to do this, but it's not here and it's not now."

We sit together quietly, staring at Stephanie as she sleeps. Every so often, she makes a face as if she's in pain. I'm not sure if she is physically in pain or experiencing a dream of the attack.

The others begin to arrive. They take our lead and remain quiet while finding seats. Aryan and Dexter aren't back yet and no one has heard from them. I have no appetite so I ignore my food until Luc starts cutting it up and feeding it to me regardless of my weak attempts at protesting.

A nurse comes in to check her vitals. Stephanie begins to groan from the bed. I jump up and rush to her side to see what the nurse is doing.

"What are you doing?" I accuse.

"She's coming to on her own. I'm going to administer some pain medication to make her more comfortable. If she fully wakes up, she won't be for long."

The nurse leaves the room and everyone else gathers around the bed, anxious to see her awake. We'll probably scare her hovering like this, but we all want to be right here for her.

A line creases between her eyebrows moments before her eyes finally open. Her eyes flare when she looks around in confusion.

I put my hand on top of hers to get her attention. "Hey, baby sis, you are okay. We're in the hospital. Everything is going to be fine." Speaking slowly, I keep my tone gentle and even to reassure her. "We're all here and we're going to stay with you."

She jerks her head in an attempt to nod. Giving us a weak smile, her eyes slowly drift closed; she's asleep again.

Next time she wakes up, hopefully, she'll be able to talk to us.

Behind us, the door opens. Aryan steps into the room by himself. I glance at the clock on the wall and am shocked to see that six hours have passed since he and Dexter left. Crossing to us, he looks at Stephanie. He touches the leg that isn't injured and leans over to speak to her sleeping form.

"We got him, little girl."

I gasp in shock when I hear him. My eyes string with tears. Putting his finger to his lips, he signals us to follow him so he can tell us what happened without disturbing Stephanie.

"We went right to the station, which isn't far from here. There have been six other attacks in the past few weeks. They didn't release the information to the public; they wanted to avoid public hysteria. Steph is the first to have gotten away" He scrubs his hands over his face. "I don't agree with that decision. They had an entire office space dedicated to these cases. We started pouring over everything they had. Dex worked like a man possessed. Ten minutes in, he found the pattern in the cases. I've never seen him so fixated and I've been with him in situations that required complete and total focus or you might as well standup and ask for the bullet in your head."

"What pattern?" Tara asks him to get him back on track.

"The police were focused on finding a common link between the victims besides them all being women and dying in the same fashion. There wasn't one; the selection of victims was as random as it could get. The pattern was location of the crime. Each body had been dumped in a new location, but Dex noticed that the bodies all had tar somewhere on them. We know Stephanie was taken to a roof so we know he had a common location. The next thing was dates. When you looked at each date, though different weeks, each crime was committed on the following day: first was Monday then the next week Tuesday and so on. Serial killers don't break patterns once they've established one they're comfortable with. So we knew that since she got away from him he was likely going to try and find another victim if he hadn't already."

I used to love watching Law & Order, but after actually experiencing something like this, I'll never be able to watch it again without wanting to cry.

"We went out on a limb based off of the dump sites and went checking roof tops for evidence with the detectives assigned to the case. When we reached the area we wanted to look, we split up to cover more roofs faster. Dexter found him and his next victim."

"Oh, god. Is the other woman okay?" Hailey asks, leaning back into Micah for support.

"She's going to be okay, she was just knocked around a little bit. She and Dex are downstairs being treated now."

"What happened to Dex?" I start to panic.

"He's fine, Sis. He's just getting his hand stitched up. He returned the favor for what he did to Steph before calling back up to arrest him."

I relax again. My smile is watery. "I could kiss him for what he did."

"No, you couldn't." I put my hand over Lucas's mouth and shake my head in exasperation. For the first time tonight everyone laughs. She's going to be okay and the sick son of a bitch was caught. We needed a laugh

Chapter Seventeen

Stephanie stayed in the hospital for a week before the doctor finally cleared her to go home. The entire week we were there Steph never lacked visitors. Our grandparents came daily, Gram fussed incessantly, Pop made demands for everything under the sun until Quin and I could save the nursing staff. The Westley family has been benefactors to most major hospitals in the Baltimore-Washington metropolitan area for close to sixty years when my great grandmother first developed breast cancer. With Grand-Pops connections, Stephanie received the best medical care and was setup with the top rehabilitation specialists in the area.

Four days into the hospital stay The Aunts, as we call them, converged on the hospital. The rowdiest group of women I have ever seen and that's saying something since I've seen Gram's "crocheting club". They were the Golden Girls multiplied by two and actual sisters. I'm still not sure I can say who is who. I'm pretty sure Aunt PJ, as she asked to be called, is the tiny one that pinched the doctor on the butt when he came to check on Stephanie, or that may have been Auntie M? No, that's not right. Auntie M is the one always cleaning everything. Aunt PJ reminds me of Tara and doesn't take crap from anyone. Now I remember! It was definitely Aunt Ger, she winked at me when she caught me looking then asked me if I ever got a chance to read that Fifty Shades book. I can't say that I have, which I'm glad for because I'm not sure I was up for that conversation. Aunt Elaine, Gina, and Adele round out The Aunts.

Gram and Pop were there when they arrived. I'm not sure what I expected for our first encounter as a combined family unit, a show down may have been a part of my over dramatized imaginings. That never came to pass thank goodness. The Aunts are a warm, loving, kind family and a clear indication of where Quincy and Stephanie get their dispositions. They adopted us Westleys into their family and treated Gram and Pop like treasured parents.

After a unanimous vote by the group for Quincy and Stephanie to move into the Brownstone, which was then backed by The Aunts, my sisters moved in with me and the girls. The Aunts want my sisters to get to know our side of the family and were gracious enough to support the move; of course an open invitation was extended for them to visit whenever they please. The move went smoothly, especially with all of the guys taking two days to handle it while we were still in the hospital.

I kept the information I learned about my parents from the attorney to myself. I don't think it was something any of us should have found out. It would cause the others unnecessary pain and poses more questions than answers it could provide. I do plan to eventually take a more in depth look into mental illnesses and personality disorders and see if I can discuss with my grandfather on providing funding for facilities and research.

After a quick google search, I was able to find out the symptoms of Borderline personality disorder and Narcissistic personality disorder. They were all there in some way or another. As a child I wouldn't have noticed, and as I got older I never felt any affection towards my mother so I would not have even looked for any of the signs or symptoms of an issue. I could always ask the Freemont side of my family to see if there is a family history, but I haven't seen them since the funeral. No great loss to me though; they were as cold and uppity as my mother.

Spring warmed up quickly. The weeks since my sisters moved in were very busy. Aryan kept us informed with information he found out about Stephanie's attack and Steph filled in the blanks on her end. Her attacker was convinced that he was recreating an occult ceremony that had specific sacrifice requirements. When he attacked her in the alley, he knocked her unconscious before dragging her up to the roof top. Before he could begin the ceremony, she regained consciousness and was able to make it to the side of the roof and jump off into a dumpster. When she jumped, her attacker got a hold of enough of her hair not to stop the fall but change her trajectory, causing her leg to catch the side of the dumpster and break her leg.

Stephanie hasn't brought up dancing and I don't think anyone else is willing to broach the subject of how this is going to affect her future. After that night in the hospital, Dexter disappeared. Aryan said he's on an assignment and unable to contact us. I hope that's true and they aren't hiding that he had more injuries to recover from. I still want to thank him for what he did since I wasn't able to that night. He was in the room for two minutes at most only to check on Stephanie quickly before leaving.

In the four weeks that have passed Lucas has been back and forth between the East and West coast. He's beginning to show the signs of jet lag. He spends more time on the west coast handling whatever this issue is, but he comes back home every chance he gets. On one trip back to the east coast, he took me with him for two days to New

York City to attend a charity function. The man sure knows how to wear a tux.

Besides not being with Lucas there have been other down sides. The paparazzi have been flocking outside my front door to catch pictures of me. The media has been in a frenzy over Lucas's harem on the east coast, which is what they're calling the Brownstone and the girls. His movements on the west coast are tracked as well, littering the television with pictures of him and Lissandria at various functions and out eating. Speculation is flying about his relationship status and his coast to coast activities.

I've gone with him twice to New York City now for business trips, yet he hasn't asked once if I'd like to go with him to Los Angeles. Like a moth to the flame, despite not wanting to see the pictures every night that he's not with me, I turn on the T.V. and see what the new photographs and rumors are. I haven't asked him about what is going on and he hasn't told me.

With so much time on my hands now, free time that I never minded having, I have finished all of the pictures needed for my show in a few days and all of my commissions. I finally answered a phone call from Chelsea, my agent, with my news. She's floating on cloud nine and finishing up all of the final arrangements. I've decided not to take any more commissions and focus on what I want to paint. I was shocked that Chelsea did not argue with that.

All of the other guys have regularly stopped over to check on us with the obvious exception of Dex. Maddox almost lives here; he spends so much time in our kitchen and hanging with girls.

It's as if I only have to think of him and he appears. Maddox pops his head in to my studio and scans the room looking for me.

"Hey there you beautiful busy bee. Ready to come out of your lonely hive and interact with everyone? We've missed you at dinner the past few nights." He accuses me like I've done something wrong. "Tara is making pancakes for breakfast, and there's a stack with your name on it." He cajoles me like a five year old. He can be so amusing.

I admit when Luc is gone I'm not very sociable.

"You're right. I'll be there as soon as I clean up and change."

I rush through everything to get down to the kitchen before the pancakes get cold. I walk in and stop in my tracks. I'm not sure why anything surprises me anymore.

"Maddox, what are you doing sitting on top of the island?" I almost hesitate to ask.

"I found my spot." He continues to eat his pancakes sitting Indian style in the middle of the island.

"What do you mean your spot?" I still can't believe I'm having a conversation about this. Isn't not sitting on the counter something you learn when you are five or six?

"You know what I'm talking about, Sheldon Cooper, Big Bang Theory. This is my spot. My zero, zero, zero." He looks up briefly but remains focused on shoveling pancakes in his mouth.

I continue into the room. "Zero."

"What's that?" He finally looks up and gives me his attention.

"You forgot the time parameter. It's zero, zero, zero, zero," I state matter-of-factly.

Grinning broadly, he winks at me. "See! I knew you would know what I was talking about."

Rolling my eyes, I say, "Regardless, get your butt off of the counter. Food goes up there." I sit down at the plate of pancakes I'm assuming was made for me.

"Relax Gen, that ass is just as edible as any piece of food we've ever set on it. If you don't agree you have spent entirely too much time moping about for Luc." Tara tosses me a banana since she knows I love to slice them over my pancakes.

"Has Steph eaten yet this morning?" I ask Hailey who's sitting next to me.

"She's coming in now."

I turn and watch Stephanie come into the room on her crutches. She's moving around much better on them. The bruising is healing and has already begun to fade. The others are watching a little more discreetly in case she needs any help. Steph hates when we jump to help her. She wants to maintain her independence, which I understand as long as she doesn't overdo it.

Alright, that's one sister, where's the other?

"Where's Quin this morning?" I ask but no one is answering me.

"Well?" I question again.

"You'll see, grasshopper. By the time you're done eating she will be back and you will bow to your sensei." Maddox uses a very poor Chinese accent.

"You are not my Miyagi. You're closer to a hemorrhoid," I jokingly snarl at him.

"Ooo. Then I'll be sure to burn you later," he says sunnily.

"Really? Can you two not discuss something so gross while we're eating breakfast?" Hailey pushes her plate away.

Before I can retort, I see Maddox leap off the island and is across the room, sweeping Stephanie into his arms.

"Put me down! I only wobbled a little," she hisses between clenched teeth.

"Quiet. Let me take the small pleasures where I can. I'm here every day surrounded by beautiful woman and not one of you has been nice enough to make use of my body." He sighs forlornly. "I may as well just stop putting in the effort to maintain my gloriously well-defined muscles."

Setting Steph in her seat, he takes a step back and lifts his shirt to flash us, waving his hand in front of his abs like he's showcasing them.

"Since you clearly aren't being appreciated by us, does that mean you'll spend more time home eating from your own refrigerator?" Tara asks sweetly with a fake smile.

"No can do, lady bug." He flashes us another one of his famous grins.

"And why is that?" Hailey asks, getting suspicious.

"I can't just be here because I enjoy seeing my ladies so much?"

"No," we all say in unison while smiling at each other.

"I'll tell one of you why I'm here, but that's it. Only one," he offers.

"That's a no brainer. Maddox Grant whispering in my ear. I'm your girl." Tara steps forward. "Take your time, enunciate carefully, and don't be afraid to use a little tongue."

I love her. I adore her brazen sexuality. I watch Maddox whisper in her ear. Thankfully he didn't take her advice about tongue. Thirty seconds into his explanation and Tara is grinning from ear to ear.

"Oh he's definitely staying, and no, I am not tell any of you why." She turns around to grab her plate of pancakes and sits down to eat.

The front door slams open.

Quincy starts ranting with each step through the house.

"Seriously, that place was swamped. If this does not cheer her up like you promised me it would I will pour it down her throat until she tells me it's the best thing she's ever had. I stood in line for over thirty minutes and forget about traffic around here." Quin stomps up to me and pushes a Starbucks cup at me.

"Enjoy." She starts handing out everyone else's cups.

Oh happy days. I can already smell the aroma of the chai tea latte. I love tea but there is something about a Starbucks chai tea latte that makes has obsessed with it. I had to cut down on my Starbucks intake. After buying so many every day to achieve a gold membership status, I began having withdrawals I was so addicted. The first sip with the foam and steam is always the best.

"So good," I moan in delight.

"Well now that we know what Gen looks like having an orgasm let's all sit down together for once." Quincy bumps hips with me as she passes, sipping reverently at her own cup.

"We all need to go out tonight," Tara announces to the group.

"What? No, we can't," I start.

"Yes, you can and you will," Steph interrupts. "You have all been hovering over me, and to be honest I need the peace. So go out, have fun, and stop moping." The last point was directed at me. "It's not like I would be going with you anyway. I'm only turning nineteen so I couldn't go even if I was physically able." Her look challenges me to argue with her.

I relent.

"Fine, we'll go out but you have to promise not to do too much. You can't risk falling and getting hurt with no one home, and since you refuse to have a home aide, I really mean business." I point my finger at her; that's the universal sign of I mean it, right?

"Of course. I'll sit on the couch and vegetate until I know you're all home safe and not wandering drunk around the city." She has a bit of mother hen in her, too.

The doorbell chimes grabbing all of our attention, yet no one moves to get it.

"Maddox sweetie, do you think you could get the door for us? We're all still eating," Hailey asks politely.

"Sure, I know when I'm being pushed out for a quick girl pow-wow." He leaves to get the door.

"Gen." Hailey brings my attention back to her and the girls. "We want you to know that we love you and understand you are going through a lot of changes right now. We know that you miss Luc and that all of those cameras outside aren't helping matters. Most importantly we want you to know we're all here for you."

I get choked up. Seriously, how could I not with them all giving me their support and love. Surrounded by them and having them all look at me with understanding and love in their eyes, I let a few tears slide.

"You all mean so much to me." I look at Hailey and Tara. "You two have always been my best friends and the sisters I always wished I had." I grab Quin and Steph's hands. "You two *are* the sisters I always wanted and in a short period of time have come to mean so much to me." I give them all a smile filled with love and affection. "It has been a lot lately. It's crazy how all of these changes have happened so fast, but it's all been the best changes in my life. I feel like I'm tackling ten years' worth of changes in just a few months. I'm in love with Lucas but all of this traveling and media crap weighs on me. We've broken so many barriers in each other but haven't even scratched the surface of this one." I sigh. "I don't know what to do."

"You go out with us. Get your mind off that Lissandria bitch and shake your drunk ass on a dance floor like you're getting paid to do it and need to make rent money, honey." Tara jumps up and starts shaking her butt at me.

We all start laughing.

"Seriously though bitch, we love you. If Lucas comes home with some shit that he's going back to that little pop singing whore whose album I so totally do not own." Out of the side of her mouth, she whispers to Hailey, "Remind me to throw that out later." I shake my head. "Where was I? If he does that we'll jump him until we beat some sense into him then track that skinny bitch and give her a beat down. Sound good, homie? We'll whip her bloody arse, just like in that fight I saw in London when I was five."

Ladies and gentleman the only woman alive that can pull off two different language slangs in one speech.

"Sounds good. I'm glad we're going out tonight. I need this, just don't let me drink as much as last time."

"You have to do a shot with me," Quincy tells me. "You missed my twenty first birthday and it is my first time out with my big sister. I thought it would take some time getting used to the idea of that, but you're so great I'm cool with relinquishing the title of oldest sister. I get to be the middle child without the middle child issues," she jokes with us.

"I can't wait to turn twenty one. I want to see Micah's club *Eloá*." Steph pouts adorably.

"What do you know about Micah's club?" Quincy asks her.

"Only what he told me. He built it from the ground up. His grandmother gave him an old run down building on the verge of being condemned and he remade it into his club. The name is so cool. He named it after the angel of sorrow born from Jesus' tears over the grave of Lazarus. She tried to reconcile Lucifer's relationship with God but instead he seduced her and escorted her to Hell to keep her with him." She lowers her voice. "When he told me the story about the angel you could tell it really meant something to him."

That is a great story. I wonder how he learned of it. Maddox finally comes back carrying a large bouquet of lilies. I don't need to ask this time who they are from. They're stargazer lilies, my favorite flower.

"It took you that long to get flowers from the delivery guy?" I razz him.

"Nope. I put these bad boys down and went pee before coming back. I even remembered to wash my hands this time!"

I get up and go over to my flowers to read the card.

Be ready tomorrow night at seven. L.

Be ready for what?

Maddox comes back into the kitchen carrying a stack of wrapped packages. I didn't even notice him leave again.

"For you." He presents the boxes with flourish.

"Oh no. What did he do?" I whisper, and start opening box after box.

Inside I find a gorgeous red dress with no back, a pair of high heels, and a diamond necklace, bracelet, and earrings. I peek into the last box, guessing what it is and know I don't want to open it in front of Maddox. I get a glimpse of black lace. I can feel my cheeks turning pink.

"Lucky, lucky girl." Tara picks up a shoe to see if it's a size she can fit into.

"I can't believe he did all of this. I had no idea he was coming home so soon. He didn't say anything."

Maddox throws his arm over my shoulder, "Who cares? Have fun. Take my boy for all he's got, and believe me, he's got plenty."

I elbow him in the ribs and shrug off his arm.

The doorbell rings again.

I groan. "Please tell me he didn't get me anything else."

Maddox sighs dramatically when no one moves. "I'll go grab the door. Again."

"Do you think he's going to pop the question?" Stephanie asks excitedly.

"No, no way. It's too soon for that," I assure her.

I look up from feeling the silky fabric of the dress. All of the girls are giving me looks like I'm crazy.

"It is," I insist.

"You know, Gen, you never told us what happened when you told Luc you didn't remember meeting him. Did he try and jog your memory with sex?" Tara laughs at her own joke.

"Shush. I don't want Maddox to hear you. I haven't told him yet. I haven't found the right time."

"Now would be a good time."

My skin goose bumps and my back goes ram rod straight. I take my time turning around. Lucas is leaning against the doorjamb with his arms crossed over his chest. His face is set in hard lines of anger and his eyes are dark, almost pewter in color.

"Lucas. I didn't know you were standing there. I mean-" I stumble over my words in shock. "I don't know what to say." My voice shakes. I can feel his anger like it's a physical being.

His relaxed pose vanishes and he stands straight. "Clearly. So when were you going to tell me? Were you going to tell me?"

"Yes, of course! I just never got the chance. Can we please go somewhere private and talk?" I plead.

"Funny, I can think of more than a few different occasions that night came up. There were plenty of chances, Genevieve." He turns on his heel and walks away.

He can't leave like this. I chase after him and catch up to him in the foyer.

"Lucas, let's talk. Please just let me explain," I beg, stopping in front of him.

He looks at my face. His eyes turn sad. "I mentioned that night to you so many times. I told you over and over again how much it meant to me meeting you that night. All the while I'm thinking we shared something special." He brings his fingers up to caress the side of my face. "But it meant nothing to you." I close my eyes, feeling the pain in his voice. He drops his hand away from my face and takes a step back. "I'm going to go for now. I'm angry and I need to leave before I say something I'll regret saying once the anger passes."

He opens the door.

"You'll be back after you can look at me again without hating me, right?" My words are filled with my own pain and anger directed at myself.

He closes the door again and comes back to me. Grabbing my face between his palms, he kisses me. Every emotion is in this kiss; it's not a kiss of desire, it's an expression telling me more than words ever could.

He pulls away, dropping his hands from my face.

"I don't hate you, Genevieve. I'm feeling a lot of things but hate is not one of them." He turns back to the door, but I stop him again.

"You are coming back," I tell him. It's not a question I'm not giving him the option.

He gets my message loud and clear. He nods his head at me and leaves.

I don't know how long I stand there staring at the door. Hours could have passed, it may have only been seconds even. He is right. I had opportunity after opportunity but I kept it to myself. I didn't want to hurt him but I did any way and even more than if I had said something from the beginning.

Arms wrap around me. I let myself be cocooned by the girls' hug. Numbly I let them lead me back to the kitchen.

"I am so sorry, Gen. More sorry than I have ever been in my life."

"It's not your fault, Tar. It's mine." My voice sounds empty even to my own ears.

I look up and lock eyes with Maddox who is standing across the island from where the girls pushed me onto the chair.

"Any brilliant pearls of wisdom you want to offer?" When an emotion finally enters my voice, it is self-pity.

He leans on his elbows across the island to look me in the eyes.

"Did you do it because you knew it would hurt him? Did you laugh about it behind his back when he told you how he felt about that night?"

"Never!" I snap angrily. "I would never do that. I didn't want to hurt him. I knew what it meant to him and I couldn't bear the thought of tarnishing that." By the end I lay my face in my hands and sob.

"Gen." Maddox is around the island now pulling my hands from my face. "That is all you need to hang on to. You didn't want to hurt him. He's a big boy. He can take the time and sort out what he's feeling. He'll see that when he calms down. You were only trying to protect him because you care." His voice is soothing.

"I don't just care. I love him. What if he leaves me for Lissandria?" The ache in my voice in unmistakable, the thought is there in my head in the fore front now.

Maddox grabs my shoulders and gives me a little shake. "Don't say something so stupid again. I know a way to get him back here in a flash." He grins at me

"How?"

"Sit on my lap. We'll take a picture and send it to him and he'll be here before you know it."

I laugh weakly at him.

"Why do you think that?" I can't help but ask his reasoning.

"Because I have what women want." He holds his arms out from his sides.

I give him a quick inspection along with the other girls.

"Nice arms?" I start, and the girls follow with their own suggestions.

"Great hair?"

"Wash board abs?"

"Dimples?"

"Nothing I can see, so it has to be a huge cock."

"Yes ladies, thank you, I do have all of that but I was referring to my swoon worthy dark eyes you can lose time staring into." He flutters his lashes comically and then hold his eyes open wide. He pulls a smile from me. He gets serious again. "I know you aren't going to like this suggestion but don't cancel your plans. Go out tonight with the girls. You need it. I'll call the guys and see who can go over Lucky's. Tomorrow you two will both have had some time to think and can talk it out then."

I look around at everyone watching me. I know it's no use arguing; there's no winning when they gang up on you.

I nod my agreement.

"I'm going to run you a nice hot bubble bath." Hailey rubs my shoulders. "Tara you work on making her tea. Quin put together some finger foods. She needs a snack for after her soak. Steph you go to the den and grab a book from the shelf. Something romantic with a happily ever after. Maddox you help her carry whatever books she picks out. Gen, go upstairs and strip down and put on that super comfy robe Gram gave you for Christmas. I'll let you know when the tub is ready for you.

They pampered me within an inch of making me feel like a prized show dog getting ready for competition. When Hailey told Steph to get me a romance novel with a happy ending I was skeptical that I would want to read that while my own relationship was spinning around the toilet bowl. It helped though. She's the master at knowing what someone needs when they don't know themselves. I'm going to get my happily ever after.

I'm going to go out with them tonight, but I'm putting my foot down at going to a rowdy club. Something low key without a crowd of people preferably.

A limo pulls in front of the Brownstone to pick us up.

"Who's paying for a limo?" I ask. I don't want them going all out for this.

"No one. It's Micah's limo. He insisted that we use it," Hailey tells me without glancing up from the text message she's working on.

"We're not going there. I can't do there tonight." I start to panic; that's where all of this started.

"No, we aren't going there. Did you seriously think we would do that to you?" Hail gives me "The Look". "You'll like this place. It's a bar and trust me when I say no one will bother us."

"Am I the only one still seeing dots from all of those camera flashes?" Quin is blinking her eyes rapidly.

The paparazzi were out in force tonight. I'm sure because of Lucas being on this side of the country and having been to our house earlier.

"Did you hear the speculation that Lucas and Maddox are sharing us and that we may or may not have wild orgies?" Tara's eyes are bright with humor. "When we get home we should act intoxicated and pretend to play rock paper scissors over who gets which guy tonight. I'm hoping we don't have to act the intoxicated part and we really are!"

"I have an idea." I start pouring glasses of champagne from the chilled bucket and pass them out. We'll start working on Tara's plan for intoxication. "I want to propose a toast. To friends that you can't imagine life without. To sisters that built a strong solid bond, by choice, and to finding the man that you know is The One, taking the bumps in the road and fighting for that happily ever after with no end."

The girls cheer and clink their glasses to mine before we down the champagne. I'm sure knowing Micah it was ridiculously expensive and not meant to be tossed back like a shot, but there's a time and place for classy and that's not here and not now.

"I'm last to join the group. I know I don't know all of the facts, but I do know you'll get your happiness. You're too tough to let this knock you down." Quincy leans across the limo to give me a hug.

"I agree. Hailey and I have known you *forever*. You have changed so much lately. It's like watching a butterfly breaking out of its cocoon. I'm proud of you. It's like watching our little girl grow up, right Hail?" Tara nudges Hailey who's nodding.

"Gee girls. Don't make me cry! Tara loaded my lashes in mascara." My heart is still heavy but they've done wonders for lightening my mood.

The limo stops in front of a bar with a brick façade. The sign reads Bottoms Up. There's no crowd outside or a line to get in. We climb out of the limo and file in. I stop just inside the doorway behind the other girls.

"Is this what I think it is?" I whisper to Tara.

"Oh yeah. Hail told you no one will bother you here." She smirks.

They brought me to a gay bar. I don't see any other women in here. I do see that most of the patrons are staring at us. They must think we're lost.

"Do you ladies need directions?" The bartenders asks with a genuine look of concern, thus confirming my thoughts.

Tara marches forward, putting her clutch on the bar. "We're exactly where we want to be." She smiles and sweeps the bar giving all of the guys her best smile. "Gentlemen, my friend here had a rough day in the love department. Think you fellas are up to the challenge of giving her some confidence to get back on the ride?"

A variety of wolf calls and "oh honeys" sound from around the bar. They've accepted the challenge. I should have mentioned to Tara the part of me wanting to stay low key.

"Gen!"

I hear my name being called and look around. Out of the corner of my eye I see movement coming towards me.

"Gen, oh my god! What are you doing here?" Brad pushes forward and embraces me.

"Brad, what are you doing here?" I'm shocked to see him.

"Really? I thought we covered that the last time we tried to have dinner." He gives me a friendly squeeze.

"Oh right," I laugh. "I'm in a gay bar. I forgot for a minute. Don't tell anyone but this is my first time."

"I won't say a word, but I will say it's obvious. Now answer my question. Why are *you* here?" He smiles down at me affectionately.

Kind of feels weird to talk to a kind of sort of ex about your new relationship, even if the kind of sort of ex is gay. "My boyfriend and I hit a rough patch today. So the girls are taking my mind off of it and making sure we don't have to worry about guys hitting on us." I decide tell him anyway.

"New boyfriend, huh? Good for you. I'm so sorry you had a bad day today but I'm happy you found someone. I was a little worried I hurt you. So I'm relieved to hear you've moved on. Who is the lucky guy? Any of your friends from your art circles?" He smiles expectantly at me like he's really interested in my reply. He must have had a few drinks already.

"You mean you haven't heard or seen the television?" I ask him a little skeptically.

"What do you mean?"

I point to the T.V. over my shoulder that has the same gossip channel on that is always airing the pictures of Lucas and me. I'm sure tonight isn't any different, especially if the photographers got new stuff today.

I get to watch his reaction when he sees the show flashing the pictures across the screen.

"Oh, mama. You are one lucky lady. You landed a big fish." He's still watching.

"No, I won't see if he needs another attorney." I didn't pay attention too much when I dated him, but it doesn't take a genius to know Brad landing a client like Lucas would open up the partnership door before they would finish shaking hands.

He finally looks at me again. "Fine, I won't beg since I still feel guilty about that situation we had."

I nod my head and accept the drink Hailey is offering me. Tara and Quin are playing darts with a few guys. From the sound of it they're exchanging fashion pointers.

The night passes quickly, Brad eventually wandered back to his group after our last exchange. It's was a rather boring seeing-the-ex-in-public experience. You always hear these dramatic stories and it definitely didn't live up to that expectation. It was good for me to see him and realize I never actually had any sort of feelings for him one way or another. He was just there to kind of pass my time with. The girls and I had a lot of fun with the boisterous crowd at the bar. The drinks were mixed to perfection, the music was perfect, and we got to dance with each other and not have to worry about grabby hands. Lucas was always in the back of my mind. I wonder what he's doing, if the guys are doing as great of a job taking his mind off things as my girls are, and I wonder if he's thinking about me, too.

When we got home I am too exhausted to deal with anything and just take everything off and crawl into bed. I look at the screen of my phone, staring, willing it with my mind to flash with a message from Luc. He hasn't tried to contact me at all. I type a quick message and waiver about whether or not I should send it. I click send and stare at the screen until I fall asleep.

I love you. <3 Your Minx

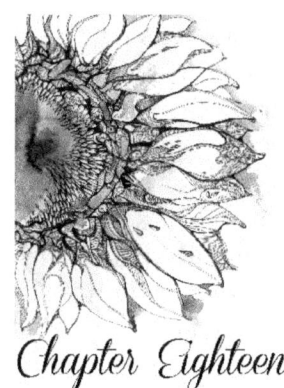

Chapter Eighteen

I wake up to my room filled with sunlight again. This time I'm not hung over. I fumble for my phone. No messages. The time says two thirty in the afternoon. Most of the day has passed already. He didn't even answer my text. My eyes sting with fresh tears. Taking a deep breath, in and out, I calm myself. He left upset yesterday, not angry. We'll work it out.

He always asks me to trust him. I will. I rush my morning routine. It's actually becoming more of a habit for me to rush my shower, brush my teeth, and pull my hair back in ten minutes flat. I'm out of the front door and in my car before anyone stops me. The drive to my favorite salon; it only takes a few minutes since it's within walking distance. They know me and take me back right away.

Three hours later my hair is styled and my nails are buffed and polished. I even had them apply some make up. Back home I dart up to my bedroom. I don't want to talk to anyone yet. I find the boxes Luc sent over and put everything on.

I stare at myself in the full length mirror. I love it. I can imagine Lucas picking out everything, ensuring that it's all just right. The diamonds sparkle in the light and are very tasteful. The dress clings to every curve, its silky sift fabric a whisper against my skin. I have long legs but the heels he bought make them go on seemingly for miles.

I smile to myself when I think about the lace panties, bra, garters, and thigh highs. I've never worn anything like this. The lace against my nipples makes them hard. Taking in the whole image again, I hope it's all that he imagined when he purchased everything. My phone that is plugged into the charger, for once, sounds the alarm I set so that I'm not late going downstairs.

As usual, everyone is gathered in the kitchen.

"I'm going lesbian," Tara calls out.

"Contemplating incest," Steph yells, then whistles at me.

I do a little twirl and stick my leg out for their viewing pleasure.

"I take it you and Luc kissed and made up?" Hailey smiles at me.

"Actually no. Not yet." I shimmy onto a stool at the island.

"Okay, but at least you're talking and still going out tonight," Quincy supplies.

"No again," I sigh. "We haven't talked yet. He actually hasn't answered the text message I sent him but he told me before that I needed to learn how to trust him and that he would never hurt me. So he sent this beautiful outfit and told me to be ready by seven. Here I am, I'm ready, and put it all out there to trust him." I smooth my hands down the skirt of the dress so that it doesn't wrinkle.

I'm doing the right thing. I know I am.

"Good for you honey. You haven't trusted a man ever. If you have faith then we have faith." Hailey's smile reassures me.

We all talk while they cook dinner. Hailey is almost done with her latest manuscript. Tara was offered another assignment that she is not sure she wants to take. Stephanie doesn't add much, she won't discuss what happened or her future. She's not ready yet. Quin decided to sign up for online college courses while she figures out what she wants to do with her career as a tattoo artist. I'm so glad I was able to make that possible for her. The conversation takes my mind off my nerves over seeing Lucas.

"Ladies, ladies ladies. Is dinner ready?" Maddox walks in rubbing his hands together greedily. "Holy tabasco sauce, Genni girl. You are looking hotter than a habanero pepper."

I glance at the clock and do a double take. Over an hour has passed and Luc still isn't here.

Maddox takes out his phone and snaps a picture of me before I can protest.

"Hey! What are you doing?" I cry.

"Gross Mad, it's so not cool to do extracurricular activities to a picture of your boy's woman," Tara jokes.

"Shut it. I'm just sending it to Lucky so that he can be jealous I get to see his lady like this and he doesn't." He looks up grinning after sending his text. His grin freezes when he sees my face.

All happiness falls from my face. I feel like I've just been hit with a two by four. I try to paste a smile on my face but it's brittle at best.

"Well." I don't know what to say.

I do my best to maintain my composure and what little dignity that isn't badly bruised and try to leave the room as quickly as possible. I skirt around Maddox, avoiding his hands when he tries to stop me, and tune out the girls calling after me.

I make it up the stairs with only a few stumbles. Apparently my dignity isn't done being beaten on for tonight.

When I reach my room, I kick off the high heels and tear everything else he bought from my body. Dumping my bag onto the floor, I scatter the contents looking for my phone.

Snatching it from the clutter, I type furiously and send my text message.

I trusted you.

That is really all that needs to be said. He asked for it and when I finally gave it he did not hold up his end. Was it too little too late?

I know the girls are there before I hear the knock on the door frame. I'm naked, kneeling in the debris from my purse, white knuckling my cellphone. I wouldn't be surprised if they're questioning my sanity at this moment.

Bubble baths, tea, and romance novels aren't going to cut it this time.

I don't fight them when they silently help me into a t-shirt and shorts. When they're done I grab my phone again to check for a message.

Nothing.

I'm hurt but anger is making its way to the forefront. I messed up, I know it, but I'm not the one completely shutting him out. I get it, he's hurt, angry, and is afraid he'll say something he would regret. How impulsive is typing a text message that you can't even reply to one saying I love you?

Turning without a word, I rush past the girls again. I fly down the stairs with them on my heels. The kitchen is empty, no one bothered to eat the dinner they prepared. I turn and head to the den. Standing in the doorway I zero in on Maddox staring out of the front window.

I stomp up to him until we're toe to toe.

"Where is he?" I demand.

"Gen, I don't want to-" he starts, but I interrupt.

"If you don't want to tell me then get out." I point to the door.

Maddox doesn't react to my anger like I would have expected. His eyes are full of patience and understanding while he studies my face.

"I care about both of you. I hope you know that. I am going to leave because I know you're hurt but so is he and I won't get involved any more than I already have been." Maddox drops a quick kiss to my forehead.

He quietly leaves after saying good bye to the others and making sure Steph is comfortable on the love seat where she's been sitting for all of this.

"Is anyone else oddly surprised at how mature he just handled that?" Tara murmurs.

"I can't believe I was that big of a bitch," I mutter before walking to the couch and throwing myself down.

"If you were going to lash out you couldn't have picked a better target. He gets it, Gen. Now what are we going to do?" Quin rubs my leg soothingly while kneeling in front of me. "Do we track him down and I tattoo dumbass across his forehead? Or do we have an anti-man night and eat the entire tub of that delicious ice cream you've been hiding in the fat free containers?"

I smile. Darn it I, knew that trick wouldn't last forever.

"I don't know what to do," I admit.

"You said that you texted him. Have you tried calling? Talking to him could make a huge difference," Hail reasons. It makes sense. Maybe something came up. I want to fix this, but how can I if he isn't giving me the opportunity?

"Can we do a vote because my vote would be for the tattoo idea?" Tara grabs a throw pillow and hits Quin with it as she passes her to sit on the floor.

Every girl needs a group of friends like this; these girls are my rocks.

I call Luc's phone. It goes right to voicemail. I'm not sure what I should do. Leave a message or no? I leave one simply telling him to call me. I honestly don't know what else to say.

"I could model a character after Lucas in one of my books and kill him off in some shocking manner if you'd like," Hailey offers up after I hang up from leaving my message.

I smile and wave her comment away. I don't want to even imagine what she could come up with.

"I'd give anything to remember that night. You two were there. Do you remember *anything*?" I look back and forth between Hailey and Tara.

"Like I said before, I left early to go home. When I came to tell you, you were sitting in the corner of the V.I.P area talking. I couldn't hear anything you two may have talked about over the loud music. I wish I could tell you something," Hailey tells me apologetically.

"I can't add too much more. I can try and help with some of the timeline so that it could jog your memory. We did the shots after Hail left to find paper to write her idea down. After that we went dancing near the V.I.P. booths. Some ugly bouncer came and got us saying we were requested. When we got up there you let Luc know what you thought of his high handedness by sending security to get us. Then once he charmed you into sitting down, I chatted up the guys he was with and talked each of them into dancing with me. I wasn't around much either but I still kept you in sight just in case, because well, you never know. You two sat together talking and kept inching closer and closer until you were practically cuddled up and whispering in each other's ear." Tara stops and rubs her hand over the back of her neck, trying to remember more. "After that a bouncer came to get me and told me we were leaving. When I got to the limo you two were already there

- 268 -

and you were wearing Lucas's shirt. He said a waitress spilled a drink on your dress. Which by the way was actually my dress and I helped you take it off from under his shirt so that I could see the damage and drop it off at the cleaners the next morning." She finally takes a breath after her long winded speech.

I shake my head. None of that sounds familiar after the point of when we got on to the dance floor.

"Can we just eat ice cream and watch movies?" My question gets nods of yes all around.

Normally I would go and paint, but I don't want to paint this feeling of hopelessness. Not knowing what is going on with Luc is driving me crazy. I need to focus on something else until he calls me back or texts me.

"Steph, do you need a pillow to prop your leg up so that you can get comfortable for the movies?"

Her cheeks redden like she's embarrassed by me questioning her comfort. "Yes actually that'd be great." She doesn't look at me when she says it.

She really is stubborn. She would have sat there the whole time rather than tell one of us to get her a pillow.

After propping her leg up, Quin and Hailey return with my secret stash of ice cream. The one I had in the car when we went to the hospital didn't survive, but Luc brought me some when he came back after the first time he left.

Tara chose a selection of movies. Thankfully none were chick flicks or involved romance of any sort. They were shoot em up action movies and one horror movie that I vetoed because I know I'd sleep with my eyes open after seeing it; that's if I sleep at all tonight.

I try my best to focus on the T.V. screen but I check my phone every few minutes waiting for a reply phone call or text message.

Beep. Beep. Buzz. Ring. Beep. Buzz. Ring. Ring. Buzz.

I wake up groggily. I recognize the sound of multiple text messages coming through all of the girl's cell phones.

I grab my phone to check my own messages. Nothing.

Siting up, I push the blanket off of me to see everyone else also waking up and checking their phones. They're all reading messages. Meaning whatever the texts are, I'm the only one that didn't get them.

Quincy swears and jumps up, running to the window and whipping the curtains closed after a brief glance outside.

I rub the sleep from my eyes and stand.

"What is going on?" I look at all of them and note their nervousness.

"Gen, you should sit down so that we can talk," Tara says calmly, which in turn makes me even less calm.

Since Quin is still over by the windows I snatch up her phone from where she dropped it when she got up. Her text messages are still open.

Kaine: *Keep Gen away from the T.V.*

Kaine: *Try and keep her from the windows and going outside, too. The paparazzi are going crazy.*

I grab the remote and turn the T.V. on. The channel is the same that it usually is in our house. The celebrity gossip station.

"The Morning Cuppa with Joe 'Getting the News while you Snooze'" is on.

All color drains from me, instantly causing me to feel clammy and nauseous. I fall onto the couch sick to my stomach and reeling from what I'm seeing.

There's video footage being played of Lucas in L.A. last night. He's carrying Lissandria out of a night club and into the back seat of a limo. The angle isn't great but you can see she's clutching onto him.

He went right back to her. Everything he ever told me about being special and not hurting me runs through my mind like a movie reel. Why? That is what I want to know, no I *need* to know. Did he think I was just going to slink away quietly after he just drops me like yesterday's trash?

Through the fog in my mind, I distantly hear the talk show host say something about Lucas boarding a plane back to Virginia in the early hours of the morning.

No more text message. No more phone calls. He's going to tell me it's over to my face.

I march from the room. My frame is rigid with purpose. I throw one of my sundresses on and go back downstairs.

The other girls are there, too. All of them are dressed and helping Steph to get dressed so they can go with me.

"No." I shake my head at them.

"Gen, you aren't going there alone. Let us be there for you," Tara insists.

"You are always there for me and I can never thank any of you enough for everything," I stress, "but I have to do this alone. I'm a grown woman. If he wants to do this to me he's going to have to do it to my face like a man." I use my words to fuel my anger. "Just be here for me when I come back."

"Always." Hailey hugs me.

They each take turns hugging me, offering their love and support.

"Rip his balls out through his nose for me, okay?"
Tara growls, ever bloody thirsty.

I stride outside and hesitate briefly when the swarm
of cameras move to block my path. This time is different;
it's not just cameras. There are microphones shoved in my
face and reporters yelling questions at me.

I ignore it all and get to the safety of my car. Slowly
I pull away. I might think they're jerks, but I don't want to
run any of them over and have them sue me.

Before going to Lucas's I take a drive past the
monuments to try and gain perspective. I live in a town that
oozes the history of our nation. The ground you walk on
has seen more things and holds more wisdom than anything
you come across anywhere else. I can come down here and
just drive by and feel like it speaks to me, telling me stories
of the past. The feeling of old knowledge invokes a deep
respect inside of me. I have always wondered what stories
the tree could tell you of the past. Before I confront Luc, I
need to find my center. Going off on shaky ground only
serves to help in your fall.

Driving by isn't doing anything for me. After
parking, I walk through the Lincoln Memorial, along the
reflecting pool, to the Washington Monument, and then
back again. I'm not walking out of here with any words of
wisdom inspired by our fore fathers, nothing spoke to me
on this walk, but I found my composure. If anything, when
this is done I'll still have my dignity.

Twenty minutes later I'm pulling down his
driveway. The paparazzi sitting at the bottom snap as many
pictures as they can without crossing onto his property.
Apparently they were already made aware of what
boundaries they could and couldn't cross. I swing my car
all the way around his circular drive. I don't plan on staying
long, I don't need to hear the gritty details, just the words
ending it all.

I stand at his door, unsure of what to do. I still have the key he gave me, but I don't believe this is a situation that I should be using it in. I ring the doorbell.

Minutes pass before I hear someone on the other side fumbling with the locks. When the door finally swings open, I stare. Anger comes rushing back at this slap in the face. Looking like she just rolled out of bed and wearing one of Luc's shirts is Lissandria. I turn and flee. There's not much room for dignity when humiliation of that level is looking back at you.

I throw my car in drive and speed back down the driveway. I hate myself for doing it, but I look back using my mirror and see Lucas running out of the house after my car. If I was Tara, I'd throw it in reverse and back over him. If I was Hailey, I would have stood there with calm reserve and slapped him before leaving. I'm not sure what my sisters would do since I haven't know them that long. I, on the other hand, am not like any of them. I finally trusted someone outside of my grandparents and best friends and look at me now, driving away like a coward with my heart strapped to the tire being run over with each rotation.

I look in the mirror again and Lucas is gone. I pull over. I'm not ready to face the cameras and have them record this moment. I glance over at the passenger seat. My phone is vibrating. The screen shows that it is Luc. I swear and throw the phone onto the floor mat.

How dare him! I turn the car back around.

I go for a different approach this time. I'll use what's worked in the past. I walk around the back of the house. When I pass the window to the kitchen I can see Lucas sitting at the table with Lissandria. I continue to the back door and enter quietly. Lissandria's hand, which is rubbing Luc's back, stills when she notices me. Lucas looks up from the phone in his hand at my approach. He stands quickly, pushing the chair back a couple feet with haste.

I stop when I'm just outside of striking distance. I don't want to be tempted.

"You have some nerve after all of this to call me. Was my humiliation of having your," I search for a word while waving my hands in her direction, "whore, shoved in my face not enough for you?"

Lucas's jaw drops with shock.

"I can see what you mean when you said things are never boring with her," Lissandria muses from behind Lucas.

I step to the side so I can have an unobstructed view of her.

"Get out!" I scream at her. "I don't give a fuck whose house it is. Leave. Now!"

Out of the corner of my eye I can see Luc shake off the stunned look and the corners of his mouth kick up into a smirk.

I round on him again ready to let all of my anger spew out at him.

I'm unprepared for when he yanks me against himself and kisses me senseless. I struggle but the attempt is weak as his lips drain away the anger and replace it with longing. He can't do this to me. I finally gather the strength to push myself away from him.

"You know, Luc, you should tell her what's going on. All of it. You could have avoided this little misunderstanding." She shakes her head and begins to leave the room. She calls back over her shoulder, "I'll meet you again sometime later, Gen." Then she's gone from sight.

I focus back on Lucas, bewildered. He starts shifting his weight from side to side and rubbing the back of his neck.

"Can we sit down and talk." He gestures towards the table.

I look at him. "I made a similar request two days ago and you walked away from me."

"No, don't think that, Genevieve." His eyes plead with me. "I walked away from the situation and I've regretted it every second since."

He turns and walks to the sitting area just off the kitchen. I follow at a distance.

Sitting on the couch, he asks me to join him.

"No thanks." I sit in the arm chair diagonal from him rather than on the couch next to him where he could touch me and distract me.

"I guess I should start at the beginning so you understand what's going on and why I didn't tell you anything." He looks at me. When I don't say anything he takes a deep breath and continues. "Back when things with my career were really rolling, I was touring and doing those online classes for my degree. I almost quit. Liss had been hanging around a lot with Kenny in those days. Our tour schedules were close and within days of each other so there were plenty of stops we'd be at each other's shows hanging out back stage. When I thought about dropping out of college when I was so close to finishing, Liss was the one to slap me on the back of my head and tell me to shut up and do it. Being who we were, my education goals didn't get much support, but she gave it to me when I needed it most. You can understand that, right? Why I would value someone in my life so much for doing that for me?" He searches my gaze for understanding.

I nod my head. I'm not sure if I do, but I need him to continue.

He looks back down at his hands before continuing. "Like I said, she was really close to Kenny so she was around that shit he always kept near. Not the heroin but everything else. She got addicted to it. When the band broke up and I started my company, her addiction got out of hand and her label dropped her. I picked her up and made an agreement that the details of what really happened not be made public. So there I was with a new label of my own and one of my first artists was a good friend but also a drug addict. I wasn't even sure how I was going to handle this situation. I didn't have to. She came to me and asked for help kicking the drugs."

He slides down the couch until he's within reach and cradles my hands between his own.

"I got her the best treatment available because of her career and the fact we wanted to keep it on the hush. I began escorting her to every event and ceremony. The media didn't waste time with slapping a label on us as a couple, and we didn't bother to correct them. When she was clean for a year, I took her to Disney Land for her first time as a sort of celebration. I stopped going to every event with her, but we are still close friends so we would often go with each other to functions. We were never ever anything more than friends. I need you to know that." He stresses each word.

"Okay." I nod my head again. "What about now?" I need to know what has been going on now.

He looks unsure again. "I'm going to tell you what I can. I won't tell you Liss' history, even with her approval. It's her story to tell to people she chooses. Something happened involving her past and for whatever reason instead of talking to anybody, she tried handling all on her own. When the stress became too much she picked up some of her old habits. Her manager at the time didn't tell anyone what was going on. Once I found out I talked to Liss to figure out what was going on and replaced her manager with one I trusted."

I can feel his hands tighten on my own with the tension entering his body.

"Once Nick, the new manager, started reporting back what was going on, it was so much worse than I initially thought. Even worse than the last time she was addicted. Her behavior was becoming erratic and unpredictable. I was on full damage control and doing everything possible to keep things quiet and under control."

He jumps up and starts pacing.

"I fucked up on both fronts, Gen. When I was here with you, I was busy with everything in L.A., keeping you out, and causing you to think that you aren't the most important person in the world to me. When I was in L.A. I wasn't giving the situation my complete focus because I wanted to be here with you instead. Last time I went everywhere with her. This time I tried to split my time and focus. Everything went to shit." He runs his fingers through his hair in agitation.

"I agree. You did mess up," I say. I can't argue with a sound observation. I do feel better knowing the other side of the story. I just wish he told me from the beginning and trusted me to be there for him.

His shoulders slump and he sits back down. I get up and take a seat next to him.

"You tried to do everything by yourself. Instead of treating me like a partner in this relationship, you kept me in the dark and had me agonizing over what could have been going on. You asked me for trust and made it as difficult as possible to give. I did though. I put myself out there, trusting you'd pick me up at seven so that we could fix what I know I messed up. You have no idea how badly it hurt when I realized you weren't coming. You didn't even call or text me back. You let me wake up this morning, see the reports, and have the reporters bombard me." My hands are shaking by the time I'm done ranting at him. I can feel my throat tighten as I try to choke back tears.

"I know, Gen." He holds my hands still. "I knew it the second I left that day. I was hurting and angry. Most of all I hated myself. That's why I didn't call or text you. Not because of what you did but because of what I did. You deserved better than that"

I don't understand what he's talking about. "What do you mean?" I'm lost now and need to get on the same page as him.

"I walked away. Just like I walked away from my parents and just like when I hung up on my father. I felt like shit each of those times and regretted it, but when I did it to you I hated myself for leaving you and not knowing where we stood or staying to fix it. I don't know why I always walk away, but I promise if you can forgive me I'll never leave an argument again. I'll never have you doubting my love again."

I don't know why, I definitely couldn't help it, but I start laughing and continue to laugh until tears are rolling down my face. Lucas is bewildered again. I know it's not a normal reaction but it's the one I'm having.

I wipe the streaks of moisture from my face and try to get a hold of myself enough to answer the question written all over Luc's face.

"Sorry, it's just that we're both damaged goods in our own ways and I swear we both spend more time apologizing because of it." I meet his answering smile with one of my own. "I guess we both have to work on our issues more. I should not have been feeling that level of anxiety over your trips to L.A. I should have said something and gotten answers. You should not have walked away, but I forgive you because I know I'm going to be busy stopping you from beating yourself up over it. Tell me what happens now with Lissandria?"

He pulls me closer and closer until I'm perched on his lap with his arms wrapped around my waist and his head buried in my shoulder.

"Well I want you to know I did plan on coming to you last night, but I got a phone call from Nick saying Liss slipped his watch and he couldn't find her. I had to go, I couldn't let something happen to her." When he pauses I nod my head in understanding. "I don't know what set her off yesterday, I didn't get to talk to her yet, but when I found her she was so drunk and high she couldn't even stand. I talked to Nick and we decided it was time to get her professional help again and to get her away from the scene out there."

"Why was she wearing your shirt?" I growl more forcefully than I intended.

Luc chuckles. "Nick's shirt, Minx. No other woman but you can get into my clothing." He starts placing little kisses up and down my neck, inhaling as he goes like he can't get enough of my scent.

Something else is plaguing me about what he said.

"You said she was friends with Kenny and hung around him a lot. Is she-" I trail off, not wanting to finish the question.

"No. Thank god. They were never like that and the needles weren't her thing. He was just easy access to what drugs she wanted," he murmurs, still pressing his lips against my skin.

I exhale the breath I was holding in relief. I don't like her right now, but I would never wish a person into that position.

I stop him from kissing my neck and pull his face away so that I can look him in the eyes. "I'm sorrier than I could express for hurting you. I never wanted that to happen. I knew that it would and that's why I didn't say anything at first and then every time it came up it got harder to tell you." His eyes soften for me.

"I know, Minx. I never thought you did it intentionally. It just hurt that something we shared, something that changed me so fundamentally, held no meaning for you the next morning." His strong gaze is steady on mine.

"That is my greatest regret." I lift my hand to his cheek.

"It's fine. I can just tell you about it." He tries to make me feel better.

"No." I shake my head.

He's shocked by my reply. "You don't want to know?"

I shake my head and smile gently at him. "I want to know more than anything. I'd give anything to remember that night. You telling me would not be the same as me remembering. That night meant so much to you and I can feel deep down it meant as much to me too, but I don't want to cheapen your memory of that night by having to tell me what happened."

I know that seems odd, but I know he gets it.

"I've missed you. I've missed this, holding you in my arms breathing in your scent until I ache to have you. Pressing my lips against the sensitive spot behind your ear and feeling you shiver for me. Cupping your breasts in my hands and feeling their weight and the warmth of your skin against my palm." The huskiness of his voice rasps out as he does everything he describes. I didn't realize how much I missed him moving his hand through the top of my dress.

It's becoming harder to breathe with his lips moving over my flushed neck, his hands gently squeezing my breast and then brushing his thumb over my nipple.

"Luc," I breathe out. "We should go somewhere more private."

He has me thrown over his shoulder before the haze of my arousal clears enough for me to realize what he's doing. I clutch the back of his pants for hand holds. When he starts running up the stairs, I close my eyes, afraid he's going to drop me.

A door up ahead closes.

"Well I guess you two are madly in love again," I can hear Lissandria say as we approach her.

When we pass her I get a glimpse of her smiling at us.

She can party hard all night and wake up the next morning as fresh as a daisy, if a daisy had bloodshot eyes. That bitch.

Simultaneously I hear her laugh and cool air against my bottom moments before Luc's hand comes down with a stinging crack.

"Behave yourself, Minx," Lucas scolds.

Shit, I said that out loud. Damn, now I'm going to have to apologize later. We're almost to his bedroom door. Luc is still rubbing the sting out of my bottom but all it's doing is making me hotter for him. I want to tell him to push my panties aside and rub his fingers against my damp lips.

I moan my frustration.

"Just a minute longer and I'll have you moaning for another reason," Lucas laughs at me.

Finally we're in his room and he slowly lowers me from his shoulder, rubbing my body down his the entire way, setting me right next to the bed.

"Fuck, Gen. You feel so good against me. My dick is so hard it feels like it's going to break through the zipper." He pushes his hips into mine letting me feel his hard length at the junction of my thighs.

I drop to my knees in front of him and make quick work on the fastenings of his jeans. I purr in the back of my throat when the material parts and he springs out. I'm a big fan of no boxer briefs. One less layer separating me from what I want.

I wrap my hands around him and lick my lips. When he growls I look up and lock my eyes onto his. Slowly I bring my lips to his head and lick away the moisture already gathered there from his excitement. I never take my gaze from his. I get to see the heat in his eyes as my tongue grazes his tip.

I love having the power to torment him. I get almost as much pleasure torturing him as he does from me doing it. When I finally take him into my mouth, it's fast and without warning, causing a gasp and groan to mingle in his throat while he spears his hands into my hair, pulling it from the quick ponytail I put it in earlier.

"If you don't stop I'm going to blow in your mouth and that's not how I want this to end." He pulls his hips back, sliding out of my mouth.

I pout at the loss. "None of that. Get up here." He helps me to my feet.

He kisses me, driving his tongue into my mouth to duel with my own. Unzipping the back of my dress, he slides the straps down my arms, letting the dress fall to the floor. I press my body against his and moan aloud my displeasure at the amount of clothing he still has on.

Having mercy on me, he breaks our kiss and takes his shirt off.

"There's no need to rush. I have many things I plan to do to your body. I'm going to slowly lap at your pussy, driving you wild with every swipe of my tongue until your head is shaking from side to side and hands are clenching the sheets while moaning my name, begging for more. Once I get that I'll give you what you want and ravish your clit and you will explode screaming my name."

I rub my thighs together, trying to relieve the ache he's causing. I can feel the moisture of my passion pooling there at his words.

He removes my bra and panties as he continues in his smooth as whiskey, husky voice. "After I feel the last tremor against my tongue, I'm going to kiss my way up your body, only stopping to give attention to the most beautiful breasts I've ever laid eyes on. I need to show my appreciation and worthiness of them before moving on. Once I'm over you and my body lines up perfectly with yours, as it always does, then I'll slide into your haven, pausing to revel in the feel of your slick heat hugging me and welcoming me back where I'm meant to be. While I'm making love to you, you won't be able to tell where I end and you begin, we'll become one entity with one purpose, to give our all to each other. When I finish, you'll never doubt again that we complete one another in every way." His lips whisper the words against mine making them tingle for more.

I step away from him and lower myself down to the bed. I move back until I'm in the middle. I prop myself up on my elbows and part my legs so that my entire body is on display for him.

"I can't wait for you to do all of that, Lucas. Just hearing you say it has me seconds away from climaxing without you even touching me. I want that and promise I'll hold you to your words, but right now I want you to let go of the leash on your inner caveman and come claim your woman by fucking her until she forgets how to speak." I get a little bolder and spread my legs a little wider so that he can see how ready I am for him.

It has the desired effect. A predatory glint enters his eyes and he slowly finishes removing his pants. He climbs onto the bed kneeling, and he stalks me like prey, eyes never leaving mine, body tense to react in case I try to run.

Silly man, I'm not going anywhere. I blink and he's on top of me in one swift move of his agile body. He enters my body in one firm stroke.

Wrapping my legs around his hips, we slide closer. His pelvis presses into my clitoris sends sparks of pleasure throughout me. One of his hands fists into my hair, pulling my head to the side, exposing my neck to his ravenous mouth, while his other hand squeezes my hip, surely leaving bruises from each fingertip. His pace quickens and becomes more ferocious with each stroke. My nails scratch at his back, each finger curling into claws with pleasure.

The sensations of heat, pulling, squeezing, excitement, and thrusting combined build until my mind blanks of all but them. Lucas growls his own pleasure into my throat before biting my neck. I explode around him. I moan deep in my throat, and my orgasm triggers his own. We strain into each other, milking our pleasure. When it all eases, Luc is smoothing his fingers through my hair, gently rocking into me still, and whispering his love for me in my ear.

I smile into his neck. That was perfect. I'm exhausted now and I can already feel my eyes drooping. A short nap and we'll be ready to go for round two.

Chapter Nineteen

My art show at the gallery is a success. I've always had successful showings but tonight is different. Not just in the way the room is buzzing with excitement over the art on display but with how I am viewing the experience.

I got to walk through earlier with Lucas before the show started and watch his expression as he took in each piece. I got to laugh when he argued with me about not being allowed to buy every piece. The best part was being able to watch him mingle and the blatant pride displayed on his face as he discussed the art work and made sure to mention the artist is the love of his life. I did notice that was said mostly to men.

"Look at you, Genni darling." Vivian slips next to me, pulling me into a brief hug. "If that's not happiness on your face then I don't know what is. I don't ever remember seeing you smile at these things." She's fishing and I'm more than willing to bite.

"Well Viv, that's because I didn't have your son in my life before. Now I find myself smiling at a lot of things." We share a smile while watching Luc make his way to his brothers.

The entire group showed up. Steph included, though I wouldn't hear of it unless she agreed to use a wheelchair so that she doesn't over-do it. She granted my wish, not wanting to miss seeing one of my shows for the first time. Tara invited a friend, but she's running a late, which is nothing new. She spends more time getting ready than anyone I know. She's a fashion photographer for a sister magazine Tara gets a lot of assignments from.

"Have you given Lucas the letters from his father yet?" Vivian asks, pulling me back into our conversation.

"Not yet. There hasn't been a moment yet that seems right." I begin to worry my bottom lip over it.

"Relax. I trust you to know when the time is right." She rubs my back. "I respect you as an artist, like you as a friend, and care about you as a person. I'm looking forward to the day I can love you as my daughter." With that, she makes a grand departure and sweeps across the room, hooking her arms into Micah and Kaine's, propelling their threesome towards a group of young ladies gathered by the refreshments.

After the show we all decide to head to a bar around the block to celebrate my success. Vivian offered to escort Stephanie home, but surprisingly Dexter stepped up and offered to escort them both home so that we can be sure they get their safely at this hour. After seeing them off, we trooped the short distance without any mishaps other than Micah pushing Maddox into the street when he draped an arm around Hailey.

It didn't take long for the girls to separate me from the pack to grill me. Last night I sent them a text letting them know I was okay and staying at Luc's house for the night. When I got home this afternoon to prepare for the showing I couldn't give them the details they wanted since I was already running late from Luc joining me in the shower I tried taking at his house.

"Spill your guts or we're liable to get violent," Tara says with her eyes narrowed on me.

I don't tell them every detail of our conversation. Some things should be kept between a couple. I do tell them about Liss answering the door and leaving, turning back around and walking in to give him a piece of my mind. I give them an abbreviated but detailed rundown of what is going on with Liss after they swear their silence on the matter. I got to formally meet her this morning over breakfast. She's not the she-devil I thought she was. She didn't make any excuses when Lucas told her she was being checked into a private thirty day clinic for substance abuse and that the car would be taking her around noon. I only wish positive things for her.

Speaking of she-devil, here comes Tara's friend, Lauren. Tara spots her as well and waves her over to join us.

"Sorry I missed your art show, I'm sure you understand a work of art can never be rushed." She leans in with her overdone face and does the air kisses that make me want to grind my teeth.

"I know art when I see art." I smile sweetly back at her. She can take that however she wants.

"Wait a second. What is this I see? There's four of you. Did you add another skinny white girl to your little group?" She gestures to Hailey and Quincy like she can't remember which one she's met before despite having been in our company a total of seven excruciating times.

"This is my sister, Quincy. Quin, this is Lauren. She's a friend of Tara's from work." I make the introductions.

"Pleasure to meet you, doll. You fit right in with these girls," she says with her usual fake smile.

"Gen girl, where is this man I've been hearing about and seeing you on my favorite show with?" She starts to look around.

I point her in the direction of the table the guys are at.

"Mmm girl. Not bad at all. However, who can tell me who that fine caramel complected gentleman is? I'll give him a moment to stare a little longer before I go over and let him meet me," she gushes, showing her enthusiasm, which is the first real action I've ever seen come from her.

I'm not at all sorry to burst her bubble. "That's Aryan, my boyfriend's brother. I'm pretty sure he's staring at Tara. He's had a thing for her since he first laid eyes on her," I say smugly.

"Please. Why would he want a skinny behind white girl when he could have all of this mahogany delight? That man is not looking to add any more cream to his coffee if you know what I mean. If you'll excuse me, I believe he's ready for the privilege of my company." She slithers off to the table the guys are at. From here I can hear her annoying voice introducing herself as our friend.

"Why do you invite her to hang out with us?" Hailey asks Tara in an accusatory tone.

"I used to think she was fun, but right now I'm not so sure," Tara says through teeth that look like she's trying, and failing, to unclench.

"GI Joe over there looks in need of saving. I've never seen Aryan so tense." Quin brings our attention to him.

"Let's go." I lead the way back to the guys.

"Nice of you girls to join us. I was just making myself acquainted with your men here," Lauren says in a sugary sweet manner while making a point of rubbing Aryan's bicep.

"Oh this is my jam!" Lauren yells excitedly. "Aryan baby, let's go dance." She gives his arm a little tug.

Aryan turns his attention to Tara who is standing next to Lauren. When Lauren notices, she throws Tara a dirty look over her shoulder.

"Don't worry, honey, I don't need Tara's permission to dance. I'm a big girl, I learned how to move my body a long time ago." Her innuendo isn't lost on anybody at the table.

When Tara remains quiet, Aryan narrows his eyes at her. His look finally gets a reaction.

"I don't mind. Go do whatever you want." Tara meets his stare then gives an equally as fake smile as the one Lauren is giving her.

Aryan's eyes take on a cold look that leaves me frost bitten, and I'm not the one he's directing it at. With that, he leads Lauren over to the clearing in the tables to dance.

Everyone left at the table is staring at Tara who is too busy to notice because she hasn't stopped giving Aryan and Lauren dirty looks since their first step away.

I guess that many stares can't go unnoticed forever because Tara finally turns back to us.

"Have you lost your mind?" Hailey questions for all of us.

"Pretty much." Tara picks up the beer she's been nursing since we got here and downs it. "I'm out of here." She turns on her heels and leaves.

Maddox sets his beer bottle down. "I'll make sure she gets home safe and doesn't throw herself into traffic." He takes off quickly to catch up to her.

Judging by the look on his face all the way over on the dance floor, Aryan has noticed this too and is glaring at Maddox's retreating back over Lauren's head.

"That was pathetic." Micah shakes his head.

Kaine also nods in agreement. "Thanks for saying what we all thinking." He tips his beer bottle in Micah's direction.

"So how do we save Aryan from the hole he just dug himself into?" Lucas asks, still studying the dancing couple.

"She looks like she's going to rub his dick off as hard as she's grinding against him," Micah observes.

"We should call it a night. It was a great idea but maybe we can all get together at the house in another day or two?" I offer since everyone did come out to celebrate with me.

Lucas lays a kiss on my forehead. "Good idea." He nods his head at Kaine.

"You go round him up before he loses a vital organ to the twister over there. Tell him someone is hurt or something and we have to go. The limo is already waiting out front to pick us up. We'll meet you out there."

When Kaine and Aryan join us in the limo, I think it's safe to say Aryan is not happy with how everything went down. Even with the few funny jokes Micah cracks he just nods his head and stays quiet.

The jostling startles me awake. I look around. Lucas is carrying me up the stairs. I must have fallen asleep when the limo started moving and slept through everyone being dropped off.

"Go back to sleep, Gen, you've had a busy couple days. You need the rest," Luc murmurs over me.

My nap was enough that when Lucas laid me down after helping me out of my clothes, I had plans that did not include sleeping.

With zero resistance, Lucas picked up on the hints I was giving off. If my hint of rubbing my body provocatively against him could be taken but any other way.

He made love to me using every part of his body. Putting the emotion into every movement, every lingering touch, brush of lips, and soulful gaze. Leaving us breathless and sated in each other's arms.

"I love you," he whispers into my ear as we spoon.

I feel the rise of his chest slow and his breaths even out as he falls asleep wrapped around me.

My gaze wanders to the painting I made so many years before now hanging above Luc's fire place. The first night I came here I thought that this is where it belonged. It had its place for a time.

"But now it's time for a change," I whisper aloud.

"Hmm? What's that?" Lucas stirs behind me.

"I'm going to change the painting over the fireplace. We need something new," I tell him.

He nuzzles my neck. "I like that, 'we'. Whatever you want to do, Minx. Whatever you want it is yours."

I smile. "I have everything I want."

"Are you sure about that?" I feel him nudge my backside.

He lifts my leg and hooks it back over his own, pressing forward to slide against my slit.

"How about now?" he questions, still rubbing against me.

"Not yet," I whisper back before angling my hips, allowing him to ease his length inside of me. "Now I do," I say on a moan.

We made love like that until the sun rose and shone its golden light across our writhing bodies.

Finally exhausted, we snuggle into each other once again.

I'll show Luc the painting I already made for that spot later.

Smiling into his chest, I let myself drift to sleep thinking about the painting he inspired that I'm calling, *More Than I Asked For.*

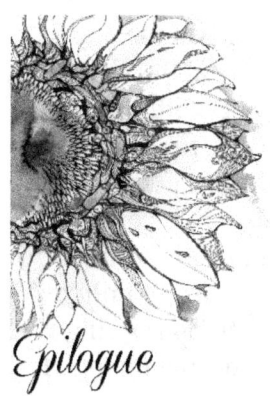

Epilogue

LUCAS

Three months later.

It wasn't a church wedding as per the usual Alexander tradition, but it was still a wedding and I cannot believe I'm standing here celebrating this day in the ballroom of the original Alexander Hotel. Six months ago I would have laughed in someone's face.

I watch Gen across the room in her beautiful dress glowing with happiness.

When I met her that night so many months ago, she told me how she wanted more from life. Her exuberance for living excited me like nothing had in so many years. I knew I wanted to be there with her, watching her experience life like a child on Christmas morning, one present at a time. I felt the possessive pull when her cheeks turned rosy after shyly whispering her confession of innocence to me. I was and still am ready to give it all just to be able to watch her, have her. I didn't anticipate everything she would give me back in return.

During a trip to New York City while sitting at our favorite spot by the lake in Central Park, she handed me two envelopes and instructed me to read the thin one first.

It was a letter from my father written on the day I was born. On those sheets of paper he wrote about finding the woman I would give my all for as he did with my mother, the joys of becoming a father for the first time, and his hope that I know what it is like to hold something so precious as my own baby and see the future in its eyes.

The pang in my chest at the thought of my father became overwhelming. I must have been a disappointment to the memory of my birth for him. Without Gen urging me to I would not have opened the second letter that changed everything.

I was astonished to see ticket stubs fall out of the envelope when I pulled the letter free. They each had different dates, times, and cities in and out of the country. They were all to Scarlet Anarchy shows. In the letter he tells me how he made every show he could when I was in the area and made a few unnecessary business trips to see others. He never missed a show, whether he was there or sent someone to record it for him, and I never knew he was there. His stubborn pride and disappointment with himself kept him from telling me while he was alive how proud he was of me.

At some point Genevieve cradled me in her arms, wiping the tears I did not know I was shedding. She was there to help heal me. She gave me something back I didn't think I'd ever have again: a better relationship with my father's memory.

Pulling myself back from my thoughts and into the present, I focus across the room to Gen. She is standing next to the bride and groom who are still holding hands and making sure that they are touching in some way. Not to be outdone by my beautiful girlfriend, the bride is alight with happiness basking in the gushing Gen is sure to be doing. The groom briefly looks up and smiles at me. I haven't seen him so content before. A few weeks ago we were able to talk and finally clear what was standing between us for so long. Since then we have becomes as close as we were in our childhood.

Genevieve made a gorgeous maid of honor. It never crossed my mind that someone in our group would be married before us, but they certainly didn't waste any time getting there. It's obvious that they're happy and perfect for each other in an unexpected way.

The ring box I've been carrying around for months now seems heavier than normal today. Watching her walk down the aisle holding the bouquet gave me a glimpse of what is in our future. I want to march across the room and slip my ring on her finger now so that the whole world knows she's mine. I've waited long enough, letting her set the pace. I want to give her everything. I'm able to give her the world and all she asks for is me.

Just like the first night I saw her, under the weight of my stare, she meets my gaze and holds it, letting the heat build between us. She takes my breath away as easily as she did that night, too. I motion for her to come to me. I wonder if this time I'll get a speech about not having manners. I almost laugh out loud at the memory of her eyes spitting fire at me and her hands perched on those luscious hips. I know that she secretly likes my inner caveman, as she calls it. She's going to experience him again soon if she doesn't agree to my plan.

She comes to me and easily slips into my arms.

"They look so happy. It was a beautiful wedding, wasn't it?" She stares at me with her bright amber eyes, lightened with joy.

"Minx, my answer is the same as it was the last time you asked. It was a beautiful wedding, but ours will be better," I tell her, smiling at her gasp and grabbing a hold of the hand she tries smacking me with.

"That is not nice, Lucas. Not everything with your brothers has to be a competition."

"Of course it does, Minx. I'd think you would know this by now." When she tries to stomp off, I pull her back and give her a kiss. "Meet me in the coat room in five minutes. I slipped the coat check clerk a fifty to make himself scarce for an hour" There's enough heat in my gaze that there's no mistaking what I want.

"Here?" she asks, acting scandalized, but the familiar flush on her cheeks lets me know she likes the idea.

I don't answer her and walk away so I can discreetly exit the reception. I love the fire inside of her that is willing to try something new and willing to take a risk. Most of all, I love that she trusts me enough to give me everything.

While I wait for her I scope out the closet. Being in here and thinking about what we're about to do has me straining against my fly. My dick is like a dog that never stays down around her. It's always jumping for attention.

The door opens and quickly clicks shut behind Gen. My heart beats faster at the sight of her. I grab her hand and pull her through the row of coats that separates a smaller room from the rest of the coat check.

"We're going to get caught," she whispers against my mouth while rubbing her hands over my abs.

I cup her breasts in my hands. "I think you like the thrill of that. Your nipples give you away, they're so hard and begging for my tongue to stroke them." With a little maneuvering I shimmy her dress down enough to have her breasts out and pushed up for my pleasure by the fabric now bunched underneath.

I lower my head, taking one rosy tip into my mouth and taking care to gently scrape it with my teeth to hear that moan deep in her throat that I adore so much.

Next to us, the door opens and closes again, the lock is clicked into place. That better not be the coat boy. I'm ready to growl. I lift my head and meet Minx's wide eyes.

Judging by the noises next to us, it's definitely not the coat checker.

The couple next to us begin to speak in hushed voices.

"I want you so badly. I've waited so long."

"You're the one that pushed me away. It's about time you've come to your sense." There's a break as the couple kisses. "It's not happening again. You're mine now."

The whispering stops.

Before things progress any further, I start to clear my throat to make them aware of our presence. The movements and rustle of clothing stops. I clear my throat again to be sure they know they aren't alone.

"Shit. Sounds like we weren't the only ones looking for privacy," he softly calls out to us. "We'll be out in just a moment. Sorry for the interruption."

A minute passes and we're left alone again. Before anyone else can come in, I go out and lock the door we were too rushed to lock ourselves before.

Behind me Gen comes out from behind the coats. Her hair is tousled enough that there won't be anyone fooled by what we were doing during our disappearance.

"Well that was interesting." She smiles at me.

I tilt my head and look at her. "Funny, you don't seem at all surprised about who we just overheard."

She starts adjusting her dress to more comfortably accommodate the mounds I'd rather have in my face right now.

"Why is that?" I'm curious as to her lack of shock.

"This incredibly sexy man told me to look at the big picture. So I did. They were actually so obvious it's sad no

- 297 -

one else has noticed before now." She beams with pleasure for finally being observant.

"Come here." I try to entice her back into my arms.

"Oh no, we've been gone long enough, Luc. People will notice." She nibbles her bottom lip which only serves to make me want to nibble her myself. "Tonight when we're home and know we won't be disturbed, then you can pick up where we left off." I have no doubt she means that. She always keeps her promises.

I love that she calls my house, home. It just goes to show that she knows where she belongs. In our house, in our bed, in my arms. Every night.

"We'll have plenty of alone time in the bedroom on the jet during out flight tonight." I watch for her reaction.

"Are we going to L.A. tonight? I don't remember you telling me." She looks perplexed, like she's trying to remember if I talked to her about our trip.

"That's because we're not going to L.A. We both need a real vacation. I already had stuff bought for you to wear and it's all waiting for us to board the plane." I give her a quick kiss to silence her before she can protest.

"Just me and you on a beach in Tahiti. Think of the sun, crystal blue water, and me in my swim trunks." I let my voice dip into the husky tone I know she cannot resist.

Her sigh of pleasure signals the end of whatever resistance she may have put up.

"Let's go say bye to everyone now." I start to pull towards the door.

"Lucas, we can't just leave. You're the best man and I'm the maid of honor. We have to stay. Your mom would be mad if we just took off half way through the reception." Her protest was expected. She's always so considerate of our family.

Too bad she isn't cooperating.

"I love you, Minx." I place a kiss against her lips again.

"I love you, too, Luc."

"Good, hold on to that thought." I lean down further and flip her onto my shoulder. "If you're quiet no one will notice our exit." I stop her from getting ready to yell at me.

Unlocking the door, I stride out without breaking step and take the nearest exit for the lobby. She stayed quiet so as to not draw attention. I won't mention to her that everyone noticed any way; hopefully her hair blocked her from seeing that.

Her hip keeps bumping against my cheek. I love her hips. I bite it through the fabric of her dress.

The ride to the airport will be just long enough for me to check out the lace confection I know is hidden underneath her dress. There is nothing wrong with getting a jump start on our vacation.

The limo is exactly where I instructed it to be. Lowering her into the back, I climb in behind her and pounce.

No ride to the airport has ever been so pleasurable.

Part Two
Genevieve

"Another grape my queen?" Lucas holds the juicy, cool fruit to my lips.

I part them just enough to let him slip it into my mouth and nip his finger when he draws back.

I see the look in his eyes and put a finger to his chest.

"Ah. Ah. You'll be rewarded later for good behavior. Right now I want to enjoy you fanning me with that palm leaf and the bowl of grapes you are hand feeding me while I'm enjoying this private beach and sparkling blue water." I smile in pleasure, closing my eyes and settling back into the lounger Luc placed on the sand for me.

"Minx," Lucas calls, his voice sounding more distant then from where he is next to me.

"Minx," he calls again. "I wonder what is going on in that pretty little head that has you smiling so."

I turn towards the voice and open my eyes. Lucas is squatting next to my lounge chair, no palm leaf or grapes in sight. My mind clears a little more. Of course I was dreaming. I could never imagine Luc becoming my love slave in reality. Maybe in bed for a few hours, but even then he would be suppressing his desires to lead. He does a poor job of letting me set the pace as it is. I was unsure at first but now, I find his drive to push for more and take what he wants exciting.

We haven't discussed living together again, but every time I sleep over, I leave something behind. He is always taking something and putting it 'where it belongs', so he says.

"Well sleepy head, you've been languishing out here for a while. The sun is starting to set. Ready to go inside?" He rubs his hand up and down my thigh.

Standing up, I walk closer to the water. The sky is purple and orange of the most vibrant shades. Lucas wraps me in his arms from behind, sharing the beauty of the moment with me.

"This is perfect," I sigh.

"It is." He places kisses against my neck, working his way up to take my earlobe into his mouth.

I push my hips back against his, feeling his length cradled between my cheeks. My top is removed, baring me to the warmth Tahitian sunset and the heat of Lucas's hands. I clutch at the arm wrapped around my waist holding me in place when his hand slips into my bikini bottom and dives between my folds to feel the desire he stirs in me. I press myself back again, wanting to bring him pleasure as well, but I'm still holding on, using his arm to stay steady on my feet, fearing that my knees will buckle.

"This is for you, Genevieve. Move with me. We're going to go down on our knees." His breath is warm on my ear.

I nod and do as he says. Once on our knees, he tugs the string on my bottoms and exposes the rest of my body. Wrapped in his arms with my back against his chest, his fingers move over me, working magic until they build me up and send me crashing, riding the waves of an orgasm.

I sag against him, letting him take most of my weight. Nudging my knees further apart to open me for him, I feel his abs flex against my back as he smoothly enters me.

"Mine," he growls. He lifts my left arm over my head "Say it. Tell me you're mine."

"Yes," I sigh, becoming breathless from his claim. "I'm yours."

Before glory of the sunset, I let Lucas take possession of me. Body, mind, heart, and soul. The only man I've ever let have me and he has all of me.

Moving harder and faster, he hits the spot inside of me, and my body seizes with pleasure. My vision blurs before going black and dancing with bright flashes. Behind me Luc quickens his pace. Moments later, catching the end of my own release, Lucas presses deep, groaning as he empties himself into me.

Lucas lowers my arm from above our heads. On my third finger is a gorgeous yellow diamond, surrounded by small white diamonds, placed in a rose gold setting. I didn't even notice him placing it on my finger. I stare at it, unable to speak yet.

"You were right. This is perfect. Nothing I could have planned would have been as perfect as this moment for making you mine." His hand slides down my arm and lifts my hand out in front of us. "Do you like it?"

I hear a hint of uncertainty in his voice.

"We can always have something else designed for you," he offers when I don't answer him.

I start shaking my head more and more adamantly. "I love it." I breathe out, releasing my pent up air. "It's everything and more."

I turn in his arms. Sunset or not, there is nothing more gorgeous than staring into the eyes of the man you love and realizing that you're ready to run head first into your future, welcoming what may come.

"That night you told me you wanted to experience sex on a beach," he tells me.

I told him I did not want him to tell me about the night we met so that he could always feel the specialness of the memory. He found a way to keep that night special for him and make it special for me.

I'll randomly find a little note waiting for me with a new fact of something that was said. Occasionally, like just now, after we've done something I told him I wanted, he'll tell me so that I know I said it and that he remembered.

"The girls are going to shit a brick when they find out." I grin.

"About the sex on the beach?" he says, trying to look naïve.

I roll my eyes and smile. "With them that's probably assumed. They're going to die when they find out we're engaged."

"Especially when they remember we won't be home for another week for them to see the ring." He gives me a grin of his own.

I cup his face and kiss him. I pull back and stand, doing my best to drag Luc up with me.

My smile turns wicked "Let's go torture them."

Raised on the shores of New Jersey, T.J. began reading romance novels at the age of fourteen when she picked up Elda Minger's *The Dare*. From that day forward she hasn't stopped reading romance novels of all subgenres. She focused on her career, working in a corporate office during the day, and read a novel every single night. One day when pausing to breathe between novels, T.J. found herself married and pregnant! After being laid off and giving birth to her son, she threw herself into being a stay at home mom.

During the day T.J. focuses on her household that is overrun with testosterone; one beefcake husband, one son that takes after beefcake husband, and two male dogs. In the evening she taps away at her keyboard letting her mind play. Be sure to follow T.J. on Facebook for updates.

www.facebook.com/authortjtims

Don't miss the next story in the More Than DC series coming fall of 2014.

www.ingramcontent.com/pod-product-compliance
Lightning Source LLC
Chambersburg PA
CBHW070651180626
46817CB00006B/2317